THE LOST TRAVELLER

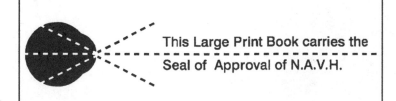

This Large Print Book carries the
Seal of Approval of N.A.V.H.

A COUNTY CORK MYSTERY

THE LOST TRAVELLER

SHEILA CONNOLLY

WHEELER PUBLISHING
A part of Gale, a Cengage Company

GALE
A Cengage Company

Farmington Hills, Mich • San Francisco • New York • Waterville, Maine
Meriden, Conn • Mason, Ohio • Chicago

GALE
A Cengage Company

LIBRARY OF CONGRESS CIP DATA ON FILE.
CATALOGUING IN PUBLICATION FOR THIS BOOK
IS AVAILABLE FROM THE LIBRARY OF CONGRESS

ISBN-13: 978-1-4328-6355-5 (softcover alk. paper)

Published in 2019 by arrangement with The Quick Brown Fox & Company LLC

Printed in Mexico
1 2 3 4 5 6 7 23 22 21 20 19

Ar scáth a chéile a mharaimid
We live in each other's shadow

CHAPTER ONE

The front door of Sullivan's Pub flew open, letting in the scent of summer and car exhaust from the main road that ran in front of the building. It was a beautiful day in June: the sun was shining and the tourists were flocking — or at least trickling — to Maura Donovan's pub, Sullivan's, whether it was for the authentic atmosphere (which meant that nothing had been changed in roughly fifty years, although it got cleaned occasionally these days) or the lively contemporary music that flourished several nights a week, something that Maura had revived only a few months earlier. She didn't care why the customers were coming; business was steady, with a mix of visitors and locals. The rest of her life was going pretty well too (Maura superstitiously knocked on the scarred wooden surface of the bar), with friends and with her relationship with Mick Nolan, which she refused define, and with plans for the future. None of this was what she had expected when she'd arrived in Ireland the year before, but she wasn't going to question her luck.

The new arrivals she could easily label as tourists: mom and dad and a sulky teenager who would rather be anywhere else than in a funky pub in a small town in some part of Ireland she'd never heard of. Maura amused herself trying to guess where they were from and what they were looking for in Ireland — a game she was getting better at by the day.

The mom glanced quickly around the place and decided it wasn't menacing: no guys with tattoos or women with sprayed-on dresses looking for a "date." There never were — that wasn't the kind of place Maura was running. She had inherited the pub from someone she had never met, but she hadn't changed much in the place. It worked the way it was, so why mess with it?

Having decided the place was acceptable, Mom approached the bar, with Dad trailing behind. Daughter turned and stared out the window, trying to pretend she didn't know them.

"Can I help you?" Maura asked.

Mom looked startled. "Oh, you're Ameri-n?"

"I am," Maura said. "Born and raised in Boston. Would you like something to drink? Are you lost? Looking for someone?"

Mom looked unsure. "Well, some of each, I guess. I'd love a cup of coffee. Marv, what about you?"

"Sounds good to me, sweetie. Jannie, you want a soft drink?"

The girl at the window didn't turn but merely shrugged, which Dad — Marv — chose to interpret as a yes.

"Okay, two coffees and a soda," Maura said. "Why don't you all sit down and I'll bring them over to you when they're ready?"

The small group dithered until they decided on a table in the corner overlooking the road. Daughter Jannie sat half turned away from them and pulled out her cell phone, ignoring her surroundings. Maura set up two coffees and waited for the coffee maker to work its magic.

She was shorthanded at the moment, and it was only partly her fault. Rose Sweeney was in Skibbereen, taking a cooking class, but she'd be in by noon. Her father, Jimmy, had just gotten married, and his new wife, Judith, was keeping him busy on the dairy farm she owned. His absence was a mixed blessing: he'd been pretty much a slacker when he'd worked in the pub, spending

9

more time talking with the patrons than actually serving drinks, but his halfhearted efforts had been better than nothing. Mick was up at his gran's, near Maura's cottage, but he'd arrive shortly. Still, here she was alone, and while there wasn't exactly a flood of customers, there would be more coming in as the day went on. The problem was, she had no idea how to recruit more employees, either full or part time. Right now that was at the top of her to-do list.

When the coffee was ready, Maura carried the two cups and a bottle of soda and a glass for Ms. Sulky over to the table. "Anything else I can get for you?" she asked.

Mom cleared her throat nervously. "Do you have a moment to sit? We've just got here and we have a lot of questions. Oh, sorry, we haven't even introduced ourselves. We're the Albertsons — I'm Linda, this is my husband Marvin, and that's our daughter Janice."

"Jannie," the girl muttered without turning around.

Maura pulled out a chair and sat, keeping one eye on the door. "Is this your first trip to Ireland?"

Linda nodded vigorously. "This is our first trip anywhere out of the country. We're from Indiana."

So, somewhere in the middle of the country. Maura herself hadn't left Boston until the year before and was a little fuzzy on where most states in the U.S. were. "Why did you pick Ireland?"

Marvin smiled. "Well, you speak English here, for a start. And I've always heard you people are friendlier than the folks in England. Got a good deal on flights, too. So here we are."

"Any personal connections? Relatives?" Maura asked.

"Not that we know of. We just wanted a pretty peaceful place that wasn't too expensive. But we were so busy we didn't have a lot of time to do our homework. Jannie's just out of school for the year, and Linda and me, we both have jobs, and we weren't even sure what we're looking for. We knew we didn't want to be in a big city like Dublin, but that was about as far as our planning went."

"You have a place to stay?" Maura asked, although she was beginning to think she knew the answer.

"Nope. Never quite got around to finding one. Got any ideas?"

"What're you looking for?" Maura asked.

Marv looked confused. "What're the choices around here?"

11

"How fancy do you want to go?" Maura asked, hoping part of Marv's answer would include how much they expected to spend. "There are some nice hotels not far from here, and of course the one right across the street, but that's pretty small."

Marv shot a glance at his wife. "I think we want something that feels a little more, well, homey than a hotel."

"How about a B and B, then?" Maura suggested. "They usually have only a couple of rooms, but you'll have a host to tell you what to see, if you want. If you were planning to stay longer, you could look into a cottage rental. Oh, and I should ask, how do you feel about cows? Because there are a lot of herds around here, and if you don't like the smells or have any allergies, you might want to stay away from the farm B and Bs."

"I never thought about the cottage idea," Linda said wistfully. "It would be nice to have someplace private."

"Sure, sweetie, but then who'd we talk to?" Marvin said, glancing at her. "We're here to get to know the place, not to spend our time between four walls." Marvin turned back to Maura. "We wanted Jannie to see a different country before she headed off for college. I love our home state, but it

12

can be a little, well, insulated from the rest of the world."

"I know what you mean," Maura said. "I'd never been anywhere but Boston before I got here last year, and it took some getting used to. But I'm staying."

"Well, that's good to hear. What do you suggest?"

"I think a B and B might suit you — it's kind of private, but there are people around who can help you figure out what's what and how to get there. You okay with the driving on the left?"

"So far. Nice highways. Haven't seen much of the small roads yet."

"Well, they are pretty narrow, but people are usually polite about passing, as long as you pull over to the side as far as you can, and there really aren't that many people on the smaller roads anyway. Are you looking for a place for tonight?" When Marvin and Linda nodded like bobble head dolls, Maura went on, "For how long? And how much are you willing to pay?"

"A week, maybe? We figure on spending two weeks in the country, but we might want to try some other parts of it." named a figure that Maura thought sour reasonable by local standards.

"Let me check around. Actually

early in the season, people tell me. It doesn't get busy until next month, and even that's not really busy. If you want peaceful, you've come to the right place."

Jannie gave a deep sigh as she stared out the window.

"So why don't you look around, maybe grab some lunch, and I'll see if I can find you a place? Two bedrooms? Private bath?"

"Please," Linda said quickly. "Where's good for lunch?"

"There are a couple of places right here in Leap. Have you seen Skibbereen yet?"

"That's the next town over?" Marvin asked. When Maura nodded, he said, "Nope, not yet."

"Well, there are some good restaurants there, and the hotel near the river. If you're okay with driving, why don't you head that way, find a place to park there, and just walk around until something looks good? It's not too big to walk. Then come back here and check in with me and see if I've found a place for you to stay. Or give me your cell number and I'll let you know what I've lined ⸢u⸣p. Okay?"

⸢"⸣That sounds great. Maura, you said your ⸢nam⸣e was? You've been real helpful," Mar⸢vin sa⸣id, "and we thank you. We'll talk to ⸢you in⸣ a bit. How much do we owe you?"

He waved vaguely at the now-empty cups on the table.

"The coffee and soda are on the house. My way of welcoming you to Ireland — I want you to like the place."

"Well, then, we truly appreciate it. We'll be back. Jannie? Let's go."

Jannie sighed again, got up reluctantly, and followed her parents out the door. When they were gone, Maura had to smile: they were so very . . . American. Clueless, maybe, but willing to experiment. She was running through her mental list of possible B and B choices for the Albertsons when Mick walked in. He'd be a better person to ask.

He smiled — she was still getting used to seeing a smile on his face, and it still made her feel warm. She smiled back. She had no idea where this relationship might end up, but right now it was pretty nice. "Who were they?" Mick asked.

"That was the Albertson family from Indiana. They decided they'd never been anywhere out of the U.S., and they wanted to show their daughter there was a bigger world outside of Indiana. Of course, they didn't get around to booking a place to stay. I said I'd check around. You know anybody who's got a couple of rooms vacant for a

15

clueless family?"

"There's a place past Gillian's with a nice view of Ballinlough, and I think I saw a vacancy sign outside this morning. Want me to ask?"

"If you would, please. They want their own bath, two bedrooms for a week, and not terribly expensive."

"I'll call now, before it gets busy here."

When he went into the back room to make the call, Maura marveled at how she'd adapted to the way things got done in West Cork. Need a place to stay? Don't head for a computer and search — just ask the next person who drops in who lives nearby. And she was pretty sure that if Mick didn't score a place for them with the first call, he'd know somebody else to call, and keep trying until he found one.

Mick was still on the phone when Billy Sheahan walked in. "Good morning, Billy. How're you doing?" Maura said. Billy, most often known as Old Billy, was an eighty-something fixture of the place. He'd been a friend of the prior owner, the one who'd left the pub to Maura, and he'd been living in a small flat at the other end of the building, rent-free, for years. Maura wouldn't think of asking him to pay: he was good company, he knew everybody and everything in West Cork, and Maura had quickly come to regard him as the grandfather she'd never had.

"Well enough. You've had luck with all the sun. I'm guessin' yer business has been good?"

"I think so. As much as the two and a half of us can handle."

"Rosie bein' the half? It's a good thing yeh're doin', lettin' her learn some skills while she's still workin' here."

"I don't want to hold her back — she's a smart kid and she works hard. Are you ready for a pint?"

Billy reflected. "Seems a bit early yet. Could you do me a coffee? I look forward to me first pint a bit later."

"Coffee coming up."

When Maura slid behind the bar, Mick returned. "What luck?" she asked him.

"They're set. It's a nice place, and good people."

"Thanks, Mick. I'm glad to be able to help people, because so many people helped me when I got here and I was even more confused than the Albertsons. The Albertsons will be back after lunch, and you can explain to them how to get where they're going. How's your gran doing, by the way? I haven't stopped in since the day before

17

yesterday."

"Bridget's grand. She loves the summer months, when it's warm and she can tend to her flowers. And more people pass by her cottage and stop by. Gillian's been by a time or two, with the baby, which is a treat fer me gran."

Bridget lived down the hill from Maura, in the tiny townland of Knockskagh; Gillian lived almost the same distance on the other side of the hill. Bridget occupied the same small cottage her husband had brought her home to when they married, while Gillian and her partner Harry had moved into the old creamery only after their baby had been born, with Maura's help. "That's something else on my to-do list — help Gillian find a nanny, or day care, or whatever it's called around here. Is it 'child-minder'? At least Harry's working now, so they've got some money, but Gillian's going stir-crazy with nothing to do but talk to the baby. She wants to paint again, and she's got kind of an open-ended commission for paintings for the Crann Mor hotel in Skibbereen, but she can't do it if she's got only a couple of daylight hours a day to work." Maura stopped there, because she really didn't think Mick would be the right person to ask

18

about available nannies in the neighborhood.

"Yeh might want to talk to Rose about somethin' like that," was all he said.

One more item to put on Rose's already full plate. The girl was not only working part time at Sullivan's but also taking cooking classes in Skibbereen, planning the overhaul of the seriously out-of-date kitchen at Sullivan's so she could actually use it, putting in her shifts at the pub, and now Maura wanted to hand her recruitment responsibilities for pub help and nannies? And the poor girl had only begun to enjoy her freedom, now that Jimmy had moved over to his new wife Judith's house, and heaven only knew where she could fit in friends or a love life. Maura was going to have to find a way to weed down her tasks, because Rose hadn't said no to anything yet.

As if summoned, Rose walked in the door. She held up a greasy bag. "I brought lunch! If you don't mind eating my less-than-perfect first tries. Have I missed anything?"

Maura smiled. "I for one will eat anything you make — it's got to be better than my own cooking. So far the only excitement has been the arrival of an American family on their first trip abroad. Parents and a daughter who's probably about your age.

Mick's set them up with a B and B, and they'll be back after they've had their own lunch. Maybe you can talk with the girl — she's making it very clear she doesn't want to be on vacation with Mom and Dad, much less in someplace like rural Ireland. Maybe you can tell her what there is to do around here."

"No worries. Hi, Mick, Billy."

Maura checked the time and was surprised to see it was almost lunchtime. "I came in early this morning, so I guess I'll go eat now. I won't be long."

"Take all the time yeh want — I think we can handle the crowd," Mick said, smiling again as he scanned the near-empty room.

CHAPTER TWO

Maura helped herself to some of the good-
ies Rose had brought, then wandered outside to find a place to eat. She'd been in
Ireland long enough now to know that
sunshine was to be treasured — she'd read
somewhere that it rained half the days of
the year for at least part of the day.

When she'd first arrived, she'd been
stunned to find she'd inherited Sullivan's.
And a house too. Thanks to an old friend of
her grandmother's who'd had no heirs, a
home and a business had dropped into her
lap from the heavens, and she'd worked
hard to make a go of the pub. As for the
house, it still felt like she was camping out
there, because she hadn't changed a thing
yet, but she was beginning to think about
making a few small improvements. She'd
been focused on the pub, and then bringing
the music back, and now she and the staff
had vague plans about serving food and

maybe fixing up the rooms upstairs to rent out for a little extra income.

What she hadn't realized in the beginning was that her property — she still had trouble saying that, even to herself — didn't end at the back wall of the pub. It turned out that she owned an irregular chunk of land that ran up the hill. Next to the pub, there was a long, low shed with various odds and ends in it; directly behind was another shed where the oil tank for the pub lived, along with other emergency fuel, then an abandoned two-story building that someone had told her was once a butcher shop. That one might have some future use. Rental? A shop? Not urgent, and kind of fun to think about.

Toward Skibbereen to the west, along the road, there were a couple of buildings that did not belong to her plot — including a decent lunch place on the corner that had been extended toward the back to include a large new room and now nearly reached the ravine on her side. Her property began directly across the ravine. *Ravine* was kind of an exaggerated term for the dip, at least by U.S. standards, but it had earned its fame because of that crazy Donovan who'd managed to persuade his horse to jump across it, thereby escaping pursuing British

22

soldiers. And leaving a name for the village. Not town — village. There weren't enough people living in Leap to let it qualify as a town.

In any case, now she knew she had an irregular piece of land above the pub, with a bunch of scraggly trees and remnants of what somebody had told her (a lot of people kept trying to educate her about her new home) was the "church" road, from back in the days when the English wouldn't let the Irish take the main road to church and they had to park the horses or carts up the hill here and walk the rest of the way. In any case, its bare outlines were still visible. She was wondering if it might be worth setting a few tables and chairs out here to handle the overflow at the pub, or in case someone wanted a breath of air or a more private setting. Wouldn't work in the rain, though. She was still thinking about it.

She perched on what was left of an old stone wall to eat her lunch. If she craned her neck, she could just see a bit of Glandore Harbour on the far side of the road, although in summer it was often hidden by foliage. Below she could see the road, and the stone wall of the old bridge that passed over the ravine. And at the bottom of the ravine was the small stream that over centuries had carved its way through the stone.

And there was something else, a flash of color against one of the thick stone piers that supported the bridge and the roadway above. Trash? Usually people around the area were considerate in taking their trash to the dump, er, tip. Except for the occasional tourist who didn't know the local rules. But this looked like a bigger load, and the colors were wrong for a standard plastic trash bag. There wasn't enough water flowing to have washed whatever it was down from upstream somewhere. Maura sighed. Since it was arguably on her land, she guessed she had a responsibility to identify whatever it was and then get rid of it.

Except she realized she had no idea how to get down there, some twenty feet below. She crept toward the crumbling edge and peered over. Then she stepped back and took a deep breath, and looked again. No, she'd seen it right the first time. A body. Someone dead. From what she could tell from where she stood, it looked like a man, youngish, casually dressed in jeans and some kind of jacket — his clothes were soaking wet, so it was hard to figure out the details. She couldn't see his face because he was lying facedown, his head pointed upstream, as if he'd just toppled over the bridge and fallen straight down. Was that likely?

Maura tried to remember if she'd seen anyone who matched his description at Sullivan's the night before, but she came up blank. Of course, there were other pubs in town, including across the street in both directions. Or he could have driven from Skibbereen, where there were even more. Assuming the man had been drunk when he fell. If he fell. Or was pushed. She rejected the idea of suicide: it wasn't a long enough drop to be sure of getting the job done.

Maura, it's not your job to figure out how the man died. Call the gardaí and let them work it out.

She patted her pockets and was relieved to find she'd brought her mobile phone with her — the one with garda Sean Murphy's direct line on it. That had proved useful more times than she wanted to count. *Might as well get it over with.* She turned on the phone and hit the button.

Luckily Sean answered. "Maura, how are yeh this fine day?" he asked cheerfully. Maura felt bad that she was going to have to spoil his mood.

"I'm grand, Sean, but I can't say as much about the dead guy in the ravine."

There was a long silence from Sean's end, and when he spoke, his tone had changed entirely. "Yer sayin' yeh've found a body?"

"I am. I have."

"And where would the body be now?"

"On the, uh, north side of the bottom of the bridge at Leap, pushed up against one of the bridge piers. You couldn't see it from the highway unless you leaned far over. Nobody's reported it?"

"No," Sean said tersely. "And he — it is a he? — can't have been there long, because there's guys who run a concession there, come see the waterfall and all that, and they couldn't miss it. Have they started up yet?"

"Yes, it's a he. I haven't noticed the concession guys," Maura told him. She peered across the ravine. "I don't see the big sign up yet."

"Right. Stay where you are. Don't try to go near the deceased. I'll make a few calls and be there shortly."

"Okay," she said, but Sean had already hung up. As if she could get anywhere near the dead person even if she wanted to, which she didn't. Actually, she couldn't swear whether it was male or female, in its current position. But whichever it was, he or she hadn't moved since she'd first seen him. Her. Should she tell anyone else?

26

Mick? Rose? No, she decided. The gardaí would be here soon. Maybe they'd find more information. And once they appeared, there'd be no stopping the spread of the news, and she'd have to be ready for it at the pub. She'd better enjoy the last few minutes of peace, because she knew they wouldn't last.

Maura had lost her appetite, so she thought she might as well take a hard look at the scene. The bridge was far from new, although she couldn't guess how old. There was a stone wall that ran from end to end of the ravine, about three feet tall, capped with slanted stone slabs intended to divert the water. There was also what appeared to be a fairly sturdy and recent metal fence on top of the stone portion, which made the whole thing close to six feet high, she guessed. Nobody was going to be able to slip and fall accidentally. No kids or teens would be tempted to balance their way from end to end, not with the fence in the way. And it would take a very large, strong man to lift the victim over the fence and drop him. Not likely. From the side of the lunch place across from her? No more likely. Early in the evening there would have been plenty of people inside, and there were large plate-glass windows. After dark there were exterior lights, she knew. Which kind of left her side of the ravine as the spot where the body had been dumped or flung, unless someone had dragged the victim along the stream bed to leave him in that particular spot. Last night — if that was when he'd died — it had been busy at Sullivan's, and she wondered if anyone would remember either the victim or someone following the victim and maybe leaving the pub with him.

Who else might have seen anything? Well, there was a bus stop on the bridge, although it wasn't usually very busy. She hadn't memorized the schedule, but it was posted at the stop. How late did the buses run? Then there were some much-sought-after parking spaces along the road where it widened at the bridge. All those spaces were too obvious — how could anyone stroll by carrying a body? But nobody would have been paying attention to whatever might be going on in the very dark spaces behind the pub, where she was now sitting. And getting increasingly depressed.

The bistro's view from the opposite corner was blocked by a couple of buildings. Had there been anyone staying upstairs at the inn across the street? There was a nice row of large windows overlooking the road, on the upper story. Somebody should ask Ann

Sheahan, one of the owners. Maybe someone there had seen something.

Maura, she reminded herself, *leave it to the gardaí, will you? It's their job.* The problem was, she answered her sensible self: *Yes, but it's my property, and it might be where the person died.*

She made an effort to clear her mind, and luckily she didn't have long to wait before she saw a garda car arrive, make a U-turn, and pull up in front of the bridge. Sean Murphy stepped out and spotted her on the bank, so she stood up and dusted off her pants. He raised his hands in question, and Maura pointed down below the bridge. He managed to find a way to step up a bit higher so he could look into the ravine, and finally his shoulders slumped. Had he doubted her? Maura wondered. He'd certainly known her long enough now to know that she wouldn't overreact to what might be a body. After a few long seconds he looked back at her, and Maura pointed to her left, then signaled that he should come around. Sean seemed to get the message: he disappeared toward Sullivan's, and a few seconds later he emerged to her left.

When he was close enough, Maura said, "I probably should have come to you, since I'm not sure where whatever this is happened and I'd already covered the ground from the pub to here, but I figured you'd like to get a look at the body. Down there." She pointed again.

"I saw it. I suppose there's little hope that it's a dummy?"

"You tell me. I came out here to eat my lunch, and I looked down and saw . . . that, then I sat down and called you. I haven't moved more than three feet since. I didn't tell anyone at the pub yet. Nobody else has noticed anything unusual, but it's hard to see down there except from a couple of angles. Nobody much comes out to this particular place, including me. There might be a better view from the other side."

"I don't suppose anybody knows the man," Sean said, almost to himself.

"Sean, I doubt his own mother would recognize him from here, lying the way he is. What happens now?"

"You go back to Sullivan's and burst into tears, and when everyone rushes to comfort you, you take an hour or so to spit out the story between sobs?"

It took Maura a moment to realize he was joking. "Why, Sean, you do have a sense of humor. But that won't work. For a start, I never cry. Let's see — I can stay here, or I can go back and say nothing, or I can go

30

back and tell whoever's there whatever you'll let me say. Which do you want?"

"You'd best tell them — the word will be out soon enough. You can tell them what little you know. I've got to call Detective Hurley, and he needs to contact the coroner — you know how that goes, well enough. And then all the fuss will start. Do you have anything on at the pub tonight?"

"Luckily, no."

"Then that's all right. I'd best get on with those calls — there's a lot that needs doing before we lose the light."

"Sean, it's practically Midsummer's Eve!" Maura protested. Even she knew that was the longest day — and the shortest night — of the year.

"And you know all that we'll be needin' to do. Go on back, but don't plan on leavin' anytime soon."

"Got it. Let me know if your guys need anything. Like coffee."

Maura picked her way carefully back toward Sullivan's. She hadn't gotten around to asking Sean whether he thought the mystery man might have met his end on her land, but he'd only just started. And she really didn't want to know the answer.

When she walked in the door, everyone stopped what they were doing and looked at her — it was an odd feeling. Mick spoke first. "The gardaí?"

So they'd seen the car. Might as well not sugarcoat it. "There's a man dead at the base of the bridge."

"Who is it?"

"I have no idea. He was too far away for me to see him clearly, and he'd landed on his face. And that's really all I know. Sean's there, and he's calling in whoever else he needs."

"Could yeh tell if he'd been there long?"

"You mean, was he, uh, decomposing? Not that I could see. Look, Sean's going to come by here when he has time, and he'll want to know if the man might have been here last night, or if there were any scuffles, or a bunch of strangers. Or if any of you recognize him, if Sean can get a clear picture of the face. So try to remember if anything odd happened or if anyone didn't fit."

"There weren't so many here last night, Maura," Rose pointed out gently.

"I know. And no one's saying the man was here. But Sean's got to ask."

"Of course." Rose nodded.

Maura had no idea what to do next. She'd never gotten to eat her lunch, but she wasn't hungry anymore. She didn't need any more fresh air — she'd just come in. Maybe she should talk to Billy, who was watching her from across the room. He didn't exactly cheer her up, but he usually made her feel better. "Rose, can you fix me a coffee? I'm going to talk with Billy."

Rose nodded and got back to work, and Maura walked over and dropped into the armchair next to Billy's. "You heard what I said?"

"I did. How are yeh?"

"Okay. You know, when I first saw him, I thought he was a bag of trash. Took me a minute or two to realize he was a person and he wasn't moving. Stupid, isn't it?"

"Yeh see what yeh want, or mebbe I mean, yeh don't see what yeh don't want. I'm sorry it's fallen on you again."

"So am I. Weird, isn't it, that this keeps happening to me? I'm hoping it doesn't have anything to do with us or with Sullivan's. I mean, why would it?"

"That I can't tell yeh, but I'll keep hopin' fer the best."

CHAPTER THREE

Maura looked up when the door opened and the Albertsons bustled in. Linda and Marv were carrying an assortment of paper bags and looked very pleased with themselves. Jannie was still dawdling along behind them, but she looked slightly less sulky.

"What a sweet little town!" Linda exclaimed. "We had so much fun — once we figured out which way to go and where to park." She appeared not to notice that everyone else in the pub looked glum.

Maura got up from her seat and manufactured a smile. "Did you find a place to eat?"

"We did! And we saw a couple more we'd like to try. Did you have any luck with a place for us? Please don't feel bad if you didn't, because we're feeling a lot more comfortable with getting around. I guess we were just suffering from jet lag or something."

"I'll let Mick tell you about it." Maura glanced at Mick and nodded, and he answered, "We did, if it suits you. It's only a couple of miles from here, overlooking a lake, and yeh'll have no trouble findin' it. I know the people who run it — they won't drive you mad askin' questions, but they'll give you whatever help yeh need if yeh ask. Breakfast's included, but yeh'll have to manage yer other meals. Shall I draw yeh a map, or would you rather think it over a bit?"

Linda and Marv exchanged a glance. Linda was the one who answered. "I think it sounds perfect. Let's say we try it for a week? And if we want to do something different, we can look again later. Right, Marv?"

"Whatever you say, Linda. So, Mick, is it? How about that map?"

"I'll give yeh one of the official maps, but it'd be simpler for yeh if I just sketch it for yeh. It's only two turns from here anyways."

The two men retreated to a corner table with a pad of paper Mick had miraculously found, and they bent their heads together over the diagram Mick was drawing. Linda came over to the bar and asked, "Could I get something soft to drink? Juice, maybe?" She turned around and called out to her daughter, who was huddled over her cell phone in a corner. "You want something to drink, Jannie?" The girl shook her head without looking up. Linda turned back to Maura and said in a low voice, "I do hope she snaps out of it soon. I wanted us to enjoy a nice family vacation, but she's barely said a hundred words since we arrived."

"Problems?" Maura knew very little about what "normal" teenagers worried about, but she thought she had to try to look sympathetic. "She having problems at school? Or with a boyfriend?"

"None of those, or at least, none that she's told me about, which isn't the same thing, now, is it? I keep hoping it's just the age and she'll grow out of it soon. She was such a happy child." She sighed.

Maura set a glass and a bottle of orange juice in front of her. "There you go."

"Thank you." Linda took a sip. "Was that a police car I saw?"

"It was. We call them gardaí in Ireland — guardians of the peace. Somebody reported that somebody had dumped a bag of trash or something into the stream, so they're checking it out."

"I thought everything looked very clean here. Well, except for a few plastic bags. Those things will outlive us all, won't they?"

"Actually, the Irish government started taxing plastic bags a while back, and that cut their use by about ninety percent. Really reduced the litter."

"What a good idea. I'm glad it worked. So, what else should we see around here?"

"Depends on what you like. Although it might be harder to entertain Jannie than you and Marv. The farmers market on Saturdays, in the middle of Skibbereen, is really popular, and they sell all sorts of stuff there. There's a lot of history, like stone circles. Or you can go whale watching. Why don't you talk to the people at the bed-and-breakfast and see what they recommend? Looks like the guys have figured out where you're going." Maura nodded toward Mick and Marv, who had stood up. Maura leaned in toward Linda. "How's Marv's driving?"

"Don't worry about him — he can handle driving on the left, or so he says. Better than I could, at least. And it's good that it stays light so long these days. I can't imagine getting lost in the dark around here."

"You'll be fine," Maura assured her, although she wasn't sure she believed what she was saying.

Linda drained her glass as Marvin came over. "I think I've got it nailed," Marv said firmly. "There's only a couple of turns, and

Mick here tells me there's a sign for the important one. Ready to go?"

"I am, dear. Jannie? We're leaving now," she told her daughter.

Jannie stood up silently, slipped her phone in her pocket, and waited by the door for her parents. Then they headed out the front door, only a few moments before Sean Murphy came in.

Maura was relieved there were no patrons so they could talk freely. "What's happening, Sean?"

He glanced around but saw only Mick and Billy. Maura could hear Rose clattering around in the kitchen in back. "Well, we've made a start. The coroner's on his way. The photographer's been and gone. A couple of men are digging through the muck — we try to keep things clean, but a lot blows in or falls into the ravine there. Always has. Could I get a coffee?"

"Sure. So you've gotten a look at — was it a guy?"

"It was. Somewhere about twenty-five years of age, give or take a few."

"Who was he?"

"Ah, now there's the problem in a nutshell. No ID on him. No scars, no tattoos — although this was just the first look at him. Mebbe when the coroner's done we'll

38

know more. But to go on, his teeth weren't in the best of shape, but he'd had no work done on 'em."

"You have a picture?" Maura slid his coffee across the bar.

Sean slumped. "And there's the next problem: when the man fell, he landed on his face, on the rocks below. Or the bridge footings. Or for all we know, someone worked hard to bash his face in before dropping him in. His own mother wouldn't know him in his current state."

"Ew." Maura grimaced. "So it was the fall that killed him?"

"Uh, no. A couple of bloody great gashes in his chest did the job."

Maura felt a chill. "So it was murder?"

Sean nodded. "Unless he stabbed himself and then flung himself over the six-foot fence, I'd say so."

The room fell silent for a long moment. Finally Mick spoke. "Was he a tourist, do yeh think?"

Sean shook his head. "I can't really say. Tourists don't dress up these days, and he was my age. What he was wearin' is what I'd be wearin' on me day off. Denims. A plain jacket. Trainers, not new. His hair was neither long nor short. He was clean, so most likely not a transient. And before yeh ask, no one's called the station lookin' fer him. But it's a main road there — he could have come from anywhere."

"What do you do now?" Maura asked.

"Collect evidence, if there's any to be had. Check the Missing reports. Problem is, we can't post his picture without scarin' all the children in the country, and half the adults, so we can't set up a countrywide alert for him. We might find some tags on his clothin' that would tell us something, but there's so much trade across borders these days that the tags could be all but worthless."

"What does Detective Hurley say?" Maura asked. She'd met with the man on several occasions and knew he was both experienced and fair. And persistent and open-minded. She had no doubt that if anyone could solve this puzzle, he could.

"It's early days yet. He says we go by standard procedure fer now. Check to see if there's an unclaimed car nearby. Ask around to see if anyone recalls seeing a young stranger. That's why I'm here now — fer the purpose of interviewing those people nearest to where he was found."

"Not at Ger's, on the corner? They'd have a good view from there." She and Rose often bought sandwiches there, so she knew the view well.

"The timin's off. Ger's was closed by the time the man went over the bridge. Might be he was in the place earlier in the day — the coroner will tell us when he ate last. Besides, I'd rather talk to your lot here."

"Not a problem," Maura said. "You've already had my story, so why don't you talk to Mick and the others now? I'll cover the front. And don't forget Billy — it may not look like it, but he's always paying attention when he's here. Use the back room."

"A grand suggestion, Maura." Sean turned to Mick. "Mr. Nolan, sir, will you accompany me to the back for your interview?"

Mick swallowed a smile. "Certainly, Garda Murphy. I am at your disposal. Not that I've got much to tell yeh."

"Let me be the judge of that." Sean gestured toward the pub's back room, and Mick led the way.

Still no customers in sight. Maura hoped that things would pick up later in the day. If word of the murder got out, no doubt it would, because everyone would want the inside story, and they'd come to assume Maura would have it. Which she usually did, though she still wasn't sure how that had come about.

She wandered over to where Billy was sit-

41

ting and dropped into the chair next to him. "So, we've done it again."

"Well, yeh're in thick of it, sure enough. You didn't kill the man, did yeh?"

"Of course not. Besides, I have an alibi."

Billy smiled. "As does Mick, I'm guessin'?"

Maura could feel herself blushing. "Yes. And that's all I'll say for now."

"It's yer business and no one else's. But you have my blessin', if it's needed."

Maura was obscurely touched. "Thank you, Billy," she said softly. "So, the dead man. Do you know, this is kind of out of the ordinary."

"How do yeh mean?"

"Well, so far when someone's died near here, somebody knew who he was, or knew who to ask. Even that guy that was found in the bog, who'd been dead, what, eighty years? We found a relative of his not far from here. Or the guy at the hotel — you knew where to look for his family."

"Maura, I wouldn't get ahead of yerself. This man in the ravine, yeh've only jest found him, and the word's not gone out yet. Surely someone will know him or will have seen him."

"I hope so. Or the coroner will get his fingerprints and find he's a criminal some-

42

where. They do use fingerprints in this country, don't they?"

"So they tell me," Billy said. "You'd best ask young Sean — I'm sure he's had the trainin.' "

"I'll do that, when it's my turn to talk to him. But let me ask you this, Billy." Maura leaned forward in her chair. "What if nothing ever turns up? No ID. No fingerprints. Nobody who misses him and is looking for him. No witness who happened to walk by him on the street. What happens then?"

"That's an interestin' question yeh're askin', Maura, and I've no simple answer. You know that if it's a murder, the gardaí will keep it an open case for as long as it takes. Mebbe somebody will find a piece of evidence in an old trunk in a ruined cottage fifty years from now and they'll match the blood on it, if there's any to be found. Or this DNA stuff. But Sean and his lot are doin' it right, one step at a time." Billy looked up to see Sean waving at him from the back. "And it looks to be my turn. Help me out of the chair, will yeh?"

"Of course." Maura extricated Billy from his sagging armchair and escorted him to the back room. When Sean had shut the door, Maura joined Mick behind the bar. "Anything interesting?" she asked.

43

"I couldn't tell him anythin' he didn't already know. But then, we weren't busy here, so there wasn't much to tell."

"I, uh, told Billy we shared an alibi. You have a problem with that?"

"Billy's a wise man," Mick said, smiling.

"And I guess I'll have to tell Sean? Or did you?"

Mick smiled. "About last night? Yes. But Sean'd be bad at what he does if he hadn't noticed that we're more than friends."

"I guess. I wish he had someone. He's a great guy."

"Leave him be — he'll sort things out in his own time. As you did yerself."

Billy came out after only a few minutes, and Rose escorted him back to his chair before going into the back and taking her turn talking with Sean. She too emerged quickly. Maura was forced to deduce that no one from her staff, man or woman, old or young, had seen anything that would help to identify the dead man. Finally Sean came out, looking depressed, and Maura went over to meet him. "Nothing?"

Sean shook his head. "More than nothing. Your lot identified everyone who came in and knew all of them by name. Not a stranger to be seen."

"What do you do now?"

44

"Go and do it all again with every other place that serves food or drink in the village. I might even talk to the priest — maybe the man went in to pray before whatever happened."

"The priest wasn't in yesterday," Mick told him, "so he couldn't've seen anything."

"Grand," Sean said glumly. "Well, cross yer fingers that the coroner finds something that will help us. Otherwise I'll be talkin' to every shopkeeper in Skibbereen."

"Why would someone from Skibbereen have dumped him in Leap?" Maura asked.

"I cannot say, Maura. I'm plumb out of ideas."

CHAPTER FOUR

A glum silence settled over Sullivan's main room, and Maura found herself torn between hoping for a crowd to arrive to distract her and hoping there would be no crowd so she didn't have to repeat the same information again and again. It boiled down to "I found a body, dead, by the bridge. Young male. No, I don't know who it was. No, the gardaí don't know who it was. Are you missing anybody?" She'd have to cut that last line, plus skip the part about his face being smashed, but she was pretty sure she'd want to say it before the night was over. *So why don't the gardaí post his picture, eh? Because he had no face.* Sean and the gardaí had better come up with a miracle.

What she did finally see was Gillian fumbling her way in. Young master Henry was three months old now, but he couldn't seem to do much beyond drool and eat and fill his diaper. Well, to be fair, he could produce a lovely smile when he felt like it, which luckily was often — it made up for the rest. Gillian had him strapped into some kind of infant carrier on her front, and she was juggling all the extra stuff that babies seemed to need, but her entrance was further complicated because she was carrying a bulky flat package that Maura guessed was a painting. She hurried over to open the door.

"Hey, stranger!" she greeted Gillian. "And little man. It's good to see you. Both of you, that is. Come in, sit down, let Henry entertain us — we're easy to please."

Gillian took a quick scan of the room. "Not much of an audience today, is there."

"Nope. We're hoping the crowd is waiting for later. But since we're short on staff, it's just as well. Can I get you anything?"

Gillian sighed. "Still no caffeine, as long as I'm feeding the young master. Juice? Ginger ale? Whatever you've got that's cold. I'm not picky. It's good to get out now and then."

"Coming up." Maura signaled to Rose. "And can I guess that our package is —"

"A painting, duh. Yes, I have finally managed to complete a painting, while Henry naps, which is rare. I brought it along so you all could look at it critically and tell me if it's as awful as I think it is."

Maura studied Gillian. She looked tired, although Maura had heard that dealing with a small baby was exhausting. Her face was thinner, but she was still a bit thick through the middle. Her clothes, which once had been cheerful and colorful, were now sort of limp, and Maura spied a few splotches she'd rather not identify. "Harry's not around much?"

"No, not that I blame him. He's spending most of his time at his new job at Crann Mor, going through the documents and budgets and such for the hotel. At least he doesn't have far to travel these days. And he's happy as a pig in . . . you know. He loves to feel useful and keep busy, and I can't complain. Except that I do. Which is why I got out my paints, but I'm having trouble finding my way back to where I was before. Here" — she passed the bundle wrapped in brown paper over to Maura — "stick this up over the fireplace and you can all tell me what you think." When Maura hesitated, Gillian said, "Go on. I need to know.

Gillian had hung paintings in the pub before and even sold a couple. She had a standing order for more at the same hotel where Harry was now working, but she had been slow to start painting again, after the baby arrived, so Maura figured she was probably hard up for cash, especially with the necessary repairs to their new home. Maura peeled off the sticky tape, propped the new painting on the mantel, and then stepped back to look at it. Billy got up from his chair and wandered to the opposite end of the room so he could see it well. Mick leaned against the bar, and Rose stood behind it. All eyes were on the painting.

After a long minute of silence, Gillian said loudly, "For God's sake, somebody say something. I'm dying here!"

"Well," Maura began, but Gillian burst out, "I knew it. You hate it. I'm fit only for illustrating comics, or maybe painting funny pictures on the walls in the gents'."

"Oh, shut up and stop feeling sorry for yourself," Maura said firmly. "Here's what I think. It's not the same as your style before, so we kind of have to refocus. It's . . . softer, somehow. Rounder. The colors are about the same, but you're using them differently."

"Next you'll be telling me I should be painting flowers and lambs. Mick, what do you think?"

"What Maura said, but that's not a bad thing. It's not as edgy as what you did before, but it's more, say, smooth. Together."

49

"Interesting," Gillian said. "Sounds kind of boring, though. Billy? How about you?"

"It's pretty."

"Ah, God, that's what I was afraid of. My brain has turned to mush after having this child. I've gone all gooey."

"Stop whining, Gillian," Maura told her. "It has a different feel to it, that's all. That's not wrong. The light's from the lake, isn't it?"

Gillian seemed to relax just a bit. "You can tell? That's good to know. But it's not too, well, dull, is it?"

"I'd call it peaceful. Is that because you feel peaceful now, or because you'd like to and this is what you're looking forward to?" Maura asked.

Gillian stared at her for a moment. "You're scaring me, Maura. When did you become an art critic? Or a psychologist?"

"I run a pub and I talk to people. Peaceful is not a bad thing. And no, you're not selling out, just because things like this would look great in hotel bedrooms. Just relax and see where it goes."

Gillian finally smiled. "I knew there was a reason why I came here today. Thanks for cheering me up. So, what's going on in Leap?"

Maura, Mick, Billy, and Rose exchanged a

flurry of glances. Finally Maura said, "I found a body under the bridge this morning."

Gillian laughed, then looked more closely at Maura's face. "You're not kidding, are you." When Maura shook her head, Gillian asked, "Who was it?"

"We don't know."

"Who's we? Your crowd here? The gardaí?"

"Nobody knows."

"Man or woman?"

"Man. About my age."

"What did he look like?"

"Very dead. Before you ask, it was impossible to make an immediate identification because the man's face had been damaged beyond recognition."

"More than I wanted to know," Gillian responded. "So of course you called your garda friends. What are they doing?"

"Investigating. Which at the moment means talking to anybody who might have seen the man after midnight and before first light this morning, anywhere in the general area. Based on a very vague description."

"Oh dear," Gillian said. Then she was distracted by a short squawk from her son. "Excuse me, I think it's suppertime. Can I use the back room?"

"It's all yours," Maura told her.

51

When Gillian retreated to the privacy of the back room, Maura turned to the others. "Well, that will no doubt be the first of many explanations that won't please anybody. I was saying to Billy earlier, most of the time someone who dies has some connection to someone else around here. Sometimes it takes a while to dig it out or put the pieces together, but that's how we've found out what happened in most cases. Think that's going to happen this time?"

Billy had been making his slow way back to his favorite chair, and when he settled in it, he said, "Give it time, Maura. It's been less than a day."

"I know, Billy, but as long as he isn't identified, I'm going to have to try to answer a lot of questions."

"And yeh'll be sellin' a lot of pints along the way," Billy reminded her.

"True, but I don't want to be called the Murder Pub of Leap, now, do I? Or the Music and Murder Place? Damn, when Seamus shows up, is he going to want to start another betting pool to see who can come closest to guessing who the poor man was? That seems kind of, well —"

"Disrespectful of the dead, yeh might say," Mick finished the sentence for her.

"Exactly. Talking things through with

Seamus and his pals last time something like this happened was useful, but to do it as a regular thing is rude, and I don't want him to get used to playing detective."

"He does buy his share of pints, yeh know. And yeh wouldn't want to keep Seamus and his pals from talking about who the man might be, now, would yeh?" Mick said.

Maura had to stop to think about that. "You're saying they might know something, or have heard something from somebody, about a fight or someone who's gone missing or someone who had a grudge. And they'll be all in one place. Should I call Sean if they show up together? It would save the gardaí from having to track them down at their homes, if they want to speak with them."

"That was my thinkin'."

The tide seemed to turn after three, and people, mostly middle-aged men, started drifting in in two and threes. Just as it started, Gillian came over to Maura. "I think I'll be heading home now. Thanks for the talk. Do you mind if I leave the painting here? Maybe someone will notice and say something, or say it looks too girlish for Sullivan's. I still need some more reactions."

"Not a problem. And if Harry comes home with some hot gossip about the murder, you'll let me know, right? I know the gardaí will be checking — heck, the man could have worked there at the hotel, or at least been looking for a job there — but Harry might hear something that the staff didn't want to mention officially."

"Ooh, I get to play detective too? Anyway, thanks for putting up with the pair of us."

"Bye, Gillian," Maura said. "You're welcome anytime — the both of you." She was pleased she had managed to cheer Gillian up, but the truth was, she really hadn't made up her mind whether she liked Gillian's new style. But Gillian needed the outlet, and Maura had faith that she'd find her way.

As she had predicted, the men who came into the pub wanted information. She had very little information and didn't know when or if she'd be getting any more. It was interesting what bits and pieces had leaked out. Everyone knew a body had been found in Leap. Fewer knew where. Even fewer knew that she had been the one to find the man. By the fifth or tenth telling, she had the dialogue memorized. The gardaí hadn't said she couldn't share what little she knew — there was nothing to hold back — so she reported what she had found. The men took a rather ghoulish interest in the details, like the state of the poor man's face, but Maura wasn't going to go there, and most didn't press her.

Sometime around six, Mick offered to spell her at the bar, which no doubt would disappoint the patrons, but she was hungry, since she'd kind of skipped lunch, and she volunteered to pick up some food for all the staff. Once outside Sullivan's, she realized how stuffy the place had become during the long day and took a moment to sit on the low stone wall on the way to the Costcutter convenience store. But she couldn't stop herself from looking back at the bridge. There was no way that anyone could have hoisted a body over the fence at this time of day without half the local population noticing, or even cars passing along the road. It had to have been after dark. But dark came late and the sun rose early, which meant there had been a very narrow — what was it called? — window of opportunity. Which should help the gardaí eliminate people with alibis for any time it was light. Maybe four hours, after midnight? The pubs would have been closing or already closed. There was rarely any traffic on the road at that time. Say a car drove up, pulled over, parked. The driver (and a helper?) got out, hauled the body out of the back seat or the trunk —

boot — and hauled him — where? Over the chain-link fence directly over the ravine was an unlikely option. which meant they had to go around, and the easiest path led right past Sullivan's.

Damn — there was a six feet high gate, but she never thought to lock it. It was more for privacy than security. If she opened up the garden for customers or food, she might have to think about putting a lock on it so people wouldn't sneak out without paying. But at the moment there was nothing to stop anyone, with or without a body in tow. But why here? There were plenty of abandoned cottages and dead-end lanes and wet bogs where someone could dump a body and no one would ever find it. Or the body could be tossed in the harbor, either at the near end or down by the other bridge, toward Union Hall. Somebody might have to know the tides, to know when the water was high and which way it was flowing, which would kind of point to a local person. But it was possible, wasn't it? Why dump it in Leap?

She didn't have any information to work with. But then, she didn't pretend to have any information about what would lead one person to kill another person, and how a person would react after the deed was done.

The death hadn't been an accident: the bloody stab wounds in the front of the body showed that. But the maiming of the face had been deliberate — she hoped it had happened after the man was dead — and so had the hiding of the body. Why?

Who was the dead man?

CHAPTER FIVE

Still unsatisfied, Maura roused herself and went on up the street to get the food she'd promised, then headed back to Sullivan's. When she walked in, something felt different. Nothing obvious, but there had been a momentary pause in the conversations, an involuntary turn toward the door. Were people that hungry for information?

She realized that might be true: these burly farmers might actually be anxious at the idea that there was an unknown brutal killer somewhere around the village, or near enough. She should be anxious too. Why wasn't she? Her best guess was that she'd blown out all her emotions when she'd first found the body, or stifled them completely, but if she allowed herself to stop and think, she thought that she should worry too. She was a single woman who lived alone in a fairly remote cottage. She was publicly identified as a friend of the gardaí. Somebody — a killer — might think she knew something or was smart enough to guess, and decide to remove her, just in case. She looked up to see Mick watching her. Was he reading her mind?

But all he said was, "Took yeh long enough."

"I got distracted — I was thinking. Here." She slid the bag of food across the bar toward him. "Anything new?"

Without speaking, Mick nodded toward a table in the far corner, and Maura recognized the new garda, Conor Ryan, recently transferred from Limerick to Skibbereen. "Does he have anything to report?"

"Nah. I think he wants to talk to yeh."

"Fine." Just what she wanted after her depressing conversation with herself about her own safety. She strode over to where Sergeant Ryan sat, an empty coffee mug in front of him. "Can I get you anything?"

"A word wit' yeh, if you've the time."

"Sure." Maura pulled up a chair and sat, leaning forward. "Do you have any news?"

He shook his head. "We've nothing to work with. The coroner confirmed what we already knew: the man was stabbed to death. The bit about bashing the face came after he was dead. He didn't drown — no water in his lungs. No identifying features.

59

In fact, the coroner said he'd never seen such an anonymous body in all his working days."

That didn't make her happy. "You going to call in a super-high-tech forensic team to analyze what his grandparents ate for breakfast or what six kinds of sand he picked up on his trainers?"

The sergeant smiled but without humor. "Wish we could, but the lads in Dublin don't think this rates high enough to call for that."

"Why'd you want to see me?" she asked.

"Two reasons, I'm thinkin'. One, we need all the help we can get, because we've nothin' to start with. That could change at any time, but at this moment we're nowhere in our investigatin'."

Looking at him, Maura guessed that asking for help, particularly from an outsider like her, was painful for him. "And the other reason?"

"Seein' as how the man was dumped at your back door, in a manner of speakin', there may be a chance that someone was sending yeh a message."

That hadn't occurred to her. "What, me? I didn't recognize the man, though I don't think anybody could. I don't know all that many people in Ireland. So if this was supposed to be a message, it makes no sense to me."

"Could be it goes back to before yer time?"

"To Old Mick? I never knew him, and I don't know anything about his life, or who might have wanted to harm him. I got the impression from talking to people that he had really slowed down over his last few years. That dead person would have been a child in Old Mick's heyday. If you want details, you'd have to ask Billy Sheahan."

"I know it's a long shot, Maura, but I'm that desperate. I've been the with Skibbereen gardai for only a short time, but I'd like to get this right. I come from one of the biggest stations in this part of the country. If I can't work out why one man died, in a village with less than two hundred people, I'll be a laughing stock across the whole of Ireland."

Maura swallowed a smile. So his male ego was involved — no wonder he hated asking her for help. "And what is it you think I can do for you?"

"We're askin' all the pub owners around, here and in Skib, to keep their ears open, see who's talkin' about the murder, or anythin' else out of the ordinary. I wanted to ask you special since yeh're the one who found the body. Mebbe whoever did it will come back to see what the people here have made of his little surprise."

This just kept getting better and better. "Sergeant, are you trying to tell me that I'm in danger? Or anyone else here?" *Like Rose?*

"I wouldn't go so far as to say that, but all of yiz here should be careful. Don't stay late on yer own. Make sure yer doors are locked. Keep yer mobiles close at hand."

"Got it." *And check out each guy who walks in who you don't know and wonder if he's a killer?* "Safety in numbers, right?"

"Maura, I'm not joking. I'd rather you were scared until we get this sorted out than that you were hurt or worse."

She looked at him carefully and realized he meant what he said. "Sorry. I'm already nervous, and having you tell me I've got reason to be doesn't help. But you're right, and thank you for thinking about us here."

"You and Mick, yeh'll be all right, I'm guessin'. What about the girl?" He nodded toward Rose, currently behind the bar.

"I'm not sure where she's living right now — her father just married and moved to his wife's place, but I don't think Rose followed him there. She'd done with school and she's on her own. Look, I'll talk to her when we close, and I can take her home with me, if nothing else. I've got a spare bedroom."

"Good idea. Let's all hope we find out what happened sooner rather than later."

"I agree. Good luck." He stood up, and Maura stayed where she was, watching him leave.

She made no effort to get back to work right away — she needed to mull over what the sergeant had just told her. She'd done a good job of ignoring the obvious: she and her staff — her friends — might be at risk. She'd thought — no, believed — that Ireland wasn't a dangerous place, that there weren't evil people lurking in corners, looking to do harm — for money, for sex, or just because they were twisted people. She'd hoped she'd left that behind in Boston, where she'd always been careful to lock doors behind her, always watched the dark places when she came home from one dead-end job or another late at night. She'd come to feel safe in Leap, and even at her cottage, isolated though it was. Now she wasn't so sure.

She could tell from the sneaky glances that the rest of the people in the pub wanted her to report on her conversation with the sergeant. They still didn't know him well, since he'd arrived only a few months earlier, and she had come from a city rather than a village like Leap. The Skibbereen garda station was nothing like what Conor Ryan knew from Limerick. Skibbereen had ten gardaí — eleven since the arrival of Sergeant Ryan — and the main Limerick station had close to a hundred, he'd once said. Of course, Limerick itself was much bigger — and so was its crime rate. But at least Sergeant Conor was trying to fit in, if reluctantly. If he was boggled by this crime, they all had a real problem.

Finally she got up and strode over to the bar, settling herself on a stool in front, and leaned forward to talk to Mick and Rose. "They have nothing new. The sergeant wants us to report anything unusual that we see or hear, like we wouldn't anyway — and he's asked all the other pubs around here. But he also said we should watch our backs — don't stay too late, don't wander around alone, make sure you lock up, things like that. Rose, are you still living where you did with your father?"

"Fer now I am, though I may find a flat in Skib to share. Why?"

"I'd be more comfortable if you had someone else staying with you, or if you could stay with me until the gardaí figure out what happened. I'd feel awful if something happened to you. Could you stay with your dad and Judith?"

Rose made a face. "I'd rather not. And it's a far way to come to get here."

"I've got a spare bedroom. You know you're welcome, and I could bring you back and forth. Think about it, will you?"

"It's kind of yeh to ask, Maura. Let me think on it." She turned away to serve a new customer.

Mick lowered his voice. "Am I welcome?"

For her safety or for other things? But Maura decided to answer him seriously. "Mick, I'll confess this has got me spooked. I've been feeling safe here, and at the cottage, until this happened, and now I realize how alone I am. So I would be glad of your company." She lifted her chin and looked him in the eye.

She wasn't sure if she expected a joking response from him, but he answered her in a tone as serious as hers. "Thank you. Like you told Rose, I'd be troubled if anything happened to you, that I could have prevented."

"Might get crowded, if Rose comes along too."

"We'll manage," he replied. "Won't be fer long."

"I hope that's true." Maura scanned the room. "Business is slower than I expected. I didn't think all the sturdy farmers around here would be spooked by a little thing like a murder. Heck, they can wrestle cows around."

Mick smiled. "Ah, yer feelin' neglected. Here yeh go and find a body and yer not gettin' the attention yeh deserve. Could be the word hasn't gotten round yet."

"So we should plan on a busy night tomorrow?" she asked.

"Mebbe. Unless the gardaí find the killer."

But the quiet spell was broken shortly after that when Seamus and his usual posse of amateur sleuths came in. To Maura, it looked like they'd made a few stops before arriving at Sullivan's. "I wondered when your lot would show up," she called out to them.

"Ah, Maura, we've been sleuthin', we have," Seamus informed her.

"And maybe doing some drinking?" she asked, smiling.

"Might be. Helps keep the talk flowin', does it not?"

"I'll have to agree with that. You have something you want to talk about?"

"Do yeh really have to ask? And a pint to go with it, if yeh're offerin'."

As Maura pulled the pints, she tried to decide whether — or rather, how much —

to involve Seamus in this crime. The last time there'd been a fatal incident, back in the spring, Seamus and his buddies had set up a pool to guess who had done the deed, with a prize of a free round for the lot of them. It had seemed harmless, and in fact the talk about it had produced some good ideas. Although nobody had managed to guess the right solution. That meant that Maura had won the grand prize, which she had declared to be: an afternoon of everybody's time to help Gillian and Harry set up their new home overlooking Ballinlough, the small lake a couple of miles inland from Leap.

This time she was uneasy. It was harmless, all right, trying to figure out who this unidentified man was, plus who might have killed him, with little to go on — it was kind of a mental puzzle. But knowing who the man was could end up pointing to who had killed him, and that person was still on the loose and might want to find a way to shut up the bettors. All right, that was the worst case; it was equally likely that the man had fled to Cork or Dublin or even England after the killing. She didn't want Seamus and friends to get hurt — she kind of liked them, and they did buy a lot of drinks. Clearly they'd already heard things at other places, and she didn't have much more to offer. Was trying to protect them even her decision to make?

The pints were ready, so she put them on a tray and walked over to the large table in the corner where the lads had settled. "Here you go."

"Ah, grand," Seamus said. "Maura, sit and talk with us. Yeh're the one who found the poor dead lad, are yeh not?"

"I am. Hang on — why don't you tell me what you think you know so far and I'll tell you how wrong you are? You know how stories change with each person who tells it."

"Fair enough. On a fine, bright afternoon you, one Maura Donovan, proprietor of this grand establishment Sullivan's, was enjoyin' a well-deserved break when yeh happened to look down in that famous ditch out there and spy a dead person."

"So far, so good. But I thought it was a bag of trash at first."

"Noted. Bein' a law-bidin' citizen, the first thing you did was call the gardaí, who arrived quickly."

"Right."

"Did you recognize the poor man?"

"No. But when I first saw him, he was lying facedown, about twenty feet below. I'm not sure I'd recognize anybody under those conditions."

"And yeh never saw him after, I assume. You know the gardaí have circulated a description?"

"Of course," Maura said. She decided to wait until Seamus asked about the condition of the body, especially the face.

"It appears the victim was a young man in his twenties, with no distinguishing marks. And little face remaining."

"Yes. I never saw anything other than his back, though."

"Little to go on there, I'm guessing. Dark hair?"

"I think so, although it could have been wet, which would make it look darker. It wasn't exactly long, but it wasn't really short either. I don't know if that helps."

"It might do. So when the gardaí, or more likely the coroner, examined the poor lad more closely, they found he'd been stabbed multiple times, from the front."

"That's what I was told. I didn't see that part of it. And nothing after that. I came back here, talked with Sean Murphy, and that's all I know. Firsthand, anyway."

"And what conclusions have you drawn from your personal observations?"

"None, really. The guy was dead. He

hadn't been dead for long. And it wouldn't have been easy to dump him there, what with the fence over the bridge."

"So how do yeh think he got there?"

Maura realized she hadn't thought ahead when she answered. "I figured he had to have been dumped from my property, out behind the pub."

"Aha!" Seamus crowed. "There's our first new piece of evidence, right, lads? The deed couldn't be done from the road! I think that calls for another round."

CHAPTER SIX

Maura signaled to Rose for another round of pints, then turned back to a triumphant Seamus. "I told the gardaí all this, you know."

"Of course yeh did, but it's the first we've heard of it. Around the back, eh? That's where our intimate familiarity with your fine pub is useful. Am I right, lads?'

Nods all around. "I'm guessin' the gardaí don't spend as much time here as we do," one of the others said.

"You'd be right about that," Maura told him. "But they *have* been here before." Rose brought over the drinks and handed them out, then retreated. "So what do you know that's helpful?" Maura asked.

"Fer a start, we know that yeh never lock that gate on the side," Seamus said.

Just as she'd feared. If Seamus knew, so did a lot of other people. "What, you guys have been sneaking in? Or out?"

"Us? Never. We've only noticed someone doin' it a time or two. It's dark and quiet if yeh go out that way, or yeh're looking fer a bit of fun with yer girl."

"I'll keep that in mind — at least until I get a lock put on. What else?"

"The door on t'other side's visible from the street, so it's harder to slip in and out. Yeh could argue that a strong person could carry a bloody body — excuse my language — all the way round the back to the ravine and pitch it in, but it wouldn't be easy. Would yeh know what the poor man weighed, Maura?"

"No, and I didn't ask. He wasn't large, though. And he wasn't a kid. Kind of average."

"So let's fergit that door. Say the killer came through the gate near the ravine and sneaked his way around. It'd have to be late, no? A man hauling a body over his shoulder along the street would surely be noticed from the road, unless it was late. And the sun's up early these days."

"Seamus, the gardaí have already figured this part out," Maura said impatiently. *And so had I.*

"Well, sure and they have, but I'm just after makin' sure we're all on the same page here. Late at night and full dark, good-sized

72

man appears carrying a dead body. He spies a gate and checks to see if it's locked. Saints be praised, it opens for him, and he slides through, along with his burden. Now he's inside, with not a soul to see him. What to do with the body? He can't just leave it layin' there — it'll be found at first light. He hasn't the time nor the shovel to bury the man. So he looks around and he sees the famous ravine, and he hurries over and unloads the man with a mighty heave."

"Great story, Seamus," Maura said, trying not to sound snide. "And of course the body lands at the least visible place, right under the bridge, so nobody will notice it right away. I don't think anyone at Ger's could see it from inside, and I wouldn't have except I wanted a quiet place to eat my sandwich. Now, the guys giving tours of the waterfall, they would have noticed pretty fast, but they're not open in the middle of the night, are they? It would've been morning before they noticed anything."

The guys around the table looked at each other and shook their heads.

Maura realized that this little chat was actually kind of interesting. "So, tell me this, detectives: was the killer trying to put the body someplace where it wouldn't be seen right away? Or was he from somewhere else and in a hurry to get rid of the body and get away?"

Seamus shook his head. "Nah, if he wasn't from here, then he wouldn't've known about the ravine. Yeh don't go looking fer a place to hide a body with a tourist guide in yer hand. Let's say fer now that he was a local man, or he'd been here long enough to know what was where. And he had to get rid of the body fast, and get himself back to wherever he came from and set up his alibi."

"And remember, he would probably have been covered with blood, from the stabbing and from hauling the body around after!" Maura reminded the men. "So he had to change his clothes and hide the bloody ones before anyone else saw him. Where's he staying, then? Where he'd have other clothes?"

"Might be he had a car. Or the dead man did and his killer took it," Seamus suggested. "Then he could go almost anywhere and jump into a lake to get rid of the blood."

"True, but how the heck do we — I mean the gardaí — look for a car they don't know exists? They've got no name to look for registrations. Hmm, unknown car belonging to unknown person from unknown place. Might have bloodstains in it. Shouldn't be hard to find." She knew she was sounding sarcastic, but she couldn't stop herself.

Seamus looked frustrated. "Ah, Maura, don't take it wrong — we're just kicking around ideas now. Do yeh want this killer to be a local man? Someone who can carry more'n a hundred pounds or so around the village and knows where a body won't be seen, and lives close enough that he can go home and clean up without a wife and six kids asking, 'Is that blood, Da?'"

Maura had to suppress a shiver: that was exactly what she was afraid of, although she wasn't sure why. If they didn't know who it was that was dead, how were they supposed to figure out who wanted him that way? "I'm sorry, guys. I guess I'm tired. I don't like finding bodies."

Seamus suddenly looked contrite. "And no more should yeh, Maura." He signaled to his mates around the table. "Boys, I think we've made a good start. Time we took ourselves home." He stood up and slapped a couple of bills on the table, then turned back to Maura. "If the gardaí don't have their man by tomorreh, you'll be seeing us again."

"I wouldn't expect anything else, Seamus. Safe home."

When they had bumbled their way out the door, Maura realized that Billy had taken

75

himself home as well, and there were no other patrons. Just Mick, Rose, and her. It was still short of closing time, but Maura didn't expect anyone else to show up this late on a Monday. "Might as well close up, I guess." She hesitated before adding, "Rose? I know you're grown up and independent, but I'd really feel better if you came home with me tonight. I don't like the idea of some guy prowling around, one who knows about the back end of this place and the gate without a lock."

Rose looked reluctant. "Why would the man come back?"

Maura shrugged. "Maybe he thinks he dropped something." *Including a body? Shut up, Maura.* "Maybe he's got another body to unload. I don't know! I'd just feel better if I knew you were safe."

"It's kind of yeh, Maura, but I don't want to get in the way of . . ." She nodded toward Mick.

Maura tried not to smile. She had always been kind of clueless about the polite way of handling, uh, bedroom activities when there was someone who could overhear, both in Boston (where her impression was that almost anything was acceptable and that was why earphones had been invented) and definitely here in Ireland. "Don't worry

76

about that, Rose — Mick can sleep on a chair downstairs. He'd be there only to make sure nobody's after me now, and I'm looking after you. I know, it's stupid, and this murder probably has nothing to do with me or Sullivan's or anything connected to us, but I'd rather be safe than sorry. Just for tonight? We can take another look at the situation tomorrow. Maybe the gardaí will have it wrapped up by breakfast."

Finally Rose shrugged and smiled reluctantly. "All right, then, I'll be yer guest for the night. I'll check the doors in the back and cut off the lights." She turned and headed for the back room.

Mick hadn't said a word but had watched the conversation from behind the bar. Now he had a half smile on his face. "I'm guessin' that all of Leap knows about us by now, and mebbe Skibbereen as well. Or even the townlands — Jimmy's not above spreadin' a bit of gossip. Does that trouble yeh — the whole world knowin' yer business?"

"In a way. I guess I'm used to being invisible, but owning a pub kind of makes that impossible. Still, I thought my private life might be, well, private."

"Too late fer that," Mick told her. "But people mean it kindly. They like yeh, and they'd like to see yeh happy. Mostly to them that means havin' someone in yer life."

"What about you? You were pretty much a loner, before . . ."

"I was that," he agreed. "But men don't chat about such things, and the few women who came in here gave up hopin' long since."

Rose came back into the main room, pulling the door shut behind her. "All closed up. Will we be leavin' now?"

"Might as well. One car or two?" Maura looked at Mick.

"I've a class at the cookery in the morning. I can take the bus to Skib if yeh drive me back here."

"We can drop yeh off, no worries," Mick said, "but yeh'll have to find yer own way back."

"As I have been, thank you very much," Rose told him.

"You don't drive?" Maura asked, wondering why she hadn't thought about it before.

"The minimum age is seventeen. Me da was going to teach me, but he got a bit busy, what with Judith and the wedding and all. I've no car anyways. The bus is fine, and I catch a ride now and then from a friend."

"We'll just have to teach you, then," Maura said. "And I know you're trustworthy — you could borrow my car."

"Maybe," Rose said. She didn't look convinced.

"So, one car, and we'll take Rose to her class before we get here in the mornin'. Done," Mick said firmly.

The ride back to Maura's cottage was nearly silent. There were no streetlights, and they saw no other cars along the way. Lights twinkled in a few of the houses they passed, and a dog came out and barked at them from its yard, but those were the only signs of life. Bridget's cottage was dark, and Mick made the turn just past it to Maura's small house. Maura never left lights on, so her place was dark too.

"Let me go in first, will yeh?" Mick volunteered, and got out of the car before Maura could respond.

Rose, in the back seat, said quietly, "He's worried."

"He is. I'm surprised — he's usually so calm. But I'm worried too, and I'm not even sure why. Okay, a man is dead, but there's no reason to think it has anything to do with us. Except for where he was dumped. But that was a convenient place, which doesn't make it personal." As Maura watched, a light came on inside her cottage.

"It was a cruel death, Maura," Rose said softly. "A lot of anger in it, but whoever did it took his time to make sure he wasn't discovered. Not just a simple fight in a pub that got out of hand. And you know how rare a violent death is here."

"I do, sad to say. So you don't think I'm just a wimp for being, well, scared?"

"If you're a wimp, I'm one as well."

Mick returned and leaned into the car. "All's clear. Let's go in."

Once inside, Maura checked the time. Approaching midnight, so they might as well get to bed, once they sorted out who was going to go where. "Rose, you're the guest, so you get the second bedroom, which is barely big enough for a cat. I think there are sheets on the bed, since Gillian stayed here a while back. Mick . . ." Maura faltered.

Rose laughed. "Oh, go on wit' yiz! I'll be fast asleep in minutes, I promise. Have you a toothbrush to spare?"

"In the bathroom. We can sort out towels in the morning."

Rose, still smiling, headed for the bathroom tucked at the back of the house, leaving Maura and Mick alone in the main room.

"Yeh're embarrassed," Mick said with a half smile.

"Well, yeah, I guess. I never dated in high school, and I wasn't into quick hookups when I was working, so I never learned the rules. And Rose seems so young — except when she seems older than I am. I feel stupid, but like I said, I'd rather have her here than wandering around in the dark."

"And I agree. Odds are we're worried over nothin', but we will be safe."

His arms felt good around her and she leaned into him. "And we'll wake up in the morning and the gardaí will have sorted it all out and we can go back to our lives."

"They will, and we can."

Rose came out of the bathroom and darted toward the stairs. "Not looking, not looking! I'm leavin' now and I'll be shuttin' the door behind me." She giggled as she dashed up the stairs.

Maura had to smile. "I guess we should go up too, after I brush my teeth."

"Together?"

"Do yeh need to ask?"

CHAPTER SEVEN

Morning brought sun and the sound of lowing cows on their way to milking and Mick in her bed. Maura knew there was something she was supposed to be worried about, but she indulged herself in a long moment of simply feeling happy.

But it didn't last. She heard sounds of movement below, and the clashing of pans and plates, and the day before came rushing back. No burglar downstairs, then — not that she had anything worth stealing — only Rose, who must be putting together breakfast, which couldn't be easy in her kitchen since Maura didn't keep much to work with in her cottage.

She slid out of bed without disturbing Mick and pulled on a shirt and jeans, then went downstairs. Good smells wafted up the stairs, and she followed her nose.

"Good mornin'!" Rose greeted her. "Coffee's made."

"Good morning to you. Are you trying to make breakfast?" Maura asked as she poured herself a cup of coffee.

"Tryin's the word, indeed," Rose said. "Do yeh never eat? I won't even ask if yeh cook, since yeh've all of two pots to yer name."

"I can cook if I have to — I watched my gran plenty — but I'm just not into it."

"Cooking or eating?" Rose asked as she mixed something in Maura's only bowl.

"Either, I guess. But I like your cooking, in case you didn't notice. And it's even better since you started with the classes."

"Ah, yeh're just butterin' me up because you want me to cook fer Sullivan's."

"I'd love that, but it's up to you. If the West Cork Hotel offers you a real job in the kitchen, take it!"

"We'll see. We're a long way from bein' ready to cook anything at the pub. Is Mick stirrin' yet?"

"Not when I left. He may want to check in with his grannie this morning — you know she lives right down the lane."

"I do. She's a grand lady, isn't she?"

"She is. And a good friend."

"What does she think about you and Mick?" Rose asked, toasting what Maura recognized as the last of her bread. She'd

83

better do some shopping soon or she might actually starve.

"I think she's happy about it. You know, we may be friends, but it's her grandson who comes first, and I think she's glad he's finally found somebody. Although she's promised not to meddle. What time do you have to be at your school?"

"Ten. And I can get to the pub by noon, after — there's only the one class this morning, and we clear out before the lunch service. We've got the music at Sullivan's Saturday, right?"

"You tell me — you set up the reservations system."

"I did, and I'm going to teach yeh how it works, when we can find the time. You've no computer here, I see."

"Nope, never had one. Never wanted one. Don't I need some sort of connection for it anyway? I've barely got electricity here."

Rose sent a disapproving look her way. "Maura, yeh're a business owner now — yeh can't afford to be without one. There's wireless in the village, no problem. We'll talk about it later."

"Is that before or after we talk about how the kitchen planning is coming along?"

"The two together, mebbe — we could set up a website and do a big announcement when we're ready to start servin' food."

"Well, you know where to find me when you're ready."

"I do." Rose slid a plate of what looked like French toast in front of her.

"Did I have eggs?" Maura asked, not sure if she was joking.

"A few. Enough. It's the last of your jam on top. And have yeh never heard of spices?"

"Only if salt and pepper count." Maura speared a forkful. "Wow, this is good!"

Mick stumbled down the narrow stairs while she was still enjoying her first bite. "Good morning, Mick. You'd better grab a plate fast or there won't be anything left."

"Mornin'," he said. "Coffee?"

Maura pointed. "Rose did all the work."

He filled a mug without comment, while Rose fixed another plate. Then he sat at the table, took a long swallow of coffee, and tasted the French toast, and Maura and Rose watched with amusement as he perked up almost immediately. "Wow."

"Ditto," Maura said, grinning. "The girl can cook, right?"

It took only a few minutes to consume everything Maura had in her pantry, which was basically one shelf's worth of supplies. At least her coffee stash was holding up —

she always made sure of that.

When she checked her watch, Maura was surprised to find that it was barely eight o'clock. These long summer days were confusing. After a moment's thought, she said, "You know, since we're all together and we have a little time, we should talk business."

"Meanin' what?" Mick asked.

"Mostly finding some new staff. Jimmy's gone, and Rose is taking classes — with my blessing, Rose! — and we've got the music a couple of days a week, and we're talking about serving food. Face it — it's too much for the three of us to handle, seven days a week."

"What're yeh thinkin', then?" Mick asked.

"I really don't know. I may have been here a year now, but I don't know where to look for people to hire. Are there agencies? Do I just ask around and see who's looking for work? Who can I trust? I don't want to hire someone and have them bail out on me two weeks later. And what kind of person and skills am I looking for? I mean, at least I had some experience working in bars when I got here, but I've been doing it for a while. How long does it take to train someone who's never pulled a pint? Should I check if they can count well enough to make change?

Do I want men or women, girls or boys? And how many for the crowds we've got, and what if we get more people coming in over the summer?"

Rose and Mick exchanged a glance, and Maura thought they seemed amused, which ticked her off. "What? I'm not supposed to think about this?"

"Of course yeh are, Maura," Rose said. "I know there's classes at the school on restaurant management and how to staff a place. But Sullivan's is small. I think three or four people works for us, but only if we're all there at the same time, more or less. Which doesn't give anyone any time off." She looked at Mick again. "Maybe two more people, full time? Then we could juggle our schedules for the busy times."

"Seems about right," Mick replied. "Old Mick got by with the three of us and himself, but at the end he had few customers to deal with, so it didn't matter."

"I agree with what you've both said," Maura spoke up. "But where do I find people?"

"I'll ask at the school," Rose volunteered. "Though there the people in the classes might be hopin' for a kitchen job rather than just in a pub. But a lot of those jobs have already been filled fer the summer, so some might take whatever they could get. Are yeh willin' to pay the goin' rate?"

"Is that what I'm paying you now?"

"Close enough. But those that don't know you might think yeh're a bit cheap."

"Great," Maura muttered. "Well, ask around and see what kind of answers you get. Maybe one guy and one girl — sometimes it's good to have a man around in case things get crazy, but other times a pretty face is worth more to us."

"I'll ask," Rose said. "Would you be takin' me da back, if he asked?"

"Ah, Rose . . ." Maura sighed. "You know he never pulled his weight — he was happier sitting and talking with his pals instead of working the bar. It wouldn't be a good business decision. Why, is he looking to escape Judith already?"

"He hasn't said as much, but he's never liked cows. Don't worry, I won't be invitin' him back, fer yeh're right about him, but he may come round askin'."

"Thanks for the warning." Maura finished the last of her French toast. "Rose, tell me something. You finished school a year ago, right? What do most kids your age around here do when they're finished?"

"Are yeh askin' to see how many of us there are who might want a job?"

"In part. But I'm curious. I guess I don't know any families with kids in their teens and twenties. Do they stay around? Do they leave as fast as they can?"

"A bit of both. There's those who go to university if they can. Or go to Dublin and room with a bunch of other kids and take whatever job they can find there. There's some that decide to take a year off and travel around Europe, since fares are cheap to get there. There's some who are needed at home on the farm. And there's some that look fer local jobs — and that may be the smallest lot."

"That's not encouraging, for me at least. Mick, do you know anything different?"

"I don't know any more than Rose here, nor have I been lookin' fer new hires fer the pub. I might add that it's mostly word of mouth, yeh know? Like, yeh're sending Rose here to ask among her friends, and if they're not interested, they'll ask their friends, and so on down the line. Not the best solution for the long term, but yeh're lookin' to get through the summer now, am I right?"

"Yes, more or less. We were doing fine until recently, but I'm afraid we're going to get swamped for the next couple of months. Or maybe I'm hoping we will, but we still need more people." Maura thought for a moment. "What about newcomers?"

"Whaddya mean?" Rose asked, bewildered.

"Well, so far, for most things we've talked about asking somebody we know, who might have a relative or a friend he could talk to. And that works for a lot of things. But now it sounds like maybe that pool of people is drying up, because kids are so much more mobile these days, and if they're looking for a short-term job, they'd rather be in Dublin or Cork or someplace more interesting. And that's fine — I think everybody should have a chance to live their own life. But that means those kids or even older people aren't around to fill the jobs that are here."

"Maura, what're yeh getting' at?" Mick asked impatiently. "We've still got to get to the jobs we've got this morning, so could yeh hurry things up a bit?"

"Okay, whatever," Maura said. "What about immigrants? Refugees? People looking for asylum? Do they need or want jobs? And can we give them jobs without jumping through legal hoops or hiding them when a garda walks in?"

Mick and Rose exchanged a look. "To be honest, I don't know," Mick said. "Rose?"

"I don't recall that it ever came up when I

was in school. Maybe there were outsiders coming in then, but they weren't at school. I can't say as I know any."

"So does that mean there aren't any sort-of-young people looking for work, or only that you haven't met any?"

"The second, I'm thinking."

"Okay!" Maura slapped both her hands on the table. "Rose, talk to the people at your cookery school and see what they know, officially or otherwise. We'll keep the whole immigrant idea on the back burner for now." Then another thought hit her. "How about this? Maybe not everyone who's here under unsettled circumstances will want to pull pints, but I'd bet that some of them could help out with the kitchen repairs, even if it's just the heavy construction and painting and stuff. It might get done faster that way."

"That's a grand idea, Maura — so long as it's legal," Mick said. "And yeh might want to talk with Sergeant Conor, since no doubt he's seen more people like that in Limerick and knows the ropes."

"Definitely. As soon as they get this murder thing sorted out and he has the spare time." Another thought hit her, and she debated about bringing it up and then decided against it. Could the dead man be an immigrant, legal or illegal? That would explain why nobody knew him. And if that was true, maybe nobody would ever admit to knowing him. But it was up to the gardaí to look into that side of things, not her. Right now she needed help behind the bar.

"Mick, you going to go see Bridget?" she said, changing the subject.

"I should do, but I won't be long."

"Can I grab a shower while you're there? As long as you promise to give her my regards."

"I'll do that."

After Mick had left, Maura looked at Rose. "Have I now corrupted the morals of a minor? Is that a crime here? Wait — how long are you a minor in Ireland?"

"Till I'm eighteen, unless I want to run for the Dáil, or what you might call your Congress — then it'd be twentyone. Yeh're talking about you and Mick? Yeh're two healthy adults who seem to care about each other. Now, if yeh were takin' all the male customers into the back room for a quick snog or more, that would be different." Rose dropped her joking tone. "Look, Maura, I've known Mick since I started working at Sullivan's. But lately he's as happy as I've ever seen him, even if he doesn't let it show much. So if yeh're askin', I'm happy fer ye both."

"Rose, sometimes I wonder if you're older than I am. I just didn't want to offend anyone here — the rules are kind of different."

"Just don't rub anyone's nose in what yeh're doin' and yeh'll be fine." Rose stood up and started clearing the table of the few dishes. "Shouldn't we be getting to work now?"

"As soon as Mick comes back. You know, I ought to try that restaurant of yours and see what they're teaching you."

"You'd be welcome. Yeh know, you've room fer a garden here."

Maura laughed. "There may be room, but there's no time!"

"Maybe when yeh can find some more staff, you can find the time."

"Let's hope so."

CHAPTER EIGHT

Mick came back quickly and reported that Bridget was fine. "Does she know about the death?" Maura asked.

He nodded. "Friends have told her. Mebbe it seems a bit ghoulish, but some of the older country people have little to entertain them beyond stories of other people. And crimes. At least no one seems to know the man yet, or so she's been told."

"So there's no one to mourn him, and he's fair game for gossip." Which seemed oddly wrong to Maura.

"Yeh could say that. They don't mean to be hurtful. Are we ready to leave?"

"Please," Rose said. "Maura, yeh've no food in the house, so I'll stop by Fields on me way to catch the bus and stock your pantry."

"Rose! You don't have to do my shopping for me."

"Do I not? Take a look at yer shelves —

there's nothin' there. Tell her, Mick."

He tried not to smile. "Well, they do look kinda empty."

"And how do you feed yourself when you're at home, Mick Nolan?" Maura demanded. She didn't like that they were laughing at her, even if they were right. She'd survived a year without starving to death, hadn't she?

"The Costcutter up the road in Leap has plenty of basic food, and some of it's good — I stop by now and then. And I shop fer Bridget as well."

Maura was out of excuses. "Fine," she mumbled, then raised her voice. "Unless this is just an excuse to get me to hurry up with the pub kitchen so I can eat there."

"And would that be a bad thing?" Rose asked, trying to look innocent.

Maura sighed. "Let's get moving, or we'll all be late."

Mick drove, dropping Rose off in the center of Skibbereen, then heading back out of town toward Leap. "She's quite a girl," he said.

"That she is. I bet her father misses having her around, if Judith gives him any time." She swiveled in her seat to look at him. "Mick, am I trying to do too much all at once, with the pub? The music is pretty

95

much established now — maybe we should sit back and enjoy that for a while before we jump into something else."

"Has Harry run the numbers?" he asked, watching the road ahead.

"You mean, how much additional income serving food might mean? After we get done with paying for the construction and appliances and permits and so on? The people who follow the music come to hear the music, not to enjoy gourmet food."

"Rose can stick to high-end pub fare," Mick suggested.

"What makes it high-end?"

"Let her explain it to you. But I think her heart's set on local foods, whatever ends up on the plate."

"Well, I'm counting on you to tell me if I trying to juggle too many things."

"That I can do. And so far it's goin' well."

The crime tape was gone from the bridge, so Mick pulled into a convenient parking space. "Yeh don't mind parkin' so near — ?"

Maura finished his question. "The scene of the crime? No, it's okay. We'd better get inside."

The usual morning cleanup took no more than half an hour, and Maura left the front door ajar to signal that they were open for business. She was surprised to see Old Billy approaching — he was not usually the first to arrive. "Good morning, Billy. You're early today."

"I am that, and it's too soon fer a pint. Could yeh fix me a coffee? It's Rosie's mornin' at the school, am I right?"

"You are. Coffee coming up."

Mick was still busy in back, so Maura started Billy's coffee, then decided to make one for herself. When they were ready, she went back and sat down next to Billy. "Is something bothering you, Billy? This is early for you."

"Ah, yeh see right through me, Maura. I'd have to say, it's the dead man. His killin' doesn't sit well with me. It troubles me that none of us seems to know who he is, where he came from, who his people are. Was he one of us?"

"What do you mean?"

"Was he Irish?"

Was she one of that "us" now? She struggled to give Billy an accurate answer. "Since his face was damaged, the gardaí didn't have much to work with, you know. I didn't see anything that made me think he *wasn't* Irish. Dark hair, not too tall, pretty well muscled, so I wouldn't guess he was a vagrant or a druggie or something. I don't know if it's odd around here *not* to have tattoos or other markings. Back in Boston, probably half the guys his age would have some ink. But Boston's a city. Where's the nearest tattoo parlor, anyway? Skibbereen? Cork city?"

Billy smiled and sipped his coffee. "That I cannot say. Could be that Rose might know."

"I'll ask. So, no jewelry, like an earring. No fillings in his teeth. Maybe he dropped from Mars. Maybe I should be asking people if they've seen glowing green lights in a local field." She looked up to see Seamus and some of his buddies standing in the doorway. "Excuse me, Billy — looks like I've got customers."

She walked over to where the men stood, shifting from foot to foot. "Wow, I don't think I've ever seen your lot here so early," she told them. "Did you set your clocks wrong? And don't you have work to go to?"

"We've been talkin' about yer dead man," Seamus said sheepishly, "and we thought we'd do better if we put our heads together. Yeh remember our bettin' pool, back a few months?"

"Of course I do," Maura told him. "I won, didn't I? What's that got to do with anything?"

"Well, when we all got together and talked

98

it over then, we came up with, what, a dozen ideas about who might've killed the man. We thought we might have a go at it this time, only tryin' to figger out where this man came from rather than startin' with the killer. We know *how* he died, but why was he worth killin'?"

Maura considered it for a moment. "Not a bad idea, Seamus. Is there a bet this time?"

Seamus waved that idea away. "Nah. We thought we'd help the gardaí out. Can't hurt to have a credit with them, so to speak, in the rare event we might find ourselves in a bit of trouble with them."

Maura smiled. It seemed there was almost always more than one motive for any good deed around here. "So not just out of the goodness of your hearts. Well, I don't see why you shouldn't try. Settle yourselves at a table, and I'll throw in a pot of coffee."

When she went back behind the bar to set up the coffee, Mick asked. "What's that about?"

"The crime solvers gang is back at work. What do these guys do for work, anyway? They're in here a lot, and at odd times of day."

"Some have farms, and the mornin' milkin's done. Some of them do the odd construction job now and then. No one

99

thing, I'm guessin'."

"Well, as long as they pay their tab, I won't complain. Could you bring the coffee over when it's ready? We might as well lay out what we want to know now, in case it gets busy later in the day."

"That I will. Are yeh gonna tell the gardaí what yeh're doin'?"

"If we figure out something, sure."

Maura went back to the table and took the last chair. "Coffee's on its way. So, where did you plan to start?"

Seamus, as always, took the lead. "Well, we've no idea who the man is, fer a start. None of us claims to know every man of his age in the county, and it could be a visiting relative or some long-lost kin, just arrived, but nobody's reported anyone missin'."

Hadn't they already covered all this? "Seamus, we've already covered the basic facts. You have anything more today?"

"We've had a night to mull it over, haven't we? There's no abandoned car reported, and the man had no bus ticket on him. So how did our man arrive in the area?"

"Maybe he lost his bus ticket when he was killed. Or since his pockets were all empty, he could have been robbed earlier walking to . . . somewhere," Maura said.

Seamus sat back and grinned at her.

"Maura, yeh're a grand devil's advocate — isn't that what they say? Yeh'll argue just about any point, but that's a good thing because it makes the rest of us think. And yeh're right: he might've been robbed, although the force of the attack on his person went far beyond what would be needed to pick his pocket. If the wallet was all that was wanted, a whack on the back of the head would have been sufficient."

"True," Maura agreed. "Do people hitchhike around here?"

"Sure and they do." A man Maura recognized as part of the usual group from Seamus's last effort at detective work, and whose name she thought was Jerry, spoke up for the first time. "Mostly the gardaí look the other way, and there's plenty of folk willin' to stop and pick up someone if he looks decent. Or she."

Maura nodded. "So he could have been a hitchhiker. But nobody's found a bag or backpack for him. Wouldn't he be carrying something?" *Like a change of clothes? A good book?* Maura thought irreverently, then felt ashamed. She had to keep reminding herself that the man was dead, and this wasn't a game.

"He might have done," Seamus agreed amiably. "So he could have been Irish, or he could have been from somewhere else. It's not clear he knew where he was going. In fact, we don't even know whether he was traveling on the main road out there, or through the countryside, or even which way he was headin'. But we can guess that whoever killed him and hid his body *did* know his way around here, because he picked a pretty good hiding place, at least for a short stay. Jerry, it might be wise to make notes of our ideas, so we're sure to follow through."

Jerry dutifully fished a tattered pad from a pocket, located a pencil, and set to work. "Irish or not? Did the killer know the village well? And how? Have I got those right?"

"That's grand, Jerry."

Maura interrupted. "Do you think the killer wanted the man to be found, or was he in a hurry and dumped him at the first likely place he came to?"

"A good point, Maura. I'd guess a bit of both. It's a public road, with shops on both sides, so he was bound to be found soon enough, but I'd wager the killer wanted him to be found — after he'd had time to make his escape. Have yeh got all that, Jerry?" Jerry nodded.

"Guys?" Maura broke in. "Can we speed this up a bit? Sometime today I need to run my business. Let's assume that if the dead man was Irish, the gardaí have a better chance of figuring out who he was, okay? It he *wasn't* Irish, it's a harder problem."

"How's that gonna help us?" Jerry demanded.

"Well, let's widen the pool just a bit. Say he's not local, and he's not Irish. Who else do we have wandering around this part of Cork?"

"Ah, I see where yeh're headed with this," Seamus said. "Who's here long enough to make enemies, yet still be no more than passin' through?"

"Exactly," Maura told him. "It's summer, so there are lots of strangers around, or short-timers. But who?"

"Travellers, fer one," Seamus said firmly. "If they're not the settled ones."

Maura looked blankly at him. "Huh?"

"Ah, yeh've not heard of the Irish Travellers? They're kind of a roving group, mostly. They have caravans and the like, and in the warmer months they, well, travel, from place to place, often with a set route year after year. In the colder times they settle in one place or another, so the kids can get some schooling."

"Kind of like Gypsies?" Maura asked.

"Don't yeh dare say that to a Traveller!

Different races, and I do mean by blood. And sadly, the Gypsies aren't quite honest — they're often petty thieves, or they drum up cash by fakin' road accidents. The Travellers may follow a path that seems similar, but they're more often honest. And they're Irish by blood, although it goes back a ways."

"Wow, I've never even heard of them. Are there any around here?"

"Not precisely in this area, but there are some larger settlements — they're often called halting grounds — up near Limerick, and others around Cork city."

"And are they violent? I mean, would they be likely to kill someone?"

"Mostly they travel as families and mind their own business. Which is not to say that yer dead man wasn't one of them, who ran afoul of a local man who bore a grudge or just didn't like them. Let the gardaí look at that side — they do keep an eye on the Travellers, which is not the same as sayin' they hassle them. Live and let live, as long as there's no trouble."

"So they go on our list?"

"They do. Only to see if there were any around this week. They may be on the move."

Maura put the idea of Travellers away to

think about later. "Okay, any other surprises? And before you laugh at how ignorant I am, remember that I don't get out of this place much, and it's usually late when I do. So there are probably lots of people I never see at all."

"That's why yeh have us, Maura," Seamus said cheerfully.

CHAPTER NINE

Maura noticed Seamus checking his own watch. "You have somewhere to be?" she asked.

"I told the missus I'd move some hay to the upper field, and she'll skin me alive if I don't do it today. But I wanted to be sure we all know who we're lookin' for, casual like. Am I right, fellas?"

His cronies nodded. "We're not lookin' to do the job of the gardaí," Jerry said, "but we talk to different folk than they do, and we hear things. People might not mention the word *murder,* but they might know if there've been any fights lately. Apart from the ordinary, that is."

"That makes a lot of sense, Jerry," Maura said. "Seamus, if you've got to go, let's finish our list."

"Right so," Seamus said briskly. "This may be unlikely, but in the summer the blow-ins arrive — yeh've run into them in the past, Maura."

"What, you're saying some English or German or Belgian couple or family comes over here looking to try something different this year, like murder?" She hoped she was joking.

"Ah, surely not. But some of 'em have people workin' fer 'em that they bring along, and it's too much bother to get them visas, if they even need them, so nobody knows they're here. Could be somebody's gardener or driver got into some trouble, and it was easier to kill him than to get into a big legal mess."

Maura was horrified. "Seamus! You're not saying that someone with a summer cottage would kill someone who works for them just because he's inconvenient?"

Seamus shrugged. "Wasn't it one of yer American writers who said 'the rich are different from you and me'? I'm not goin' to pretend to know what they're thinkin'. I'm only sayin' it's possible. We're lookin' fer people who're invisible to most of us who live here. That kind of hired person fits the bill."

He had a point, one she hadn't thought of. "Well, put him on the bottom of the list. Who's next?"

"Students."

"You mean college kids? Do they still just come over and hang out, and take the odd job when they need cash?"

"Yes and no, I'd say. If yeh're not Irish but yeh're takin' courses or spendin' a year at university here, you can work summers and holidays all proper and legal — there's a visa fer it."

"I hadn't heard about that." Maura made a mental note to check that out — it would fit her need for extra help in the summer very nicely if the kids were allowed to work in pubs, and if it wasn't already too late to set it up this year. "You're saying the dead man might've been a student? He looked sort of old for that, but it was hard to tell. Still, wouldn't someone have missed him by now?"

"It's summer. He might not have bothered mentionin' his plans to his friends or family. He might've just said, 'Oh, I'll be workin' on a farm in Kerry this summer.' Though with everybody havin' a mobile these days, someone could be expectin' to hear from him. Do yeh know if the gardaí found his mobile?"

Maura shook her head. "Not that I've heard of. The gardaí haven't said whether he had one, but I'm not sure if they know how to find out. If he did have one, I can't

108

imagine that anybody would be dumb enough to keep it, so it might be smashed or be lying at the bottom of the harbor, and I doubt the gardaí have looked very hard. It's kind of hard to look for something you aren't sure exists."

"That's fer the gardaí to look into."

"Right. They're certainly better at stuff like that than we are. Anybody else?"

Jerry spoke up suddenly. "Foreigners. I'm not sayin' that in a bad way. There'd be tourists, sure, but there's also immigrants, legal or not, and those who come here hoping for asylum."

The whole problem was becoming more complicated than Maura had expected. "But don't they have to register or something? I mean, when I got here, I didn't have to do anything more than show my passport. Oh, but it was an Irish passport — my grandmother made me get one."

"Most often people from other countries do, especially if they hope to stay, but I don't think they check in daily with whoever's handlin' their paperwork. So once again, who's to know they're missin'?"

If the poor guy hadn't been dumped literally in her own yard, Maura thought she would have given up about now. Too many groups of people who might fit the description of the dead man. Too many she'd never even heard about, or who would take the kind of hunting and searching that she wasn't any good at and didn't have time for anyway. And the gardaí were probably already tramping all over this ground.

She looked up to see Seamus watching her sympathetically. "It's a lot to think on, Maura. Nobody's tellin' yeh that yeh're the one who has to sort this out. But the gardaí and the rest of us are all startin' from the same place this time. Let them do what they do best — follow up on things like immigration. All I'm suggesting is that we keep our ears open and see what news we pick up."

Maura smiled. "And might that mean stopping in a few extra pubs? Just to listen, of course."

"Only to gather information, to be sure."

"You're not still thinking of a new betting pool, are you?"

"We haven't worked out the details, but the day is young." Seamus finished his coffee. "I've got to get back to dealin' with me cows, and I'm sure these other lads have their own chores. Let's plan to gather at the end of the day here —"

"After milkin' time," somebody said quickly.

"Right so," Seamus said, "and see if we've

got anythin' new fer the gardaí. If that suits yeh, Maura?"

"You know you're always welcome. But you've got to pay for at least some of your pints."

"Ah, yeh're a hard woman, Maura Donovan," Seamus said, but with a smile.

"And one who has to make a living. Good luck to all of you."

Rose arrived just as Seamus and his posse were headed out the door. When she crossed to the bar, she asked, "What was that about?"

Maura smiled. "You mean, why was that crowd here so early in the day? They're looking to help the gardaí with their investigation."

"You mean the poor dead man? Whyever do they think they can help?"

"Actually it's not a bad idea. Look, you know we and the gardaí have got zero information on the guy so far. Seamus and his pals hang out at a lot of pubs and know a lot of people. All they're suggesting is that they pay attention to what people are saying. It's less formal than a police interrogation, right? So maybe it won't scare people off. Shoot, I should have told them to talk to their wives too — women talk to each other in a different way, and in different places. They might pick up information too."

"So long as they don't go about pretendin' to interview people," Rose said, looking unconvinced.

"It's not exactly an organized thing — it's just people talking. Like you can talk to the people in your classes. Are they local? Are they Irish? Has one of their friends gone missing?"

"I could do," Rose agreed. "But mostly we talk about the food." She changed the subject. "No other people this morning?"

"Nope. Let's hope there's more tonight. How was your class? Was this a food one or a management one?"

"Management. I'm tryin' to take more of those up front. I can handle the food and even experiment with dishes, but I've no knowledge about how to run a place. Would Harry be able to give me any information on how to estimate costs?"

"Maybe," Maura said. "I admit I can't explain it to you. If you talk to him, let me know — I should listen in."

"I'll tell yeh if it happens. Yeh need to know, Maura, if yeh're going to keep this place running and in the black."

"I know, I know." Maura sighed. "It's just that I never seem to have the time. I'm here like at least twelve hours a day, and the rest of whatever time I have left, I have to eat and shower and sleep. Did you have any luck asking if any of your classmates need a part-time job?"

"Not as yet. I might talk to the instructors, see if they have any ideas how to find people. But they're pretty much rushed off their feet as well. Have yeh had lunch yet?"

"No, Seamus and the gang took up an hour or so of the morning."

"If they're comin' back later — which I'm guessin' they are — do they get free pints?"

"Maybe. I told Seamus I'd have to charge them at least some of the time — this is a business, after all, not a social club. Check with me after the first round, okay?"

Rose sighed. "I'm glad we're not rushin' into gettin' our kitchen here together — we're barely handling the things we've got goin' now."

"You think getting the kitchen going is a bad idea?"

"Not at all, Maura. But we need to know what we're lettin' ourselves in for and be ready, not just shut our eyes and jump blindly. And havin' more people workin' here, even part-time, would make it easier fer us all."

"I know, Rose. I think I should make you manager here, and I'll just keep pulling

113

pints and chatting up the guys. You can run the business side."

Rose smiled. "That's a grand compliment, Maura, but I'd really rather just cook. And watch people enjoy what I've cooked fer 'em."

Maura was getting ready to go out in search of food for herself when Gillian appeared at the door, with Henry riding along in his sacky-thing. "Hey, Gillian! What brings you here two days in a row?" Maura greeted her.

"A craving for adult conversation. You know, the kind that uses words and doesn't involve drool. Do you have any on hand?"

"I might. Have you eaten?"

"He has" — Gillian looked down fondly at her sleeping son — "but I haven't. Where do you want to go?"

"I've had enough of Ger's lately." Maura didn't mention the dead man. "And the Costcutter. The bistro's a bit pricey for lunch. Rose? Do you mind if we head over to Union Hall for a bite?"

"Sure and yeh should go!" Rose said firmly. "It's a grand day, and we're not too busy — now that we know Seamus and friends will not be back fer a few hours. Hi, Gillian — how's the little one?"

"Growing like a weed and always hungry.

114

We can chat later, because I'm hungry too, thanks to him."

"You want me to drive?" Maura asked.

"Only if you've got that kiddy seat in your car," Gillian said firmly.

"Oops, I forgot. You can drive and I'll play with Henry."

"That suits me." Gillian led the way out to where she'd parked and spent a couple of minutes getting the baby strapped in and settled. Once they were on the road for the quick ride to Union Hall, Gillian asked, "So what's new in your world? Anything on that poor man?"

"Nope. Seamus and the lads came by to volunteer their services to identify him."

"Seriously? What is it they think they can do?"

"It may not be a bad idea, actually. We're all starting from the same place, as Seamus pointed out to me. The gardaí have their own ways of looking at things, but Seamus and friends hang out in a lot of other places — pubs, of course, but also feed stores and hardware stores and places like that — so they hear different things. Besides, why discourage them? They might come up with something, and I don't think they can get into trouble."

"Are you so sure of that? Your man died

in an awful way. I mean, multiple stab wounds? That means his killer has a temper and may have been angry. But he was also smart enough and cool enough to plan on where to leave the body — he didn't just dump the man and run."

"Gillian, you're depressing me. You're right, of course, but I hope that Seamus and the gang have enough common sense not to go blundering into places and asking people if they've killed anybody lately or seen someone hiding a body. Or even if they've seen a pool of unexplained blood. From the way they were talking, I think they're going to do more listening. You know, somebody says something like, 'I thought cousin Denis was coming for a visit, but there's no sign of him and he's not answering his mobile.' I'd guess the guys can ask some innocent-sounding questions, like, 'Was he the one from over Bandon way?' They certainly aren't going to ask if he hangs out with thugs or foreigners."

"I can see your point. I just don't want to hear of anybody else getting hurt or disappearing."

"Neither do I! Seamus and friends make up a large part of my business, and I don't want to lose them." Maura realized they'd already reached Union Hall. "The Coffee Shop?"

"My thought exactly."

already reached Union Hall. "The Coffee
Shop?"
My thought exactly.

CHAPTER TEN

The small restaurant and bakery in Union
Hall was nicely filled, which pleased Maura
— she wanted the place to survive because
she was addicted to their house-made
pastries, even though she rarely had a
chance to buy them. She and Gillian found
a table for four in the corner, where they
could park Henry's carrier easily. If they
had thought they wouldn't be noticed there,
they were wrong, because half of the women
in the place, both staff and customers, came
to coo over Henry, who slept through all
the attention.

Maura watched with a smile until everyone had taken a turn, then asked, "Does
that happen everywhere you go?"

"More or less. I assume it won't last
forever. But he is adorable, isn't he? You
don't have to answer that — I know I'm
just a bit prejudiced. What do you want to
eat?"

"Something I don't make at home, which is mostly scrambled eggs or cheese sandwiches."

Gillian shook her head. "Ah, Maura, you really must improve your diet. You work hard — you need to keep up your strength. Are you still thinking of opening the kitchen at the pub?"

"Yes, but it hasn't gone beyond thinking. Rose is taking cooking and restaurant management classes in Skibbereen, and I'm waiting for her to get a few of those under her belt before we think about the kitchen — but I'm guessing she's already got some good ideas. Besides, we're busy enough with the music for now. By the way, Rose asked if I had talked to Harry about the financial side of serving food, and I had to tell her no. Would he mind talking us through the basics? I know he's busy with the hotel."

Gillian waves her hand. "Of course he'll help — we owe you enormously. And your place isn't exactly large or complicated, so Harry would have no problems. I'll run it by him and we can set up a time. Rose will want to be there too?"

"Of course. She's a smart kid, and she'll probably understand it better than I will. I'm really glad she's out from under Jimmy's thumb. And that he's someone else's problem now." One of the owners came over to take their order, and Maura decided on a salad with a lot of unfamiliar ingredients. What the heck — she needed to eat more greens. If the stuff in the salad was actually green. In the sample in the chiller cabinet, some of it looked red, and there were some purple leaves lurking.

When the owner had gone back to the kitchen area, Maura asked, "Has your family come around yet?"

"Not really. We had Henry christened in church, to please the family, and my mother and father graciously came, since we were doing what she would consider the right thing by the child. But she's still miffed that Harry and I aren't married. They didn't hang around after the ceremony."

"I'm sorry to hear that — it must make things hard for you. Funny, isn't it, that Bridget, who's twice your mother's age, can be so open-minded about it, but your mother can't."

"I know — Bridget's a special person. But Harry and I are good, with or without my parents' support. How're you and Mick doing?"

Once again, Maura couldn't hide her blush. "Fine. I think. I have nothing to

120

compare to. He smiles more than he used to."

"He never used to smile at all, whenever I saw him, so that must be a good sign."

"We're taking things slowly. I've made enough big changes in my life in the past year, so I'm not in a hurry." Still, it was nice to know that Mick was happy, or at least happier than in the past.

"I'm not pushing you in any direction, Maura. But you're a friend, and I want you to stay around. Oh, and I want you to be happy too, but if that doesn't include Mick, that's all right. It's your life."

"Sometimes I wonder." Maura smiled at Gillian. "None of this kind of stuff used to happen to me back in Boston. Anyway, enough about me. How's the hunt for a childminder going?"

Gillian's face fell. "Terrible. I started out with high hopes, you know. There are all sorts of agencies listed on the Internet, but when I started looking at the details, most of the girls or women wanted full-time, live-in positions, in or near a city. None of which can I offer. I didn't even dare look at how much salary they expected to receive, beyond room and board and a day or two off each week. I wouldn't mind offering a room, or at least subsidizing one. Has Rose had any luck finding someone for us?"

"Gillian, we only asked her to ask around yesterday, and she's been to exactly one class at the cookery since. So no, no results. You know, she hasn't been there very long, and she's usually at the pub when she's not taking classes or putting in time in the kitchen there, so I'd guess she hasn't had a lot of time to get to know the other people. And she's been so busy that she hasn't been able to keep up with her local friends from school, most of whom seem to have moved on anyway. What kind of a schedule are you looking for? Or maybe I should ask, what do you think is the best you could hope for?"

The waitress delivered their lunch and stopped a moment to coo at Henry, who, miraculously, was still asleep and looked angelic. When she'd gone back behind the counter, Gillian resumed, "Well, I know I can't be as flexible with my painting sched-ule as I was before. You know — getting lost in the work and trying to capture the last of the light, and then looking up to find that ten hours have passed."

Maura laughed. "No, I don't know. I run a pub, remember? It has set opening and closing hours and we're always short of staff. But to get back to you, in the real world, what do you want?"

Gillian reflected. "Well, I'd settle for maybe four uninterrupted hours at a stretch, three days a week. If I'm inspired, Harry can fill in now and then. But I don't know where I can find someone with that irregular a schedule."

"At least that gives me an idea of what you're looking for. Now, as far as I know, twelve hours a week isn't going to support much of anyone around here, unless you're offering a lot per hour. Of course, I don't have any idea what the going rate for much of anything is. I mean, Rose and Mick kind of came with the place, and I asked them what they'd been making under Old Mick and they told me, and that's what I've been paying them. Which for all I know is completely unfair to them."

"Do you know what the minimum wage is in the country?"

"Uh, no. I assume you do?"

"Of course I do — I'm married to an accountant, remember? Since 2017, an experienced adult worker is entitled to at least nine point two five euros per hour — and that term 'experienced' is pretty easy to meet. The rate goes down from there, based on age and experience. Which means, you can hire someone younger and unskilled for less."

"Huh," Maura said, feeling stupid. She'd never liked math much, but she did have a responsibility to the people who worked for her, and she needed to know this kind of stuff if she was going to hire more people, which might mean she'd have to increase what she paid Mick and Rose too. And then take a hard look at her budget.

"Do you pay yourself?" Gillian asked, interrupting her thoughts.

"Uh, sort of. I mean, I have the house, and I don't eat much, but I do have to buy gas and insurance and stuff. But it's not exactly a salary I can count on."

Gillian was shaking her head before Maura finished talking. "I think I need to get you together with Harry when you have some free time."

"Yeah, I know. But I never expected to run a business, so I didn't prepare for it. I mean, I took a couple of night classes on budgets and accounting, but I guess I didn't take them seriously — I just thought they'd help me get a job. But can we please get back to the problem right now? I need to find more staff, you need a part-time some-one to look after Henry. What do we do?"

Gillian poked at the food that remained on her plate. Without looking at Maura, she said, "Well, there are some other options, if you're not too particular about the legal side of things . . ."

"What, hire somebody undocumented?"

"It doesn't have to be someone who's in the country illegally, but some don't qualify for work permits and the like right away if they're waiting for a green card or a visa or permanent status. And they may not have family or friends around to support them while they wait."

"Oh," Maura said. "That sucks. But — the gardaí are in and out of Sullivan's all the time. How could I hire anybody who's not quite legal without them noticing?"

Gillian shrugged. "I don't know, but I may find out when I get truly desperate, and I don't get a lot of visits from the gardaí. I love this child to distraction, but I'm forgetting who 'me' is. I need some outside help, and my family's useless."

"I do understand, Gillian — really. Like I said, it sounds like we have the same problem but for different reasons. You need to find some time to keep you sane, and if I look hard at it, I'm probably going to burn out if I try to keep doing everything at the pub myself. So somehow we have to find a hidden group of part-timers with flexible hours who can fill in when we need them."

"Or we could share one person and make

it up to fulltime hours. Half barmaid, half baby-minder."

"Worth thinking about!" Maura said. "Are we having dessert?"

"Need you ask?" Gillian grinned.

They managed to make it back to Sullivan's in less than an hour. By that time, Henry had begun to make little whimpering noises, so Gillian elected to take him home to feed him his lunch. As she was leaving, she told Maura, "Let's think some more about what we talked about. And talk to Rose — she probably has a better idea of what the other students' schedules are like. And if we come up with an arrangement that suits, it doesn't need to be forever. Things do keep changing — even babies."

Maura smiled. "I'd make a bad pun, but I don't think you need to hear it."

"Oh, sorry. I guess I'm used to it. See you soon!"

CHAPTER ELEVEN

Even after a full year and more, Maura was still trying to figure out the crowd patterns for the pub. Actually, *crowd* was kind of an exaggeration, since sometimes — usually midweek, midafternoon — the crowd might be only three people, each buying one and only one drink. But she couldn't open and close by the hour, could she? Maybe that one person who arrived and found the door locked at three o'clock in the afternoon would be the one who could have changed her life, but he went to the Harbour Bar only a few steps away instead. Although, come to think of it, she seldom saw more than one person working the bar there, and they served food. She really needed to work out a plan for staffing.

The next arrivals were the family she had met the day before — she struggled a moment to remember the name. It started with an A . . . Albertson, that was it. American.

Mom, Dad, and sulky daughter. Mick had set them up with a friendly B and B not far away. Right now the Albertsons looked kind of nervous, and Maura guessed that they'd heard about the death.

Mom — Linda? — took the lead. "Hi, remember us?" she said, advancing tentatively into the room.

"Sure," Maura said promptly. "You're the Albertsons. How's the place working out?"

"Oh, it's very nice. Peaceful too. I didn't realize there'd be so many cows around here."

"County Cork is a major dairy region. I'll bet you even get Cork butter in the U.S. these days. Can I get you something?"

"I, uh — could we talk for a minute? You don't look too busy."

"No problem. You sure I can't get you something? Coffee? A Guinness?"

The husband — Marv, Maura remembered — finally spoke. "I haven't had a Guinness since we got here. Give me a pint. Please."

Linda laid a hand on his arm and said anxiously, "Oh, Marv, should you be drinking so early in the day? And you're driving."

"Don't worry, Linda," Maura reassured her. "It's not that strong, and he doesn't have to finish it, if you're worried. But he's

128

right — everybody should try it in Ireland. If you've had it back in the States, it's a very different drink."

"Okay, I guess." Linda didn't seem convinced. "But let me have a coffee, please. Jannie?" she called out to her daughter. "You want something to drink?"

Jannie tore herself away from the array of old music posters and souvenirs on the walls and said, "What sodas you got?"

So the girl actually could speak? "Of course. Coke? Pepsi? Or juice, if you want."

"Whatever," Jannie said, trying to pretend she wasn't connected to her parents.

"Coming up. Why don't you sit down at a table and I'll bring your drinks over?"

"Great!" Marv said with forced heartiness. "This way, ladies." He shepherded his little family to a corner table overlooking the street.

While she poured the drinks, Maura told Mick, "They seem worried about something, and I said I'd talk with them. Either they hate their B and B or they've heard about the body. If it's the second one, I have to figure out how to tell them that this is about as safe a place as you can be in Ireland. I'll bet Indiana has a higher crime rate."

"Could be, but it's not what they were

129

lookin' fer in a happy holiday," Mick said.

"True. Could you do me a coffee while the pint settles?"

When the drinks were ready, Maura carried them over to the table, handed them out, and sat down. "So, what can I help you with?"

Linda took the lead, after a glance at her husband, who was enthusiastically sampling the Guinness. "We're sorry to bother you, but I thought that since you were American, you'd understand."

That could mean any number of things. "Is it something about the B and B? I don't know the people who run it, but Mick does and he vouches for them."

"Oh, no, no, it's not them. They've been very welcoming, and the place is lovely — simple, but it has all the necessities. But we were in the town, and I overheard someone say something about a murder?"

Maura had guessed right. "We don't know officially if it's a murder yet, but yes, a body was found yesterday — he'd died the night before, it looks like."

Linda looked down at her coffee and swirled it around with her spoon. "It's just that we came to Ireland because we thought it was peaceful. No crime, you know."

"And it is," Maura said firmly. "Look, I

grew up in a kind of rough part of Boston. I knew plenty about crime there, and I knew people who committed them. This place is nothing like that. Ireland isn't like that, and this corner of the country is about as crime-free as it gets. I won't sugarcoat it. You go to the cities — Dublin, Cork, even Limerick — and you'll find crime, because that's the way the world is these days. Yes, there are gangs and drugs, and people get into fights. But not once you get outside of the cities. I'm pretty sure you can look up the numbers on the Internet for Cork. It's too bad this guy had to die, but nobody's even sure how or where it happened. Please, don't think it's normal for around here. And I know some of the guys at the police station — that's in Skibbereen — and they're good people. Does that help?"

Marv spoke up in a hearty voice, "See, Linda? I told you you were worrying about nothing." He turned to Maura. "She worries a lot, you know. She's sure I'm gonna run headfirst into a car because I forget which side of the road I'm supposed to be driving on. Or I'll give somebody the wrong bill and blow the budget."

"Hey, don't worry about that — people around here are honest. You overpay, they'll tell you. As for the driving stuff, just take it easy until you're used to it. A lot of the local roads are too small to worry about which side you're on — just don't go too fast, especially around curves. On the bigger roads, like the one out there" — Maura nodded toward the road that ran in front of the building — "you might have noticed that there are dotted yellow lines along the side in some places. That means you can pull over there and let someone behind you pass. If they really, *really* want to get by, they'll flash their lights. Just take it slow."

"Good advice just about anywhere," Marv said. "Doesn't seem too crowded anyway."

"Mostly it isn't. But don't try to drive through Skibbereen on a Sunday morning when church is letting out."

He smiled. "I'll remember that."

"Anything else I can tell you? What brought you to this part of the country? What kind of things do you want to see? This time of year, there are a lot of small festivals going on that might interest you."

Jannie spoke — the first time Maura had heard her put together two sentences. "Hey — those posters and stuff on the walls. They for real?"

"Yeah. The guy who used to own this place probably had all those bands here in the past, going back a long way. We're try-

132

ing to bring that back now, with current bands, although things are really different now."

"Cool. Can anybody come? I mean, would they let me in?" For once, Jannie looked almost excited about something.

"Janice!" Her mother protested quickly. "A bar? At night?" She turned to Maura. "I assume this music takes place at night?"

Maura hid a smile. What kind of a place did Linda think she was running? "Yes. But look around, will you? This is not some grungy bar full of scruffy characters. Anybody is welcome, if you pay the cover fee, which isn't very high. Before you ask, Linda, no, we do not serve alcohol to minors, and my staff knows that. No exceptions. Heck, you probably saw Rose the first time you came in. She's seventeen, and she's been working here longer than I have. She knows the rules, and she doesn't drink. As for the music, I'd guess the average age of the audience falls somewhere between you and your daughter, but we don't allow any kind of violence. No fights. We want people to have a good time."

"You got anybody coming in this weekend?" Jannie said.

"Sure. Check the poster on the door — I have trouble keeping track of the band names."

Jannie flashed a brief smile. "Dad? Can we? Come some night, I mean?"

Marv looked conflicted, and then glanced at Maura and seemed to come to a decision. "Yeah, why not? That's why we came to Ireland, right? To see what the place is really like." Linda looked worried but didn't say anything, but Maura assumed Dad would win out.

"Hey, if you're worried, why don't you talk to Rose? She's just come in." Maura nodded toward the bar, and Rose raised a hand and waved.

"She looks like a perfectly nice girl," Linda said dubiously.

"She is. Go talk to her, Jannie." Maura stood up quickly. "Oops, gotta go — customers."

The place filled up gradually over the next hour or so, and Maura didn't notice when the happy Albertsons slipped out. She wondered why they had really come to Ireland. People who just wanted a change of scene usually went to the beach somewhere, like Florida. Whose idea had it been to come all the way to Ireland? And why not England? Maybe there was a story there, but Maura didn't have time to worry about it. Despite the Albertsons' reaction to the death, most local people came for information, to trade gossip, to catch up on local news. It wasn't ghoulish; it was just normal human curiosity. And, lucky for her, most people wanted a pint to go along with the gossip.

At some point, Maura joined Rose behind the bar. "You saw the Albertsons, right?"

"I did that. They seem a bit out of place, do they not?"

"Yes, I guess they do. They seem scared of their shadow. The first thing they asked about was the dead man here."

"Maybe they came here to get away from things like that back home?"

"But I wouldn't have thought they'd get so upset by one event. I'll have to ask where they come from exactly. They said Indiana, but there's a lot of Indiana, I think, and some of it's kind of rough, or so I've heard. Never been there."

"Rougher than yer Boston?" Rose asked, polishing a glass.

"Maybe in a few parts, but not in general. If we see them again, maybe you could talk with Jannie? I don't know if it's true in Ireland, but I've been told that in the States, traveling and hanging out with your parents is the kiss of death, even if you get along well with them. I feel sorry for Jannie —

she's just too old to enjoy that part of things. Or that's my guess. What do I know about cheerful families on vacation?"

"I'm thinkin' yer right, Maura. She's just actin' her age, I'd guess."

"Which is pretty close to yours, Rose, but you act a lot older."

Rose shrugged. "I had no choice. Da was a mess when me mum died, and there was no one else to step in fer us."

"How're your classes going?"

"Good. It's harder work than I imagined, but it's great to learn what really goes on. You should eat there sometime."

"Like, go out to dinner?" Maura smiled. She could count on one hand the number of times she'd done that, and one of those had been with Sean Murphy, on an official date that went nowhere. She was grateful that she'd managed to keep him as a friend. He was a good guy, and she kind of hoped he and Rose might get together at some point — something she'd never mentioned, because she wanted Rose to have a life outside Leap before she settled down with anyone.

"I know that's not yer style and nights are busy here, but maybe you could come over for lunch and I could introduce you to the staff? Oh, didja have lunch with Gillian like

136

you planned?" Rose interrupted her day-dreaming.

"I did. She's still stuck trying to find a childminder so she can get some work done. But she doesn't know a lot of people your age or even my age around here who are looking for that kind of work, and all she can find online are people who want a lot of money and more besides. Have you had a chance to ask anyone at the cookery school?"

"Sorry, no, but I will. In summer I'm guessin' it's not hard to find someone, but Gillian's going ta want someone past that, and people go back to school. I'll kick it around with some of the girls I've met — maybe they have sisters. Or even mothers, lookin' for a little cash."

Maura noticed that Rose was avoiding her eyes. "And all your own friends have gone off to do something else, right?"

"Yes. Internships, study, some to uni, some to jobs in Cork city, living with six other people in a flat."

"Would you want to do that?"

Rose shook her head slowly. "I'm not sayin' I'd mind a chance to see a bit of the world, but I've always been the one to look after things. I wouldn't know how to put me first."

Maura sighed. "I hear you. Neither of us seems to have had a chance to be young and enjoy it."

Rose looked up and flashed Maura a brief smile. "Are yeh complainin'?"

"With all that's been handed to me in the past year? Of course not. But you have a chance to plan, not just wait for something to fall into your lap."

Rose stepped back and put her hands on her hips. "Maura Donovan, are yeh tryin' to get rid of me?"

"Heck, no. You're the one who brings in the younger men, and some of the older ones as well. I'd lose money if you left."

"Good to know I'm needed."

CHAPTER TWELVE

When Maura had a free moment, she leaned toward Rose and said, "Did Jannie talk with you?"

"No more than a few words. She's only lonely. She wasn't happy about coming along on this trip, and there's been little to change her mind. I told her I'd take her to talk with some kids her age, maybe hang out a bit. If her parents will let her out of their sight."

"I guess they haven't traveled much, or at least not outside the States. And — I know I sound ridiculous saying this — kids grow up so fast today, and I think they haven't noticed that. I hope they relax and find a way to enjoy themselves."

"No worries," Rose said, polishing the bar top.

Maura turned away to clear the table in the front and saw Sergeant Ryan coming in, wearing his usual expression, which was grim. She seemed to recall having seen him smile — once or twice — but she assumed he was in work mode now. "Sergeant." She nodded to him when he was close. "Can we get you anything? Or do you have news for us?"

"No to the both of yer questions. I'd like to ask some more questions. Can we go somewhere more private?"

Was that good or bad news? Maura wondered. "Let's go to the back room, and we can shut the door. You've seen where the body was found?"

"I've had a quick look at the place, but I just want to make sure my information is correct."

"I did talk to Sean Murphy, you know." Maura wondered if it might be a mistake to bring him up — she wasn't sure if the sergeant had figured out her working relationship with Sean yet, since Conor Ryan hadn't been part of the Skibbereen station for long. But she didn't want to waste anybody's time repeating the same information.

"And I've read his notes. But it never hurts to have another eye look at the facts."

"Fine." Maura led him to the back room, where the music happened. Right now it was empty, and she walked over to one of the tables at the far end. Not that anyone would try to eavesdrop on their conversation. "What do you want to know?" Even though she kept her voice low, the sound echoed off the high ceiling, since the large room was empty of other people.

Sergeant Ryan pulled out the standard pocket-sized note pad and leafed through it. "You called the station to report you'd found what you believed to be the body of a man at the base of the bridge at approximately one o'clock on Monday. How did you come to find him?"

Why was it that all of Ryan's questions sounding vaguely like accusations? And she'd already reported the details to Sean. But she swallowed her resentment and said, "It was a busy morning, and I wanted to get some air and find a quiet seat to eat my lunch. I went out the back and sat down, and then I noticed something at the bottom of the ravine. I thought somebody had dumped a bag of trash there, but when I looked more carefully, I realized it was a person."

"Do people often dump things there?"

"Not that I know of. Of course, I've only been here a year, so that's all I can speak of. But I understand that the fencing on the bridge there is kind of new. I don't know

141

who put that up, or why."

"What is the extent of your property?"

What did he mean by that? Maura wondered. "On this side of the ravine? Well, there's the pub itself, and the land goes up the hill for a bit — I've never looked for the end of it, since nobody's using it. There's a small building there, you know, but it's empty now. There's maybe ten or fifteen feet toward the east, where the steps are that lead down from the balcony up there." She pointed to the corner above. "In the other direction, toward Skibbereen, there's the couple of buildings right on the road that don't belong to me, but behind those, I guess I own the land to the edge of the ravine. I don't know if I have any responsibility for keeping the ravine clean or clear of trash — nobody's ever asked me to do anything about it. You could ask Mick, since he's worked here longer. But the guys across the way have been working to make a tourist attraction of it, in the summer. If they'd been around on Monday, they would have found the man first." *If only.* "Did you talk to them?"

"Sure and we did, but they were long gone when the death happened," Ryan replied, scribbling something on his pad. "But . . ." Maura waited. "How many means of access

142

are there to your side of the ravine?" Ryan finally said.

"I can't say for sure. From the back of this building, for one. Probably from the property on the other side — there's no fence. Maybe even down the hill from above, although I've never seen anyone coming from that direction. I don't know what's up there."

"And yer gate to the street," Ryan said bluntly. "Is it always open?"

"Yes. I never bother to lock it because the only place it leads is to the pub, and those doors I do keep locked when we're closed. I've never heard of any break-ins along here."

"Yeh're usin' the space round back?"

"Some of it, when we need it. Mostly for overflow — I can put a couple of tables out there when I need to, and there are some lights, but it's kind of thrown together. There's a storage shed too, where we keep the fuel and stuff. The idea was that people would come in the front and get their drinks, and if they got hot or thought it was too crowded, they could go out there and cool off. It hasn't happened too often — more often recently, I guess, now that it's summer. Why do you want to know?"

Sergeant Ryan cocked his head and studied her silently for a few moments. "The other gardaí tell me yeh can be trusted, so I'm willin' to tell yeh. Yeh probably already know that we believe the man was brought in through that gate of yers. Which says several things. One, he knew it was there and he knew where it led. Am I right?"

"Makes sense. You've see it — you know it's not marked. So he would have to have known or at least guessed what it was, which means he must have been here sometime. That's what you mean?"

"In part. He knew he could get behind yer buildin' here, and then he'd be out of sight, him and the body. The question is, was it no more than luck, or did he know about the gully there?"

"You mean, did he figure it would be a good place to hide a body, where it wouldn't be noticed for a while? That's hard to say. I don't know if you've been around here long enough to hear the story about O'Donovan's Leap, which is what gave this village its name. But knowing the story and knowing what the layout actually is now are two different things. Sure, the bridge has been there for a very long time, but how would someone know how visible something at the bottom would be? I mean, I work alongside it, but I don't go out there much, and I hardly ever look down, so it was simple chance that I noticed anything. Something or someone could have been lying there for quite a while." Maura thought for a moment. "Look, let me ask you a question. How do you know that it wasn't a couple looking for a private place for, well, what people do in summer, and things got out of hand and the guy ended up dead?"

"Nice try, but there's reason why that wasn't what we think. Fer one, the man was stabbed, more than once. All right, that might've fit yer idea, but then there was a blood trail from the street, so he was already bleedin' when he was brought to yer back yard. Second, his face was bashed about, so someone didn't want us to recognize him. Third, it would have taken a strong person to pitch him over the edge and have him land smack in the middle."

Maura hadn't noticed the blood trail, but she'd been behind her building or inside the pub after finding the body. "Okay, I see your point. At least you can say that whoever killed him didn't come through the pub but from outside. I'm happy to hear that."

He nodded, but then added, "But that's not to say he hadn't been here in the past, maybe snooped around a bit. Have yeh had much turnover in yer staff?"

Maura stifled a laugh. "Not since I've been here, which is just over a year now. Maybe he's worked at some of the other pubs or businesses here and been in this place? So he'd know the layout?"

"We're askin' everyone, of course. Do yeh have any enemies? You inherited the place, am I right?"

"Yes, from someone my grandmother knew. I never met him."

"Is there someone who thinks he should have gotten it, not you?"

"Not that I know of, but I have kind of a short history here. My grandmother said he had no heirs, and his will was pretty simple. You could ask Billy Sheahan — he lives at the end of the building, and he knew the former owner for years. Before you ask, he's over eighty, and a pint is about all he can lift. There's no way he could dump a body. On the other hand, he's in the pub most days and nights, so he might have seen something."

"And might I find him at home?"

"Probably. He rarely goes anywhere except to Sullivan's. He doesn't have any family. I haven't seen him today, so I'm sure he'll show up soon. By the way, he's a great resource for local history and all the families around here, if you need information about

146

things like that."

"I'll keep that in mind. So there's no one that comes to mind who might have a grudge against you, personally, or the place itself?"

Maura shook her head. "Not that I know of, but I'm still the new kid. Have you heard anything like that?"

"Nah, but I've just started talkin' to people." He shut his notebook with a crisp snap.

"Can I ask you something else?" Maura said quickly.

"Is it about this death?"

"Kind of. Look, you transferred here from Limerick, right? I haven't been there, but it's a city, isn't it?"

"That it is. With the crime that goes with a city, if that's what yeh're askin'."

"Not exactly. It must be very different for you to try to investigate in a small-town setting, where everybody knows everybody else's business."

"I'd say that cuts two ways. The good thing is, people notice anythin' out of the ordinary."

"Like somebody sneaking around carrying a body? By the way, was he just slung over somebody's shoulder, or stuffed in a duffle bag or a suitcase? Rolled in a rug? I

147

mean, somebody with a body would be kind of obvious if anyone saw him."

"That's a fair point, but nobody's mentioned either. Could be he was dumped in the wee hours — well after yer closin' time — when nobody was about."

Which I had already deduced. "Which makes it even more likely that whoever was carrying him around had checked out this place by daylight. No way would anybody figure it out in the dark, in a hurry."

Maura realized she had more questions, and she'd better ask them quickly before Sergeant Ryan went on to his next interview. "So nobody knows who the dead man was yet?"

"That's right," Ryan said, then stopped.

"How are you hoping to find out?"

He sighed. "By talkin' to people like yerself, I guess. There's no hard evidence. Worst case, it was a pub fight between two people who'd just met, and we might never know. Maybe it wasn't even the winner of the fight who took care to clean up the scene, but someone who didn't want any trouble at his own place. Or maybe it was a personal thing, with no witnesses. We can only ask, which is what I'm doin'."

"Then I won't keep you. But one more question. There's an American couple who just arrived, and they're staying not far from here. They've heard about the death, and now they're wondering how safe this place is. I have to say, they're kind of timid, and they haven't been abroad before, but I tried to tell them they didn't have anything to worry about. Is that fair? I mean, I'm American too, and I've lived mainly in a big city, so my view of what a 'lot' " — Maura made air quotes — "of crime is is kind of skewed."

Ryan smiled for the first time. "As is mine. But this is a safe part of the country, by anyone's standards. They're more likely to run their car into a cow in the road than to be the victim of a human crime, far less a violent one."

Maura smiled back. "Can I quote you?"

Ryan stood up. "I'd best be on my way. I've others in the village here to talk to. Let me know if you see or hear anything that troubles you. I've been told you've a good eye and ear for crime."

Maura stood up as well. "Probably because I'm still kind of an outsider, so I see things differently. I don't see what I *expect* to see, if you know what I mean. But I hope I've helped."

"Your assistance in garda matters is greatly appreciated," the sergeant said formally. "I'll be goin' now."

"I'll see you out."

When they emerged into the main room, the crowd had grown and Mick was behind the bar. Old Billy had arrived and claimed his seat. Ryan walked out the door, and on leaving he turned right, toward the other places that served food, and Maura went over to the bar. Mick leaned toward her. "And what was that about?"

"Just the garda following up. I can't believe it was only yesterday that the poor man was found. The sergeant's asking the right questions, anyway. But there's no news about the victim."

Rose returned from collecting used glasses, and Maura told her, "Rose, the sergeant said pretty much what I told the Albertsons — this is one of the safest places around. I hope they don't let worrying spoil their vacation."

"Listen, I've been thinking — would yeh have the time to come over and see the café in Skib? Maybe in the mornin', before things get busy? You could talk to Sinéad about hirin' around here."

"Sinéad?" For a moment Maura was bewildered, until she remembered that Sinéad owned and ran the café in Skibbereen where Rose was taking classes. "That's a great idea! I'll ask Mick — he'd have to cover the pub." Maura called out, "Mick, you okay with covering for a few hours in the morning? Rose had a great idea about talking to the owner of the café in Skib."

"The mornin's dead quiet — I can handle it."

"Great," Maura said. "Rose, we're on."

CHAPTER THIRTEEN

The evening trickled on, but few new customers came in. Of course, Maura tried to convince herself, it was only a weeknight, and there was no music or other attraction. But another small voice kept nagging her: Was it because of the body? Was it because *she* was the one who had found the body? Was she becoming something like a bad-luck charm and keeping people away? Certainly it couldn't be something she had done to offend people. But apparently she had no control over the way she seemed to attract crime. If she was a religious person, she could consider an exorcism, but she didn't think that would help.

She decided to talk to Old Billy, who had returned from his small rooms after his supper and settled in his usual place. She dropped into the sagging armchair opposite him by the fireplace. "Billy, did Old Mick ever think this place was haunted? Or cursed?"

"Ah, Maura — any place that's been around as long as this one has is bound to have collected a few ghosts or the like."

"I can buy into that, but are they active? I mean, can they do anything in the present?"

"Like make trouble? Do harm to people? It depends."

If she'd been hoping for a simple "no," it sounded like she wasn't going to get it from Billy. "So you're saying there are angry spirits?"

"Could be. Tell me, Maura, do you believe in luck?"

"I guess. Some things just work out better for some people than for others. Is that what you mean?"

"Perhaps. What about coincidence?"

"You mean, things happen right when you need them? Not just any old time?"

"Yeh're gettin' my drift. Yeh haven't been here long, and yeh're young, but some of us old folk, we used to believe in all sorts of charms or spells. Mebbe *believe* isn't the right word to use, but we honored the old traditions, just in case they might be true."

"Like what?"

"Sure and yeh've heard of leprechauns and fairies and banshees and the like?"

"Well, yeah, but usually as a joke. You're

153

saying there are people who believe in them now?"

"A few, mebbe. Do you know of the fairy tree?"

"Huh?" She'd never heard of such a thing, but maybe people who visited pubs didn't talk about trees.

"Yeh've no doubt seen a few without knowin' it. If you see a tree standin' alone in a field or along a fence, yeh leave it be, fer cuttin' it down would bring bad luck — yeh'd anger the fairies. Do yeh know a magpie when yeh see one?"

"They're those black-and-white birds? Kinda big?"

"They are. If yeh see one alone, it's said to bring bad luck, and yeh need to speak to it to prevent that. There's an old poem about the magpies that starts, "One for sorrow, two for joy." Goes back centuries, I'm told. And watch what yeh do with yer salt."

"I'm guessing there's more?" Maura asked.

"Sure and there are plenty of old sayin's. But don't worry yerself, Maura — they're mostly forgotten now."

"Are there any sayings or traditions about keeping death away? Because I seem to keep attracting it here." Not at her house, thank goodness, although that could come next.

Did she have a fairy tree? Did Bridget? She wasn't planning to cut any trees down. But what if they fell down on their own?

"It's said that there are things yeh can do to bring good luck, but I wouldn't put too much faith in 'em. The best I can tell yeh, Maura, is to go on wit' yer life and keep yer eyes open."

"That's what I'm trying to do. You ready for a pint now, Billy?"

"That'd be welcome, although it should be me last of the day."

"Coming up."

She slid back behind the bar, where Mick was already filling a glass. Maura nodded toward it. "Billy's?"

"You have to ask? He have anything important to say?"

"No, mostly we were talking about folklore — and if there's a way I can keep trouble away from this place. You know any good charms?"

"I'm not the one to ask. Bridget might have some ideas. Yeh're still worried about a killer roaming about? And now yeh're looking for a charm to ward off a killer?"

"I know it sounds silly. Here I am, giving the Albertsons happy talk, and I don't know what I think myself. Tell me, does it seem weird that the poor guy has been dead for two days now and nobody knows who he is and where he came from yet?"

"It's out of the ordinary fer this place, I'll give yeh that."

"Maybe a friend or relative picked him up somewhere and drove him here. Or he came by boat."

"Has no hotel or B and B or hostel reported anyone missing?" Mick asked.

"Not that Sean or the sergeant has told me. Maybe he was sleeping rough? Is that the right term? It's warm enough."

"Could be. Hard to prove, though."

"Would he have bled a lot when he was stabbed? Nobody's reported a mess of blood anywhere."

"There's plenty of fields to bleed into, and no one would know." Mick leaned back, crossed his arms, and stared at her. "Maura, where are yeh goin' with this?"

"I don't know!" she said, more loudly than she intended, and a couple of people at tables turned to look at her. She lowered her voice to answer Mick. "I was feeling safe, even though I'm living out in the country somewhere and it's pretty dark, though there are people around. And dogs who bark at people. But now there's at least one person who's a killer. I know, there are hundreds who aren't, and they're all very

156

nice, but it takes only one person to kill someone. I don't like feeling afraid. I don't want to *let* myself feel afraid, but I don't want to get killed because I was being stupid and pretending there wasn't a problem."

"Why would anyone kill yeh, Maura?"

"Maybe they think I have money, or Old Mick left me a pile of cash buried under the fireplace. Maybe just because they can — they like killing. I don't pretend to know what goes on in a killer's head. But I want to get past this. I want to go back a couple of days, when everything seemed happy and cheerful."

Rose had been sitting with Billy while Maura and Mick talked, but now she came over to the bar. "A friend at the cookery school asked if I wanted to stay over with her tonight, fer I've got an early class there. Do yeh mind? At least you won't have to worry about me."

Maura said, "Certainly, dear, as long as you go to bed early, make sure your doors are locked, don't talk to strangers, and brush your teeth."

Rose looked startled until she realized that Maura was joking. "Yeah, Ma. But I was also thinkin' maybe you could come over in the mornin' and have a chat with Sinéad before she gets caught up with the café

lunch. I talked to her about doin' it, earlier."
Rose turned to Mick. "Mick, Maura was worried that you'd have to handle the pub all by yerself. Think you can manage it?"

He smiled at her. "I'm pretty sure I can. Not like it's the first time. Yeh'll be back by noon?"

"If Maura could be there and bring me back."

"I think I can do that," Maura told her. "What time should I be there?"

"Ten, say? I'll tell Sinéad to expect you, and that'll give you an hour or so before the meal — she opens at noon."

"Sounds like a plan. So, okay, you'll be with a friend tonight, I'll meet you tomorrow in Skibbereen at the café at ten, talk to the owner, and bring you back here after. Is there anything I should or shouldn't say? Like you want fewer shifts here so you can work around your classes? Oh, and is it rude to ask her what she pays the staff and how she figures out how many she needs?"

"Don't worry — she's pretty up-front about her place and how it works. Ah, there's Niamh." Rose waved at a girl standing outside the door. "Mind if I leave now? I can make up the time tomorrow, when we'll be busier."

"Fine, go. And keep your mobile with you."

Rose joined her friend at the door, and they went out chatting like magpies. Hmm, she must have magpies on her mind. She wasn't even sure what kind of sound they made. Did they talk to each other?

With Rose's departure, that left Billy, who looked like he was dozing, and a couple of other guys with half-empty glasses in front of them. Seamus and his gang were conspicuously absent, and she hoped they had spread out among the other pubs in the area to ask their questions. *Any bar fights? Anybody thrown out before a fight could blossom? Any strangers lurking in corners? Anybody asking odd questions? Anybody who looked even remotely suspicious? Maura, you're grasping at straws.* Plenty of things went unnoticed all the time, and nobody could see that the wrong word to the wrong person could end up with a death.

It was a slow night indeed. Maura hoped that the gardaí would come up with some answers about the death by tomorrow, or it might put a damper on the rest of the week. She turned to find Mick watching her. "What?"

"Yeh look worried."

"I told you I was. Maybe I'm going all

psychic and I sense evil, only I can't see it."

"Would you know evil if you saw it?"

"I'd like to think I'd feel it, even if everyone around me looked perfectly ordinary."

"Even in a crowd?"

"You mean, like when we've the music here, and there are lots of strangers? I've never thought about it. But I guess I feel safer in a crowd, even if I don't know the people. Like nothing bad could happen in a room full of witnesses."

"Will yeh be wantin' company tonight?" Mick asked quietly.

"A bodyguard? Or something else?"

"Yer choice."

"Yes, I think I would," she said carefully.

They closed up the pub a little early, and no one was disappointed. Outside they argued briefly about which car to take. Maura had promised to meet Rose at the café in Skibbereen at ten, but Mick had to be at Sullivan's to open. Two cars, then, so they'd have to drive to her place in Knockskagh in their own cars. No big deal, although occasionally Maura was a little spooked by driving in the dark — where it was *true* dark. The only things she ever saw, on the back road to her place, were one or two passing cars, and the eerie glow of some small animal's eyes when her headlights caught them.

Was she getting soft? She'd always been independent, mostly out of necessity. She hated to ask people for help, much less emotional support. Now she had someone in her life who offered both, although cautiously. But between them, the relationship, whatever it was, moved forward slowly and erratically. Add to that that she was unsettled by the idea that she had been involved in solving more than one crime and she didn't know how that had come about. It was nothing she had looked for, nothing she wanted. And more, she had to admit to herself that she wanted Ireland to be a safe and welcoming place, to let her figure out what she wanted from her life and what her choices were. She resented being distracted — why did she have to have been the one to find that body? Of course, it had been more or less on her property, or had at least been hauled across it, so somebody would have pointed a finger at her in any case. But why? What had she done to deserve it?

She arrived back only a minute or so before Mick. Bridget's cottage was dark, no surprise. On her small lane, her house was flanked by abandoned buildings, which were falling down. Not exactly welcoming. When she got out of the car, she could hear small

161

animals rustling in the weeds and dead leaves. In Boston they would be rats, but here she had no idea what they might be.

Mick pulled his car in behind hers and turned off the lights, then got out. He came up behind her and wrapped his arms around her shoulders and pulled her close. They stood that way for a couple of minutes. Finally he said, "Yeh're safe. I'll make sure of that."

He understood. She fought back tears and said, "Thank you."

CHAPTER FOURTEEN

Nothing went bump in the night, as far as Maura could recall when she woke up. On a bright summer morning, things looked better than they had at midnight on a dark night. Finding out who the dead man was and why he had died was not her problem. She knew she didn't know him and she hadn't done anything to him, and she was pretty sure none of the people who worked for her had. She stifled a smile at the mental image of Billy stabbing someone to death and carrying the body away to dump it. Although he knew the lay of the land better than anyone. Maybe Billy had had an accomplice. Or maybe he — or they? — had killed the man to protect her, or Rose, or because he oozed evil and had to be gotten rid of.

Ridiculous, Maura! she told herself. She could hear Mick moving around downstairs — he was surprisingly quiet for a tall man.

Neither of them had to be anywhere soon, although she should allow enough time to get to Skibbereen and park her car for her ten o'clock meeting. She felt kind of weird about talking with someone she didn't know about how to hire people, but she honestly didn't know where to start. This woman was working in the — what did they call it? — the hospitality trade, like Maura was, and most likely handling both food and drinks, offering meals throughout the day. Maura couldn't begin to imagine dealing with both at once, but Rose seemed interested in the idea. She owed it to her to learn more about what it took.

She pulled on the bare essentials in clothes and loped down the narrow staircase. "I smell food. I didn't know I had any."

"Good mornin' to yeh too, Maura. I don't know how you keep a cockroach alive in this place."

"Easy — I don't spend much time here and I don't eat here very often. And I certainly don't have company. I can fix a cup of tea, assuming the milk hasn't gone sour, but that's about it. Although from what I've seen, a cuppa covers most social occasions. There might be a tin of cookies — biscuits — hiding somewhere."

"Yeh have heard of things like flour, have

yeh not?"

"That white stuff that comes in bags?" Maura grinned at him.

"Ah, so yeh have seen it! Seriously, if I'm gonna be spending time here, I'd like to eat. And yeh need to eat as well. Yeh're on yer feet twelve hours a day, and yeh can't do that forever without takin' care of yerself."

"Got it. Note to self: buy food. The Costcutter has most of the basics, so that's easy. What do you like to eat?"

"Will yeh throw somethin' at me if I say 'meat and praties'?"

"Praties?" Maura cocked her head at him.

"That'd be potatoes to the likes of you. Yer headed fer a restaurant this mornin', are you now?"

"I am, or at least, I'm talking to someone who runs one. And cooks, I assume."

"Then pay attention, why don't yeh? If somethin' smells good or looks good, ask what it is and what's in it."

"Jeez, Mick — I'm already talking with her about finding staff and salaries. Now you want me to talk about recipes too?"

"If yeh found food yeh liked, you might eat more."

"How about I ask Rose to be my spy? And I'll volunteer to be her guinea pig."

"That might do. Tell her to share her

165

recipes."

"Can I ask her to pick up the ingredients too?"

"Yeh're pushin' yer luck, lady."

They found enough to eat, mainly a sad frozen loaf of soda bread in the small freezer, then set off on their separate ways. As she drove toward Skibbereen, Maura reflected that neither of them had said anything about spending the night together. It wasn't exactly a regular thing — more spur-of-the-moment. And it was always at her place. Maybe Mick lived in a cave, or a barn with the livestock (although in that case he would have smelled rather odd). Or maybe he just valued his privacy, much as she did. This relationship stuff was tricky.

Traffic was light in the morning in Skibbereen, and Maura had no problem finding a handy parking space behind the supermarket. She walked the half block to the corner where the café was located and saw Rose standing outside the front door waiting. Maura checked her watch quickly, but she was right on time — the class must have just ended.

"You're here!" Rose crowed as Maura approached.

"You thought I'd bail out on you?"

"I was afraid you might. Come on — Sinéad is a very busy woman."

"Lead the way," Maura told her, with more confidence than she felt. She seldom talked business with anyone, much less another woman who was running her own business. Which was dumb, she knew, because she could learn a lot from them. But she was embarrassed by how little she knew — she was kind of making things up as she went. And combine that with food, which as Mick had pointed out she knew next to nothing about, and she was worried she'd look like an idiot and people would laugh at her.

Rose must have sensed her dismay. "Maura, the woman doesn't bite. Just ask yer questions."

Maura sighed. "Yes, ma'am."

The ground floor of the corner restaurant was simple and appealing, with windows on two sides and a bar against the inner wall, and chairs and tables between. The location was good, too, on a very visible corner in the center of a busy town. Smart choice, Maura had to admit. "Where's the kitchen?" Maura asked Rose in a low voice.

"Upstairs. Alanna, where's Sinéad?" Rose called out to a woman at the other end of the room who was setting up tables.

"In the kitchen. Go on up," the woman replied.

"Thanks," Rose said. "Come on, Maura, follow me."

The stairs were narrow and ran up along the back wall. Maura had trouble imagining how anyone could go up and down with loaded trays of food without regular disasters. On the other hand, the servers would certainly be in good physical shape.

The second-floor room was the same size as the room below, but one end was taken up by a kitchen full of gleaming stainless steel. Even though lunch wouldn't start for another two hours, there were several people busily chopping and slicing and preparing who knew what.

"Sinéad?" Rose called out.

"Hang on a moment." The obvious leader of the pack, a wiry middle-aged woman with an air of authority, barked out some orders to the others in the kitchen, then turned and joined Rose and Maura at the far end. "Welcome. I'm Sinéad Lynch. Rose said you had some questions about how to manage staffing at your place? That's the old pub in the center of Leap, is it not? Oh, please, let's sit down. You want coffee?"

Maura couldn't swear that the woman had taken a breath since she started talking to them. "Coffee would be great."

Sinéad turned and issued an order to someone, who nodded and reached for two cups. Then she turned back to Maura and Rose. "You've been running the place, what, a year now?"

"Almost exactly. Before you ask, when I started I had no experience running anything, although I'd worked in pubs before, back in Boston. Luckily the staff — like Rose here — stayed on and helped me through it, so I survived. Thing is, since we're doing better now, I need more staff, and since I'm not from around here I don't know where to look. How do you manage it?"

Sinéad didn't seem put off by her ignorance. "You don't have a kitchen yet, right?"

Maura shook her head. "There is one, but it's old and I'm not sure everything works. If we were serious about food, we'd have to gut it and start over there. That's one reason why we haven't made a decision. Your kitchen here is beautiful, but it's about twice the size we have to work with."

"That's not necessarily a problem. If you can't expand the space, you shrink your menu."

"How many people — cooks, I mean — can you have working here at once, like for dinner?"

"Up to six at a time. And now you're wondering why they all don't trip over each other all the time. It's because we plan carefully, and I show the staff how to make it work. Take a look at the people in there now — what do you see?"

"Uh, three . . . kids, I've have to say. They're all young. I don't mean to offend you, but you're the oldest person in the room."

"I am, and I've plenty of experience in running a kitchen, starting when I was their age with my parents' place. I thought long and hard about how I wanted to do things when I was planning this space. What equipment we needed. What we could manage, given that the only place for the kitchen was upstairs. But I thought the location mattered more, so that was another reason to hire young servers who could manage the stairs with heavy trays. I'll admit it's not easy."

"Well, that's a couple of things we don't have to worry about — our location is what it is, and it's all on one level, with the kitchen at the back. But serving food is still in the future. Right now I need staff for the pub itself. There are only three of us working there, and we all put in a lot of hours.

Then there are the nights when we have music, with over a hundred people, and we definitely need some help then. What do I do?"

"I pull most of my staff from the local school system. Look at the age of these kids. It's summer break, so some of them work full-time and others part-time. When school's in session it's trickier, because they can't always work all shifts. So I need more people to cover the same amount of time. But I think they appreciate the chance to earn some money and the experience with working in a real restaurant kitchen. Some of them started with taking the classes, and others decided to do that after they'd been working here for a while. Look, we've been open only two years. It's working so far, but that's not to say it won't change. The restaurant business is unpredictable, and the profits are pretty thin. Plus it's hard work — you have to love it to commit to it. Rose here" — Sinéad nodded toward her — "she has the makings of a good cook. She understands food."

Rose blushed. "I like to try new things. But I'm far from ready to open a place at Sullivan's. That's why I've been coming here."

"And you're wise to know that, Rose.

There's no rush, is there, Maura? You'd have to lay out some money up front to set up your kitchen, and then you'd have to build your food business, so it would be a while before you made much from it. You could start small, with snacks and the like rather than meals. Or do lunch only. But don't rush into it thinking it'll make you rich."

"Don't worry — I wasn't thinking that. I noticed when we came in that you have a full bar. Can the school-age kids serve drinks?"

"Our ground-floor staff is a bit older. The kids can take the orders, but they can't serve the drinks. Rose here's an exception, is she not?"

"Kind of," Maura said, hoping she was on solid ground. "I asked when I first took over Sullivan's, because Rose was so young, and I was told that if she was related to the management, she could work. I never asked a solicitor, but the gardaí are in and out and nobody's ever said anything. Do I need to do anything about it now?"

"If no one's complained, I'd leave it alone. But don't hire any children for behind the bar."

"So we're back to my first question: where do I find part-time staff that's old enough to pull a pint and serve it and that won't cost the earth?"

"You're doing it right so far — asking around. I've had to turn away a few kids because I'm covered for now, but that changes all the time. Or maybe they get tired of the hard work and want to take time off to have fun. They might have older brothers or sisters who'd be interested in picking up some money before they go back to university. I'll ask my staff and some people I know around here, if you like."

"Please! And I've got some rooms above the pub if they're looking for a place to stay. Nobody's used them for a while, but it wouldn't take much to clean them up."

"That could help," Sinéad agreed.

"Uh, one more question," Maura began tentatively, "and you don't have to answer if it's a problem, but what about people who aren't students? Like immigrants? People looking for asylum? Waiting for residency or approvals or whatever it takes? Some of them must need jobs, but would I get in trouble if I hired them, either officially or off the books?"

Sinéad though for a moment before answering. "It's a question many people around here face. Many of that lot end up working on a farm this time of year, and nobody asks a lot of questions. A pub or a restaurant is more visible, and it could be a problem. Maybe you should ask a garda before you think of taking anyone on."

"Thank you — that's what I needed to know. I certainly don't want to get into trouble, or get anyone I hire into trouble. But I do need some help."

Sinéad checked the large clock hanging on the front wall. "I've got to start lunch prep. You're welcome to stay and try the lunch here."

"I should get back, but I'd love to take you up on that some other time. Lunch is probably easier than dinner for me, and maybe Rose could come with me and tell me what I'm eating."

"Ah, so you're not much of a cook your-self?" When Maura shook her head, Sinéad added, "Maybe you should try one of our classes that covers the basic skills. Ask Rose about them." She stood up. "I'll let you know if I find anyone who's looking for some work."

Maura stood as well. "Send them over! Thank you for taking the time to talk with me. It's really nice to meet someone who cares about what she's doing and is trying to do it well."

"You're welcome. Rose, see you at the

next class." Sinéad turned and made a beeline for the kitchen space, where she started issuing orders like a drill sergeant. Maura followed Rose down the stairs and out onto the street.

"Did yeh find out what yeh wanted?" Rose asked.

"Yes, and more. It makes me feel good that she approves of me thinking it through instead of rushing into anything. Like I've been telling Mick, we've already added the music, and we're still seeing how that works out. Trying to take on something else new — something that would cost money and make a mess of the place, at least for a while — doesn't make sense right now. Maybe in the winter, when things are slower. Assuming you stick around that long. Would you want to work for Sinéad?"

"She hasn't asked, but she runs a good place. But at Sullivan's, it would be me own place. Let's wait and see."

"We should be getting back," Maura said.

"Let's stop by Fields and pick up something fer lunch — save us another trip. Do yeh know the place?"

"I've been in it a couple of times, but you know I don't really cook. Mostly I buy tea and pastries."

"Then yeh're in for a treat. Come on."

CHAPTER FIFTEEN

Together Maura and Rose walked the long block to the supermarket. As she approached, Maura felt a strange reluctance, her feet dragging.

Rose noticed. "Yeh've been here before, right?"

"Yes. But I keep telling you, I don't do food. I mean, I eat enough to survive, but I really don't care what it is."

Rose stopped, her hands on her hips, "Maura Donovan, yeh're a sad case. There's so much yeh're missin'."

"I get by," Maura muttered.

"Let me ask yeh this, then," Rose went on. "Which would yeh rather do: learn a bit about food and how to cook it, or learn to use a computer for yer business?"

"That's not fair!" Maura protested. "And everybody keeps telling me I have to use a computer, so I should do that anyway. Why do I need to? I've got you, right?"

"Because yeh're runnin' a business in the twenty-first century, is why," Rose said firmly. "How do yeh think the crowds that come fer the music hear about it? It's not just the people who live nearby or stop in at Sullivan's now and then. It's how you communicate! Sure, I'm doin' it fer now, but I may not always be around. Yeh can find some school kid who knows as much as I do, but will he or she work fer yeh? Yeh can hire someone, but then you'd be payin' out money for something you could learn in a week. Yeh need to know this."

"I don't have the time. Or a computer." Maura stopped herself from adding, *I don't want to.*

Rose shook her head. "Yeh'll need to make the time, and a computer doesn't cost all that much. Stop making excuses fer yerself. The food's a different question. Yer thinkin' of servin' food at the pub, so there are things yeh need to know there too. We're here, standin' in front of the market, so let's start with this. We haven't the time to do a big shopping, but yeh have to walk through the place with me before we can buy our lunch."

"Oh, come on, Rose — this is ridiculous. I've survived this long without starving to death, haven't I?"

"Yeah, wit' yer gran feeding yeh for most of it. Who knows what awful diseases yeh're lookin' at? Scurvy, mebbe? When was the last time yeh ate a vegetable?"

"Uh, last time I bought a sandwich? There was something green on it."

"Quit yer whinin' and follow me."

Maura sighed. This was ridiculous: she was being bossed around by a child. Well, one who could definitely cook, and who knew more about computers than she did. "All right, but one condition: we start with the bread and cake section."

"If yeh must." Rose sighed dramatically.

Maura soon realized that they'd have to walk through the vegetable section before they got to the cakes, but there were few surprises there. Lots of potatoes, of different kinds according to their labels, but they all looked the same to her. Carrots. Large cabbages. Onions. Okay, so far, so good. But she kept her eye on the tables ahead, filled with a dozen kind of cakes and other sugary things. When they finally arrived there, Rose said firmly, "You may pick one. Only one."

"Uh . . ." So many choices, and they all looked wonderful. "That one." Maura pointed to a neatly wrapped small brick of a cake with a checkerboard pattern inside.

178

"Good choice — Battenberg Cake. I'll spare you the fish and meat departments — let's go find some ready-to-eat sandwiches or something close, and then we can leave and get back to work."

Maura clutched her prize and followed Rose to the sandwiches, where she picked a safe chicken salad sandwich. "Are we done now?"

"Want to take something back fer Mick?"

"I don't know what kind of sandwich he likes."

"The ham and cheese will do. There." Rose pointed.

They paid — Maura noted that Rose seemed to have some sort of frequent-buyer card — then headed out the back to where Maura had parked. Once they were settled, Rose said, "Now, was that so terrible?"

"No. But in my own defense, when am I supposed to cook anything? If I was going to stock up, I think it would have to be breakfast food and teabags and milk and sugar, because I'm never home for supper."

"A fair point," Rose agreed. "But if yeh hire a couple more people, yeh can have more time fer yerself."

"Oh. Well, yeah, maybe." Actually she had no idea what to do with free time, but she doubted that putting together gourmet

179

meals would be her first choice.

Back at Sullivan's, Maura carefully hid her cake, in case anybody got any ideas about helping themselves.

"How'd yer meetin' go?" Mick asked.

"Useful, although the woman didn't have a stash of available wait staff to spare. She says I'm doing it right, asking other employers. Rose, what did you think?"

"I think Sinéad may have the local school market locked up — the restaurant has a good name and people are glad fer the chance to work there. Yeh might have noticed that she didn't really answer yer question about the foreigners, beyond saying yeh should be careful."

"I don't want to break any laws, but I've got to find somebody somewhere."

"Mebbe yeh should talk to Sean about it, off the record, like," Rose suggested.

Maura sighed. "But Sean is such a by-the-book type of garda. Not that I blame him, because he's still kind of new to this. But how do I ask him how to avoid breaking the law?"

"Nothin' wrong with that," Mick commented. "And I'd bet he's heard the question before. There are those that want work, and those that need workers, but it's not always easy to get them together. And even if yeh do find people, yeh've got to worry these days that they get along with each other as well as the customers. There can be problems with outsiders, legal or no, if they come from different cultures or countries."

"All right, I'll talk to Sean. How much longer can I play the dumb American card?"

"Not long, I'm guessing," Mick told her. "Yeh've come a long way."

"Fine — I'll see if he has time to talk in the morning. Think the business will survive until then?"

"Might do," Mick said. "Why not talk to him tonight?"

"Because that's our busiest time. I'd rather do it in the morning." Okay, maybe she was stalling, but she wanted a chance to think about what Sinéad had told her.

Sean took the decision out of her hands when he dropped by Sullivan's in the middle of the afternoon. "Hey, Sean," Maura greeted him. "Have you solved the murder?"

He looked tired as he dropped onto a barstool. "That we have not, and we're no further forward than we were. The sergeant is itchin' to arrest somebody, but even he's havin' trouble finding a likely suspect. Can you do me a coffee?"

"Of course. Are you going to call in help from other stations?"

181

Sean shrugged. "They'd know no more than we do. Seamus and his lads haven't brought yeh anything new?"

"No." Maura slid the cup of coffee over the bar. "In fact, he's been kind of missing for the past day or two. I'm hoping they're checking out the other pubs around here to see if there's anything worth looking into."

"Are yeh sayin' he thinks the gardaí aren't doin' their job?"

"No, not at all. But be fair, Sean. People in a pub would talk differently to their own than to a garda. More freely. Seamus is good at getting information that way."

"He is that," Sean admitted. He sipped his coffee, staring at nothing in particular.

Maura gave him a minute of peace, then said, "Can I talk to you about something? Not related to the murder?"

"Official business?" he asked.

"Well, yes, legal, I guess. It's not urgent, but it's kind of important to me."

"I'm happy to help yeh," Sean said.

"Let's go into the back room so we can talk. Bring your coffee along, unless you need a refill."

"I'm good. Lead the way."

When they were settled, Sean asked, "What's troublin' yeh?"

"It's not me, it's the business. I need more

staff. Now that Jimmy's out of the picture, it's just me, Mick, and Rose, which means we're here all the time. Now that it's summer and the music is doing well, I have to find more people, but I don't know where or how to look."

"How is it yeh think I can help yeh?"

Maura smiled. "I don't expect that you run a hiring agency. I was talking with Sinéad Lynch at the restaurant in Skibbereen, and she says she uses mainly school kids who are old enough to work, both in summer and during the school year. But I think she's used up most of the supply, not that she said as much. So I've been wondering about other groups, like foreigners, or students who don't come from around here but need to work in the summer — even Americans. But to do that I need to know what's legal. I mean, you and some of the other gardaí are in and out of here a lot, and I don't want to be breaking any laws or hiding people in a closet when I see you coming."

Sean looked relieved. What had he been expecting to hear? Maura wondered. "Ah, I see. You bein' in the business of serving drinks, and maybe food down the road — you need a different staff than most of the shops in town. Can yeh pay the wage they want?"

"I'm not sure what that is, and I'm probably not paying Mick and Rose enough, not that they've complained. But I could offer to put them up in the rooms upstairs, if we cleaned them up. Is that allowed? Does that count as part of their wages?"

Sean stared at what was left of his coffee for thirty seconds or so before speaking. "I won't lie to yeh. There's times we turn a blind eye, knowin' that the shopkeepers have few choices and the employees need the work. There are some rules that apply, and I can give you that information. But that's not the only problem yeh might have."

"Oh, great, there's more than just finding people?" Maura felt deflated. Was nothing ever going to be simple?

"There is. To be kind, let's say there's those who are less than honest. They tell you a pretty story about needin' the work, and when yer back is turned they'll rob you blind and disappear. Yeh shouldn't always trust strangers."

Maura sighed — she'd heard it before. "And I do need people who will stick around, at least through the summer. Long enough to know how we do things, not that it's complicated. Maybe that's why I've been thinking of hiring students — I guess I want to believe they're more honest than some of the adults."

"It's too bad yeh have no relatives to call on. Have yeh asked anyone at Crann Mor?"

"You mean, in management? No, I've only just gotten serious about looking."

"Could be they get applicants there who don't quite suit their needs but who would be fine at Sullivan's. Talk to Siobhan — she might know some people."

"Thank you, Sean — that's a great idea. But are there any legal questions I need to ask anybody? Do they need visas, or permission to work in Ireland? Are there limits to the number of hours they can work?"

"Ah, Maura, yeh're getting way ahead of me. Let me think on it a bit and ask around at the station. Sure and there'll be people who can help yeh out. How many do yeh think yeh need?"

"Heck, I haven't even gotten that far. Depends on the shifts and the schedules. Music nights we've gotten over a hundred people here, and the three of us can barely manage. If we get any more successful it'll be impossible."

"There's many who would envy you yer success. It's a good thing that yeh're doin' well."

"I know. It's just that we're still getting used to it." She stood up. "Well, I'm sure you're busy, and I appreciate what you've told me. I do want to stay on the right side of the law, but I need help."

"I'll let yeh know if I hear of anyone who's lookin'." Sean stood up as well.

"Thank you, Sean. Let me know if you find out anything more about the dead man."

"I'll do that. Walk me out?"

Maura led the way to the front and waved as Sean walked back to his car. Rose asked, "Any luck?"

"A couple of ideas — he thinks I should talk to the people at Crann Mor."

"Sure, and why didn't we think of that?" Rose exclaimed. "And you with connections!"

"I think Sean was thinking more of people who don't quite reach the standard expected by a fancy hotel but could still use a job. Maybe I'll do that in the morning. Unless we all collapse from exhaustion."

"Just hang on a little longer — we'll figure something out," Rose said.

Or die trying, Maura thought grimly.

CHAPTER SIXTEEN

After another long day with a depressingly low number of customers, Maura dragged herself home — remembering at the last minute to grab her cake from its hiding place. She felt less guilty knowing that the cake was something she would never make, no matter how many lessons she took or how much effort she put in, so she could justify buying it. She'd be glad to match Gran's cooking skills — Gran had always made simple food that tasted good and was easy to stretch for unexpected guests, or a second meal if they were both too tired to cook — but that wasn't likely to happen.

She stumbled up the stairs after locking the front door, dropped onto her bed, and fell asleep as soon as she was horizontal.

The next morning the sun was shining — again. Wasn't it supposed to rain a lot in Ireland? Either there was some sort of drought going on, or she was spending so much time at the pub that she wasn't noticing the weather outside. Maura wasn't sure which explanation she preferred, but it must have rained sometime, because everything was very, very green. She got up, pulled on a sweater against the morning chill, and wandered downstairs. There was no more food than there had been the day before — except for the cake. All right, she'd have cake for breakfast, and enjoy every bite. Why not?

When she'd finished her sketchy breakfast, she showered and changed clothes — reminding herself that she had to do some laundry soon or she'd drive people away with the smell. She wondered how much a washer cost and if she could afford one. Not right now, not until things were a bit more settled at the pub. If they ever would be.

Fed, clean, and dressed, she decided to stop in at Bridget's cottage before heading into Leap. She didn't expect that Bridget would have any insights into finding more staff, but it was always nice to talk with her, and she did have a network of friends, some of whom might have grandchildren looking for work. When she reached the end of her lane, Maura stopped: there was a battered caravan — what she would have called a small house trailer back in Boston — parked in the field opposite, uphill from Bridget's cottage. She was pretty sure the field belonged to Bridget, though she didn't use it for anything except maybe grazing the occasional horse. But in the year she'd spent at her own place, Maura had never seen any regular activity in that field, although somebody mowed it now and then. Did Bridget know about the ramshackle vehicle? She thought she should find out.

She was still on edge about the unknown, unseen killer, she realized. Stupid, she knew, because nothing about the place had changed. Her home was still shabby, and there was nothing to steal. There was her fragile connection with the death — why had the killer dumped the body next to her property, even being bold enough to pass through her own gate? — but she hadn't even been there at the time, and she didn't know anything about the who or the why. And she hated being a weak silly woman, jumping at shadows. But she'd be devastated if something happened to Bridget and she could have done something to prevent it. She patted her pocket to make sure she had her cell phone, then strode briskly down the hill and rapped on Bridget's door. "Bridget? It's Maura."

She heard the sound of laughter from

inside — from two voices, Bridget's and a man's. Then the scrape of Bridget's chair as she struggled to get out of it, then the soft footprints as she approached the door. A smiling Bridget opened it.

"*Fáilte a Mhaira!* Come in, come in. I was just telling Peter here that I seldom get many callers here, and now I've two at once. Let me introduce the two of yiz."

Bridget stepped back to let Maura in, and Maura tried to study the other guest without being too obvious. Midthirties, shabby but clean, slight, and smiling. Not exactly threatening. Maura stepped forward. "Hi. I'm Maura Donovan — I live up the hill. Is that your mobile home up there?"

"Peter Sheridan. Yes, it is — my family's gone into the town to get some supplies, and I thought I'd stop in and say hello to Bridget here, since she's kind enough to let us use her field now and then. You'd be American?"

"I am. If you've been coming around for a while, you'd have known Old Mick. I inherited the cottage from him, and the pub in Leap as well, last year."

"How're you settling in?"

"It's been interesting," Maura told him, relaxing just a bit. He seemed pleasant enough, and harmless. And Bridget didn't seem worried.

"Shall I put on the kettle?" Bridget asked, beaming. "Have you the time fer a cup, Maura?"

"Sure. Need any help?"

"It's all but ready. You and Peter chat while I fix it. Sit down, you two."

"Are you on holiday?" Maura asked politely.

Peter smiled to himself. "Yeh haven't been around here long, have yeh? Do yeh know of the Travellers?"

"I've heard the name mentioned, but it seems like I spend all my waking time in the pub. What should I know?"

Peter seemed to relax just a bit. "Ah, 'tis a long story, but I'll give you the short version. We Travellers are a particular group of Irish, related to the rest but different, and as the name suggests, many of us have no fixed home — we travel about the country. You might have heard some of the other names people call us — pavees, tinkers, even gypsies. Though we're not gypsies, and the term is seldom used kindly. Mostly we live in or near the cities — there's a settlement east of here, although that may be closed down soon. Some of us are settled, as it's called, but many of us still roam about during the warmer months. That's how I came to meet Bridget here. We needed a place to park, and she was kind enough to let us use her field fer a time. But I'll warn yeh up front: we're not always welcome. There's those who think we steal or take advantage of those who are kind to us. If I tell yeh now that me and my family are honest people, would you believe me?"

What Peter said matched what others like Seamus had told her. "I try not to judge people too fast," Maura said. "And Bridget vouches for you, and I trust her. So I'll believe you until you show me I shouldn't. You and your people just kind of wander around the countryside? You've got kids? Do they go to school in the winter?"

"We're comin' around to that, slowly. It was only in 2017 that the government saw fit to recognize us as true Irish, and that means we're entitled to some public privileges, like health care and education, but that's been slow to take effect, for if people don't trust us, neither do we trust the government."

"I don't mean to be rude, but how do you support yourselves?"

"We breed dogs and horses. We collect scrap and sell it. Whatever work we can find, short term. But we don't want to lose our traditional lifestyle, so it's been hard to juggle the old and the new. Changing times we live in." He accepted a cup of tea from Bridget, took a sip, then asked, "So how does a lovely young American woman like yerself come to be running an Irish pub?"

"Old Mick left it to me. Bridget probably knows more of the story than I do. My grandmother was a friend of hers, before she left for America."

"The luck of the Irish, eh? You've landed on yer feet here."

"Looks like it. It's been an interesting year, but it seems to be working out."

The sound of children's voices could be heard outside, and then a woman telling them to be quiet. Peter stood and opened the door. "Nan! Come say hello to a new neighbor of Bridget's — she's from America."

Maura could hear the woman issuing orders to the children — "Now, take this back to the caravan, and we'll be there directly" — before she joined Peter at the door. She turned out to be a slender woman, taller than Maura, her hair tied back loosely. Peter said, "This is Maura Donovan, who lives up the hill in Old Mick's place now."

"Oh, is he gone? He was always kind to us. Good to meet you, Maura. How do yeh come to be here?"

"My grandmother knew Old Mick, years ago, and between them they fixed it so that when he passed away I inherited the cottage. And his pub in Leap."

"Will yeh be stayin', do yeh think?"

Nothing like coming straight to the point, Maura thought. "I hope so. Certainly for now. It's all very different than Boston, which is where I came from."

Nan seemed anxious. "Peter, we'd best get the kids fed. We said we'd meet up with the Butlers at the Carbery fair today."

"So we did. Bridget, thanks fer the tea and the chat. Maura, good to meet you."

"Will you be around long?" Maura asked.

"We seldom know. There are plenty of fairs in West Cork in the summer, and we try to follow them when we can. If we're still around, we can talk more. Let's go, Nan."

When they'd left, heading up the hill, Maura turned to Bridget. "Well, that was interesting. Have they been coming here long?"

"You mean, to my field? That they have, and Peter's father before him."

"Does Mick know about them?" Maura asked carefully.

"He does. Are yeh askin' if he's not happy havin' them here?"

"I don't know. Maybe. Look, if he has a problem with them, I'll keep my mouth shut. Are they really, like, outcasts or something?"

"They lead an odd lifestyle, but it's an old one that goes back centuries. There aren't so many of them. But I'm told there are even some in the U.S."

"And I didn't know that either. Sometimes I feel like I grew up in a Boston bubble — I didn't even get out of the city much. I certainly didn't see gypsy caravans in the city."

"Well, now that yeh know they're here, at least fer a few days, mebbe you can get to know them better. Any news on that poor dead man?"

Maura shook her head. "Nope. It's ridiculous, isn't it? Wait — you think he could be a Traveller? That would explain why people around here wouldn't know him."

Bridget considered. "It could be. Easy enough to find out — ask Peter. These folk may ramble about, but they do keep up with each other's news, mostly by talking to each other when they cross paths. Family is important to them, and you'd be surprised how news gets around among them. If I see Peter first, I'll be sure to ask. So what other news have you?"

"I'm trying to find more people to work at the pub, at least for the summer months. I don't suppose any of the Travellers would want a short-term job?"

"It's not their way of life. A week or two, mebbe, but not anythin' measured in months."

"I'm not surprised, from what Peter said. I can't believe I've never heard of them before."

"They follow their own calendar. There's usually those who pass through here every year or two."

"I talked to the woman who runs the new café in Skibbereen about where she finds staff — Rose got us together because she's taking classes at the place. She said it's mainly schoolgirls, around Rose's age. But it sounds like she's got first claim on them, and maybe they even fight to work there — Rose tells me the place is getting a good reputation. And I talked to Sean Murphy about what's legal and what's not quite legal, but the gardaí will look the other way. If you hear anything from your friends about someone who's looking for work, please let me know. At this rate, I think we'll all be worn to a frazzle in a month or two. And I can throw in a room if they need it. It'd be just for the summer, or maybe longer

196

if things work out well."

"I'll keep my eyes and ears open. Should you be on your way?"

Maura checked her watch. "Darn, talking with Peter took longer than I thought. But I'm glad I met him. Should I say anything to Mick?"

"Only if he asks, I'd say," Bridget said. "He worries enough about me without adding Peter and his lot. Even though we've known them for years and I trust Peter."

"Okay. I won't lie if he asks, but I won't mention them. Take care of yourself, Bridget. And thanks for the tea."

"Stop by whenever yeh like. And send Gillian by as well, will yeh?"

"Of course." Oops, she hadn't even mentioned Gillian's hunt for child care, but that could wait for another day. Although Bridget might be a better source than some, since she knew so many of the local people. And their children and grandchildren. "Bye now."

Maura went back to her place and retrieved her car, then set off for Leap in a thoughtful mood. As she had admitted, she hadn't known Travellers existed. She'd been living here more than a year, but she hadn't seen any caravans, or at least hadn't recognized any that might belong to Travellers.

She hadn't heard anyone mention the group. She didn't read papers or own a television, so there were probably plenty of public events, both in Ireland and in the rest of the world, that she hadn't heard about at all, unless they were filtered through the patrons at the pub. She wasn't going to pretend that was unbiased, but she had no clue which way the bias went most of the time. She had to wonder what other things she had missed in her first year.

Bridget had seemed to take the arrival of Peter Sheridan and his family in stride. Maura trusted Bridget's judgment, and she'd treated Peter like an old friend, so Maura wasn't going to start out distrusting them. She couldn't blame them for being poor and working only now and then, because she'd been in the same boat back in Boston. That they had chosen their kind of odd lifestyle, and raised their children in it? She had no right to criticize, because Bridget had suggested that the lifestyle went back centuries. To gather all the Travellers together and tell them they had to live in houses and send their children to regular schools and get normal jobs would be a wrenching change. Did the Irish government even have the right to do that? The U.S. government had kind of tried that with the Indians, and that hadn't worked out real well for the Indians, who were still struggling with the results.

Well, she'd learned something today, and it had given her something to think about. But it hadn't solved her two main problems of the moment: who was the dead man and why was he dead, and where was she going to find more people to work in the pub?

CHAPTER SEVENTEEN

Maura was surprised to find Seamus and a couple of his pals already in the pub when she arrived. They rarely if ever showed up before noon.

"Did I oversleep, or are you early?" she asked.

Seamus smiled ruefully. "It's our wives — we've been out near every night this week, talkin' to folk at the various pubs around here, and the women are a bit put out. I'm guessin' they don't believe that we're investigatin'. So we've ditched our midday chores to fill you in on what we've found."

"Which is?" Maura prompted.

"Not much, sorry to say."

Not what she wanted to hear. "Who've you talked to?"

"Me memory's a bit fuzzy after all those pints, but I think it's safe to say we've spent time in every pub in Skibbereen, and then we widened our search to Union Hall and

Glandore, and down the road as far as Ross-carbery. Me liver may never recover."

"What were you asking? Oh, wait, first tell me, had the gardaí been there before you?"

"Mebbe half the places. They're doing their best. But let's say me and me lads took a bit more time, and mebbe ordered a pint or two, to soften up the people at each of 'em so they'd talk to us."

Maura wasn't surprised, and actually it made sense to her. "A brilliant strategy. So you won't be wanting another pint until next month?"

Seamus's mouth twitched. "I wouldn't go so far as to say that, but it's still early in the day fer it."

"So" — Maura went back to where they'd started; she was getting impatient — "what have you learned?"

"Well, we can't point to a killer yet." He beckoned to one of his friends, who joined them at the bar. "Jerry, yeh're our official record-keeper. Help me out if me mind goes blank. The night of the death — Sunday that was, right? Fer it was the Monday that yeh found the poor man, Maura."

She nodded. "Yes, Monday. And?"

"Sunday's often a slow night, and the pubs are supposed to close early. Although it might be if there's a good crowd of tourists, the law could be just a bit more flexible. But no one remembered any big fights, nor small ones. Am I right, Jerry?"

"I'd agree wit' yeh, Seamus," he said.

"Tell me something," Maura said suddenly. "This place usually attracts more men than women, right? Except the nights when there's music, when it's pretty evenly split."

Seamus cocked his head. "And yeh're thinkin' that matters?"

"You tell me. Are guys, after a few pints, more or less likely to get into it if there are ladies present?"

"Do yeh mean 'ladies' " — Jerry made air quotes — "like their wives or girlfriends, or ladies they'd like to impress? Or some other kind?"

"Let's say female strangers, tourists, maybe some visiting relatives. Keep your minds out of the gutter, guys."

"If it's a mixed group yeh're thinkin' of, I'd guess there are fewer fights. It'd be in yer average tavern-keeper's best interests to keep the rowdies under control. Which makes a real fight stand out all the more in people's memories. Which none does."

Maura realized she'd been hoping there would be an easy answer, like a bar fight that got out of hand. It was nice to know that there were few serious fights around here, but it didn't help them find who had killed the man and dumped him outside her pub. "And the gardaí didn't pick up anybody Sunday night for being drunk and disorderly, if that's what you call it?"

"Depends on what yeh're thinkin' that means. Let's see, there's bein' drunk in public, which can be under the intoxicating influence of not only alcohol but anythin' else that'll do the trick, and then there's disorderly conduct, but that counts only after midnight. But the fine's more expensive than the first. Ah, and then there's the latest twist, where the gardaí can fine yeh a hundred euros on the spot if yeh're drunk, and one hundred-forty is yeh're drunk and disorderly, but neither gets yeh tangled up with the courts, so the only record would be whatever the garda wrote down."

"What? You're saying you can get away without being arrested simply by paying a fine right away?" That sounded wrong to Maura.

"As long as yeh stop making trouble when the gardaí ask yeh to."

Maura was shaking her head in disbelief. "Why don't I know all this?"

"Most likely Mick takes care of any arguments fer yeh, or he makes sure the troublemakers leave before they, well, become troublemakers fer yeh," Jerry explained patiently. "And anyone local knows yeh're friendly with the gardaí."

Maura thought for a moment. "Okay, then. If there's another person involved when someone is being disorderly . . ."

"Yeh mean, like they're fightin'?"

"Yes, or close to it. And don't try to explain to me how you can be disorderly all by yourself, unless you're seeing things. Would the gardaí just politely tell them to go their separate ways and hang around until they're pretty sure they did?"

"They might do," Seamus said.

"Would they take names or check IDs?"

Seamus shook his head. "Ah, Maura, the gardaí aren't after making trouble fer a lad who's had a bit too much to drink. It would depend, I'm guessing. If it's the first time, they'd likely send him home with a warning and keep an eye on him after that. If it's someone known to the gardaí already, fer other reasons, there'd be that fine. If that doesn't discourage him, he could be hauled off to court."

Now Maura felt deflated. "So there's no official list of public drunks or scuffles between a couple of drunks?"

"Only in the minds of the gardaí. Yeh know how many they are around here. They know who to watch. They're tryin' to keep the peace, not arrest anyone."

"You see what I'm getting at, don't you, Seamus? If there was a fight that started but the gardaí or the barkeep broke it up, then the guys could have met up later or just taken it around to a dark corner, but there wouldn't be any official record, right? So no way to identify who they might be?"

Seamus sighed. "Yeh have it right, Maura. But, see, it's seldom been a problem fer us here. We know if we fight, the barkeeps won't let us keep comin' back, and neither will our wives let us out of the house. If an outsider comes along and makes trouble, the gardaí will most likely take him to the station until he cools down and make sure he goes on his way with no more trouble."

Maura stared at him bleakly. "So right now we have no name for the dead man, and no idea who might have killed him, and the gardaí have no record of who might have been in a scuffle or have even looked like starting one, and no pub owners remember anything that helps us. You have any idea what to do next?"

"Look fer Martians?"

Seamus's expression was the picture of fake sincerity, and Maura had to laugh. "Well, you tried, Seamus, you and your gang. Maybe if we let it rest for a day, we'll see it differently."

"Don't worry, we'll keep tryin'. And we'll be back later fer a pint. Ta!" Seamus gathered up his gang and led them out of Sullivan's; then they split up and headed in different directions.

Billy was standing outside waiting for them to clear the way, and then he made his slow way in and settled in his chair. There were no other customers, so Maura went over to greet him.

"Good morning, Billy. How are you?"

"Not so bad, not so bad. Was that a committee meeting, like?"

"What, Seamus and pals? They've been doing undercover work in all the local pubs to see if they can find any suspects for our killer or identify the dead man. So far they've had a lot of pints but come up with nothing new. Am I missing something? Or should I just give up now?"

"I'd say no news tells yeh something. The lads were askin' after fights and such?"

"They were. I'm not sure what you mean — oh, you're saying if neither the gardaí nor Seamus and his crew have found any mention of a fight or anyone who was making trouble at the right time, then we're probably looking in the wrong places?"

"Exactly. Yeh started in the right place, but yeh've found nothin'. Time to take a fresh look."

"Great, but I don't know where to look. I mean, what do we know? Young man was stabbed and died. Somebody didn't want him identified and didn't want anyone to know where he died, so he fixed it so the man couldn't be recognized and he carried him here to the bridge and dumped him. The only odd bit is that he knew about the back way through my gate. Which kind of suggests that he's been here before."

Billy nodded. "Could be. Could be a regular, or could be someone who'd stopped in a time or two. Or could be our killer thought it would be easy to toss the man over the edge of the bridge in the dark and found a fence in his way, so he scrambled around in a panic lookin' fer another way in and found yer gate."

"Billy, you're right on all counts, but that doesn't help anything. How the heck do we find him?"

"I'm jest tellin' yeh what ground's already been covered. Nobody's heard talk of a fight. The poor lad wasn't dressed like he had any money, so a robbery seems unlikely. Somebody wanted him dead. Why would that be?"

"I don't know! Let's take a look at how he was killed, okay? He was stabbed, not just once but many times. That kind of sounds like somebody who was angry, out of control. If it had been planned, maybe it would have been only one stab."

"Could be," Billy agreed amiably. "Have yeh got a 'why' in yer back pocket?"

"Billy, I haven't a clue why anybody kills anyone else. Money. Love. Hate. Insanity. Take your pick. Does this sound planned to you?"

"Not the deed itself, but as yeh've said, odds are the man knew this place, or knew of it."

"Sullivan's has been here a long time. If the guy was older, maybe he knew it when Mick was running it. I haven't changed much."

Billy sat back in his chair and looked at her. "Maura, why is it yeh care so much? Yeh didn't kill the lad, did yeh?"

"Of course not! And even with his face bashed in, if I'd known him I probably would have recognized him somehow. But whoever dumped him kind of pointed a finger at me, whether or not he meant to. I don't think I've ticked anyone off, not enough to try to drag me into a murder, but it could have happened. Should I give up?"

"Ah, it's early days yet. Could be somebody will let somethin' slip and the whole thing'll start up again."

Maura wasn't going to hold out a lot of hope for that. "Can I ask you something?"

"Sure and yeh can, if yeh'll get me a pint."

"Oh, of course. I'm sorry — I've been distracted by all this. I'll just be a minute."

Maura stood up and went over to the bar, where Mick was polishing the top. "Could you pull a pint for Billy?"

"That I can. The two of yiz seem to be dccp in conversation, although I can probably guess what yeh're talkin' about. Seamus and his lot have had no luck?"

"Nothing obvious jumped out. And in some ways I trust them more than the gardaí when it comes to asking questions, because they're not official and they can get people to talking." She watched as Mick filled a glass partway, then set it down to settle before topping it off. "What if this really is a random thing? I mean, what if the dead man and his killer didn't come from here? What if the poor guy was killed in Cork or Dublin, and his killer stuffed him in the trunk of a car and just drove until he thought he was far enough away from where it happened, and then he started looking for a good place to dump a body and here we were?"

"Mebbe, and if that's so yeh may never know who either one was. Are yeh worried that someone wanted to point this at you, or Sullivan's?"

"People could think that, whether or not it's true. I mean, maybe the killer didn't know Old Mick was dead, so he left the body here to send some kind of message to him?"

"Unlikely, I'd say." Mick pushed Billy's full pint across the bar. "The last few years, he did little business here, except among his old friends. It was more like a club than a business, but he didn't care. I don't recall that he ever spoke of any earlier life that might produce bodies so much later."

"Okay, so let's cross off anybody who might have a grudge toward Old Mick. Cross me off, for why would I do this to my own business? And you, and Rose. Jimmy I'm not so sure about, but he hasn't been around much, and I think all that stabbing and lifting and carrying would seem like too much work for him. Besides, he's pretty well fixed with Judith and her cows now. Unless some shady character from *his* past showed up and wanted a piece of that land."

"He may talk a good line, but he's never really strayed far — I'd count him out as well. And I'd guess that Judith would hold on to her land and give up Jimmy." Mick nodded toward Billy. "He's waitin' fer his pint."

"I know. But one more thing." Maura lowered her voice. "Say none of us comes up with a likely killer or victim. Say they aren't from here, but they've been around here for a while, long enough to know what's what. Where do we look for them?"

"Like those who are just passin' through, or workin' fer a time before movin' on?"

"Maybe. It's summer — isn't there short-term work available?"

"Let me think on it. But, Maura? A word of warnin'. It's not yer problem, and yeh shouldn't be pokin' yer nose into others' business. They might not take kindly to it."

"I know that. But I want to know what happened. I — we — can't afford to lose business, and I may if nobody finds the killer."

CHAPTER EIGHTEEN

Business dragged through the day, and Maura was beginning to feel panicky. Had finding the body so close really had that big an impact? Or had all the tourists suddenly decided that West Cork had lost its charm and gone somewhere else, or decided to stay in Dublin? Was it because Rose wasn't around as much, and all the male patrons came in only to see her and chat? (Maura wondered fleetingly whether wearing makeup herself could possibly make a difference.) This was the peak season, wasn't it? Tomorrow night, with a middling-hot band scheduled, would be the real test.

But now she was at loose ends. Rose was at the café in Skibbereen, picking up some hours serving, and she'd be in after the lunch rush. That left her and Mick to cover the bar. Could she duck out on him again? She felt she was doing that an awful lot lately, but now she wanted to go talk to

Siobhan over at Crann Mor about how they recruited staff there. Of course, the luxury hotel wanted a higher class of servers than she did, but maybe they'd be willing to direct the rejected applicants her way.

Better do it now, in case it got busy later. "Mick? Do you mind covering for an hour or two? I want to run over to Crann Mor and ask how they find their staff."

Mick looked around the room: the sole customer was Billy, although it was still short of the lunch hour. "I think I can manage. Take yer mobile and I'll give you a ring if a busload of people show up."

"Thanks. Rose should be in after two, but I'll be back by then."

She hurried out to her car and pointed herself toward Skibbereen. She'd discovered the back way to the Crann Mor road, which made getting there simpler and faster. Plus, it was a prettier drive, and she wasn't in a hurry . . .

Maybe she should have called for an appointment. Or maybe the hotel used some sort of recruiting agency, which would be great for them but wouldn't help her at all. Or maybe every person in the county already had a job if they wanted one and wasn't looking for a new one, and she was up a creek. *Stop it, Maura!* she chided

213

herself. *There are people around here who need jobs — you just have to find them.*

She arrived at the hotel after ten minutes and walked into the lobby. Since the JBCo group, which had recently purchased the hotel and land and was busy polishing it up, had increased their active participation in running the place, it was looking cleaner and brighter already. She'd have to ask if business had picked up — did they advertise? How? Not that annoying Internet again — but she had to admit that from all she'd heard, that was how hotels booked their guests these days.

Luckily, Siobhan O'Mahoney was working at the front desk, managing to look both competent and welcoming. Maura walked up to the desk and said, "Hi, Siobhan. You have a couple of minutes to talk? It won't take long, I promise."

"Hello, Maura. Let me find my assistant to cover the desk and I'll be right with you."

While Siobhan tracked down the assistant, Maura wandered around the big room, peering into the dining room, which was located at the back of the grand lobby and overlooked the formal gardens behind the building. She hadn't seen the garden for a couple of months, and now it looked both lush and manicured, in the full flush of summer.

Siobhan joined her a moment later. "Inside or outside?" she asked.

"Inside, I guess. This is business and I don't want to waste your time. Although the gardens are looking lovely. Is Bernard still keeping them up?"

"He is, thanks to you. And he's got two boys helping with the heavier work. What can I do for you now? Come, sit." Siobhan pointed to the richly upholstered settee at one side of the lobby, and Maura settled herself gingerly on it while Siobhan took a matching chair next to it.

"I'll get straight to the point. I need to find more staff for Sullivan's. Last year I didn't know what I was doing, and we muddled along with the staff we had when I arrived. But now Jimmy is married and working on his wife's dairy farm, and his daughter Rose is taking cooking classes and talking about serving food at the pub, and that leaves only two of us to cover everything. But I'm not local, and I don't know how to find people, either short-term or long-term. I did talk to Sinéad at the café in town, but she hires mostly from the local school — what do you call them? secondary schools? — and I'm not sure she wants to

215

share that pool, or that the kids from there would even want to work at Sullivan's. You have any suggestions?"

Siobhan smiled. "Take a breath, will you, Maura? I see your problem. Of course, you're looking for a different kind of employee than we are here, but we do get many applications and referrals. I'd be happy to send some of those your way, if I think they'd be a good match. But I will say that many young people now are leaving the area to look for work — Cork city, even Dublin. Or they want to spend six months or a year on the Continent, or they're off to uni in the fall. It's not as easy as it once was. I feel lucky that my daughter Ellen chose to stay and work here."

It was the same story she'd heard from Rose. "That's what I've been afraid of — that's what Rose said. And more than that, it seems like everybody who's lived here all their lives already has a personal network — they put out the word with their family and friends and the problem's solved. I don't have that. And I'm not even sure what pay I should be offering them, if I want to compete with the other places around here. I do have some rooms upstairs that would be livable with a little work, to sweeten the deal if that's a problem."

"Let me think it over, will you?" Siobhan said. "And I'll ask Ellen as well. As you might guess, she moves in different circles than I do, so she might know more likely candidates. But you do know the age limitations on serving alcoholic beverages?"

"Of course — I checked as soon as I found out how young Rose was. I'd certainly stay on the right side of the law if I hire someone new."

"Good — that's important. And you're serious about adding the cooking?"

"I'm not sure yet. I'm letting Rose work on convincing me, and apart from the cooking she's looking into the business side of things. Of course, we'd have to remodel the room in the back and buy appliances and get permits and all that, so it could be expensive to start."

"We're planning to overhaul our kitchens here soon," Siobhan said. "If any of the stoves or refrigerators or work tables would fit your place, we'd be happy to pass them on to you."

"That would be wonderful! Let me know if and when it's going to happen and I'll send Rose over — she can figure out what we need and what we'd have room for. But we're not in a hurry."

"I'm delighted to help — you have to

217

know I'm grateful for what you did for us when we had that bit of trouble. The music's still going well?"

"It is, or so Mick and Rose tell me. That's part of the problem. We can handle the normal daily traffic, but when there's a good band playing, suddenly we've got a hundred and more people jammed in, and we simply can't pour drinks fast enough. Even someone to help out on the music nights only would be a big help."

"I will definitely ask around. And I'm glad you came to me, Maura. You've learned a lot in a short time, and I want you to succeed. I'm happy to help." Siobhan stood up. "Was there anything else?"

"No, not right now. Well, maybe you can tell me, has anyone here talked about that body that was found in Leap this week?"

"Not that I've heard. Are you asking if the guests talk, or the staff?"

"Either, I suppose. There's so little information available. Nobody knows who the man was, or why anyone would want to harm him, or why whoever did decided my place was a good place to leave him. None of it makes sense."

"And the gardaí are no further along?"

"No, or not that they've told me. I don't mean to criticize, but they're used to having a pretty good idea of who's responsible for crimes around here. This one's got them stumped."

"I'm sorry to hear that. All I can tell you is that we've not misplaced any guests, and all our staff is accounted for, so the poor man didn't come from here. I'm sorry that's not much help to you."

Maura laughed. "Just be glad you don't have to deal with any more deaths here."

"God willing! It was nice to see you again, Maura, and we owe Rose a good meal. Let's try to set a date."

"I'd like that. She keeps telling me I have a lot to learn about food."

Maura drove back to Leap feeling encouraged, not that she had solved anything. But she'd started the ball rolling — in two places in one day! — and she might have found a source for secondhand kitchen equipment if they decided to go forward with serving food. Was she reluctant out of fear of failing, or was she simply being a cautious business owner? Rose was doing all the right things, starting with learning cooking, the business side, and how to promote, all at once. She was really a special kid, and self-ishly Maura hoped she would stay on at Sullivan's. But she wouldn't hold her back if Rose got a better offer. Even if that left her even more shorthanded.

Mick looked up from the newspaper he was scanning when she walked in. "Have I missed anything?" she asked.

"I've guided one lost tourist toward Skibbereen. She didn't buy anything. How'd yer meetin' go?"

"Siobhan's going to keep an eye out for likely candidates, but even she admits that a lot of kids are leaving the area, either for school or to find work in someplace more exciting. At least I'm getting the word out that we need staff. I can't think of anything more to do at the moment."

"Yeh might look into foreign students at one or another uni. If they're in a regular program, they can get work permits for the summer months. Of course there's paperwork involved. But yeh might find an American or two who thinks it would be interestin' to work in an Irish pub fer a short while."

"Assuming I knew any American students back in Boston to ask," she said. It always depressed her to admit how few people she had known there. "What about refugees?"

Mick shook his head. "We take fewer than most countries, legally. I don't know the numbers for those who arrive but never apply. There's those who want to resettle here, or are looking fer asylum, but again, the numbers aren't large, and few end up in Cork."

"Mick, you're depressing me even more. And say we found one of those few refugees who wanted to stay around here and work at Sullivan's for minimum wage — would they fit in? Or would our customers have a problem with them just because they're foreign?"

"How'm I to answer that? How many outsiders have yeh seen in here?"

"I don't know! Is there any other group I haven't thought of?" She wondered if she should bring up the Travellers, but from her short conversation with Peter she had the idea that they didn't want to stay long in any one place, much less behind the bar in a pub. And she'd also heard that there were still plenty of Irish people who didn't trust them. "I guess our only choice is to keep working here until we drop."

"And who would yeh leave the place to?" Mick asked.

"I . . . don't know. What happens if I don't leave it to anyone? What's the law?"

"I'd guess they have to find a relative of a sort."

"What if there aren't any?"

"Yeh've a mother, do you not? And a half

sister and half brother?"

"I guess. But would any of them want this place, and the cottage?"

"Maura, that's a question you need to ask yerself. This place is yours, free and clear. So's the cottage. Yeh can do whatever yeh want with it. Or have 'em sold when yeh're gone and give the money to the Save the Whales fund or such a thing."

"Maybe I'll ask Harry what I should do. Or maybe I could leave everything to his son, since I don't have kids."

"Yeh're not so old — it could still happen."

"Would *you* want the place?"

He looked startled at the question. "I'd never given it any thought. Yeh know full well I've been takin' my life a day at a time fer a while now. I've made no plans fer the future. Surely there's someone who'd want it more than me. Like young Henry, as you say." He straightened up and started lining up glasses behind the bar, a fraction of an inch at a time. "There's no need to decide today, is there now? Things can change. But it's good to have a plan somewhere fer others to follow, if need be."

Maura sighed. She'd done the right thing and put out feelers for employees, but there seemed to be few around and available.

Now Mick was telling her she should plan for her death. And all that came after finding a body within sight of the pub. Maybe she should go to church and pray that things turned around soon. Or dance around a prehistoric stone circle, with the same prayer. Whatever might work.

CHAPTER NINETEEN

Friday morning Maura arrived at Sullivan's early, to make sure everything would be ready for the evening. Even though they'd been hosting musical events for a number of months now, she still got nervous about the details. She was surprised to find Rose waiting for her. "You're here early," Maura commented, shutting the door behind her. Opening time was still an hour away.

"Oh, Maura, I've made a stupid, stupid mistake," Rose said, near tears.

Maura struggled to think of what Rose might have done that had made her so upset. "And I need to know?"

"Well, yes, because it's about tonight, see, and the online booking page I set up."

"You forgot to put up the announcement? You put the wrong date?"

"No, neither. I put the wrong price fer the tickets."

"What are we asking?"

"Well, this is a pretty good band, and they've got a new recording coming out, and they said they might bring advance copies. So we decided to charge twenty-five euros, right?"

Maura honestly couldn't remember — she left all those details to Rose and Mick. "Sounds right. What's the problem?"

"What's on the order page says five euros. Which is a bloomin' bargain fer these guys."

"And we sold out? Isn't that a good thing?"

"Sure and we sold out fast. But you know how it goes. There's always those who show up hoping there'll be a few tickets held back, or a batch of people think they can sneak or charm their way in. And these lads will draw all of those, fer sure. We'll be swamped here — but we won't be makin' the money we should off 'em."

Now things were beginning to make sense. "Well, like you said, we sold out. We won't make as much money as we could, but I can live with that. So why are you so worried?"

Rose swallowed. "Well, the place will be overflowin', and there'll be people standing around, waitin' and hopin' to get in to see the band at such a great price, and there's only the three of us to manage the crowd

225

and serve the drinks. We've nothin' like a bouncer, if that's what you call it. One or another of us will have to turn people away, which is always hard. Worse, we're goin' to have to keep the drinks flowin', and there's the two bars to cover, front and back." Rose waved her hand. "Maybe I'm makin' too much of it, but I can see it happenin' and it could be a disaster."

Maura swallowed a hysterical giggle. Who was it who had said 'all publicity is good publicity'? How would that work if they had a riot and it spilled out onto the streets — correction, the one and only street — of Leap? "I think I'm beginning to see the problem. You have any ideas what to do about it? Do we honor the ticket reservations, even if the cost is wrong? Do we try to turn people away? Do we tell the gardaí so we'll have some outside help?"

Rose was looking like the teenager she was. "I don't know!" she wailed. "I'm so sorry. I didn't read over what I'd put in — I was rushing. And now there'll be a mess tonight."

With a sellout or even an overflow crowd, and only three people to manage it. Yes, they did need help. But from where? "I'm going to call Sean and see what he says." It was the first thing she could think of. And also the only thing, at the moment.

She found her phone and called the garda station, and luckily she found Sean was in. She explained quickly what the problem was, but she wasn't encouraged when he said, "I'll do what I can, but we're short a coupla men — on summer holiday, yeh know. One or another of us can drive past now and then, but there's not enough of us to put a man outside yer door. Unless they start breakin' each other's heads."

"That's what I was afraid of. You don't need to apologize, Sean. We'll just have to handle it. But if you know anybody with bartending skills, send them our way, okay?"

"I'll do that, Maura. I'll probably see yeh sometime tonight."

Rose had been watching anxiously. "No help from Sean?"

Maura shook her head. "They're short-handed as it is. We'll just have to do the best we can. And maybe pray for rain. Or a flood. We should put Mick on the door to check for tickets. If these players are as popular as you say they are, the crowd would probably trample you or me without even noticing."

Rose looked near tears. "I am *so* sorry, Maura. I was tryin' to do too much, and not payin' enough attention."

227

"Been there, done that. These things happen, Rose — don't beat yourself up over it. Do we have any stun guns in the place?"

"What?" Rose looked confused.

"Never mind — I'm joking. They're probably not legal. We'll just have to sweet-talk the crowd into behaving. I haven't been paying a lot of attention myself — how do we handle the crowd once the music starts? I mean, do any people leave so others can fit in? Or does everyone who gets in stay until closing?"

"Once they're past the door, they'll stay to the bitter end. And past, if yeh'd let them."

"We'd better make sure we watch all the doors. We don't want people to try to sneak in." Exceeding their occupancy limit wasn't too big a deal if it was only a handful of people, but if people got trapped or an accident happened, it could be disastrous.

"And which one of us is goin' to be in two places at the same time?" Rose demanded.

"Oh. Right." Too many doors, too few people. Where could she look for help? Old Billy would no doubt volunteer, but he wouldn't be able to hold off a herd of young men determined to get in. But maybe she could ask him where she could find some volunteers.

Mick walked in on the two of them. "What?" he asked immediately.

"Uh, we may have a problem about tonight," Maura said, and explained the situation. She was dismayed when he looked troubled. Had she been secretly hoping he'd come up with a magic solution? "You have any ideas?" she asked when she'd wrapped up.

"I can't say that I do. Give me some time to think. Yeh said yeh've already called the gardaí?"

"First thing. They don't have anyone to spare."

"Anyone else we can borrow fer the worst of it?"

"Mick, it's Friday night in tourist season — they're all going to be busy. And I guess if we lock the doors and turn out the lights, the crowd who's made the trip all the way here to see the band will probably start throwing rocks at the windows and anyone who's in their way."

"Yeh have a point, not that I've seen such a thing in Leap."

"Can we move the whole event out to the street?"

"Not without a permit from the gardaí, and I wouldn't hold my breath on gettin'

229

one this late."

"So how on earth to we get the word out *not* to come tonight?"

Mick shook his head. "Yeh can't."

"I'm so sorry," Rose said again. "It's my fault."

"Rose, I forgive you," Maura said impatiently. "*We* forgive you. Mistakes happen. We'll just have to muddle through somehow. Maybe we could call your father in?"

"He's off with Judith at a cattle fair."

Maura took a deep breath and squared her shoulders. "All right, we'll do what we can. Mick, how are we fixed for supplies?"

"Good enough. These folk don't come to eat, but they'll be drinking. But the kegs are full, and there's no room below to bring in more now."

"When's the band coming?"

"Suppertime, I think. You want to tell them to play slow hymns and keep people calm?" Mick was actually smiling now.

"That would probably cause a riot too. Are they a fast and loud kind of band?"

Rose nodded. "Mostly."

Maura thought for a moment. "I suppose the best we can do is tell those who come that this is a gift — the reduced price, that is — and we'll do it again, but only if they promise to keep things to a dull roar."

230

"Yeh mean, like we planned it this way?" Mick asked. When Maura nodded, he said, "Brilliant."

Maura was out of ideas. "Then let's get this place ready. And get any breakables out of the way."

The rest of the day was ordinary, but to Maura it felt like the calm before the storm. No, not just any storm — a New England nor'easter, or maybe a hurricane. Like those times when the sky used to get dark, and then the wind would pick up, and then things would get really bad. Funny — every time she looked out the windows now, she was surprised to see that the sun was shining.

Billy came in just before noon, which was late for him. Maura took his pint over to him and explained what was happening. "Did anything like this ever happen before?"

"What, a large crowd? Sure, though it's been years. Some nights there'd be a big match on the telly, and people would be packed in like sardines. And if their team won . . . well, Mick — not your Mick but my old friend — would take names, and anybody who made trouble wouldn't be allowed back fer a while. Worked most of the time."

"You think I'm making too much of this?"

231

"Nah, yeh're just bein' careful, as yeh should be. It'll all work out. But I might stay in me own place tonight. I'm not a big fan of the music these days, and I'd probably end up with a rugger player sittin' on me lap."

"I can't say that I blame you, Billy."

Billy left in the late afternoon, when people started coming for the music. The bad news was, they'd have a long wait; the good news, they'd be buying pints for all of that wait. Maura did know that if they got too drunk too soon, she could call the gardaí to remove them, under the law. Still, it was nice to see the old place fill up with happy people. She didn't know much about the music scene back in Boston, but she was pretty sure the guys playing here tonight weren't looking to stir up the crowd to dangerous levels. All they had to do was look around at the place and they'd see that — Sullivan's simply wasn't that kind of place. Maura was glad they'd reinforced the balcony that ran around the edge of the back room when they'd started with the music — and now it could hold a good crowd.

It was close to nine when things started to heat up; the band was in the kitchen, tuning up, and the show was supposed to start around ten, although Irish time was kind of flexible, Maura had found. It was hard to get through the two main rooms, and she had Rose covering the bar in the back room while she and Mick handled the front. Anyone who wanted a drink was going to have to fight their way to one or the other bar, because there was no way to take a drink to them. Just before ten, Mick stationed himself by the front door to check tickets, and Maura could hear the sound of electric guitars coming from the back room. And then the crowd thickened and clotted, and she felt a stab of fear. Could they handle this? Why had she ever thought they could? They needed more staff and there weren't any available.

For a while she was kept busy filling pints, taking money, and trying to keep people moving from the bar to the back, which was filling fast. When the band produced a recognizable chord, the crowd thinned briefly as everyone surged toward the back room. Maura took the moment to wash some glasses, and when she looked up, she was surprised to see a stranger at the other end of the bar, filling pints with a practiced hand. Clearly he knew what he was doing. About her age, dark-haired, dressed like everyone else in the crowd. And smiling. He was enjoying the hubbub. He looked over at her and smiled. "You'd be Maura, the owner?"

"I am. Who are you?"

"I'm Niall. Looked like you could use some help."

"You've done this before."

"That I have."

"We can talk later," Maura told him. The crowd surged forward again, and Maura went back to filling glasses. Only now she could manage a smile now and then, thanks to this stranger. She could get his story later, but right now she needed him right where he was, doing exactly what he was doing. Maybe he was an angel, but if he could count out the right change, she wasn't going to ask.

Closing time came and went, and Maura gave what was left of the crowd a generous half hour to empty their pints before herding them toward the doors. Mick took over that task, and she chatted to the band for a couple of minutes and handed over their pay for the night's work, including their cut from the take at the door — or more like what they'd expected to make before Rose's mix-up. They seemed tired but pleased with themselves. Once they'd taken themselves and their equipment out the door, Maura stopped to talk to Rose, who was cleaning up the bar in back. "How'd it go at this end?"

"Good," Rose said. "I guess we were worried fer nothin'. Who was the guy behind the bar in front?"

"I was going to ask you. He just kind of showed up and started in. Did a good job, too."

"Did he make off with cash?"

"No. I checked, and I think Mick was keeping an eye on him. Do you know him?"

"No, but he seemed a bit familiar, like I'd seen him somewhere, but not to talk to. Maybe it'll come to me later. I'm knackered."

"Go on home. Or crash here if you want. The mess will still be here in the morning."

"There's an old stuffed chair upstairs — that'll do me fer now. 'Night, Maura."

"See you in the morning." She turned out the lights and went back out to the front, where Mick was setting the chairs in order. "Rose is going to stay upstairs for what's left of the night. Where'd the guy who took over the bar come from?"

"I thought you'd know. Never seen him before."

"I asked Rose, but she didn't know either. She thought he looked kind of familiar and she might have seen him around. So he didn't ask you if you needed help?"

"I was kept busy at the door. I looked up and there he was, but he looked like he had things well in hand, so I let him be. I made sure he put the money in the till, and cleaned it out a couple times just to be safe."

"Gawd, capable *and* honest. And kind of cute. We're going to have to track him down. Tomorrow. Or maybe I mean later today. You going home?"

"Unless yeh've got a better idea?"

"My place?"

"Grand."

CHAPTER TWENTY

"Was that what you'd call the luck of the Irish?" Maura asked over breakfast the next morning. It was only brown bread and tea, but at least the bread was fresh and chewy and full of good grain flavor, and there was fresh milk for the tea. *Baby steps, Maura.*

"What, that heaven-sent bartender?" Mick asked. "I'd guess he looked at the situation and thought he could help. Which he could."

"Think he'll come back and ask for a night's pay?"

Mick shrugged. "No idea."

"Well, if you see him again, don't let him escape. We don't have any permanent fix for our problem. And maybe it's time I learned how to work a computer, at least for business. Do you know what Rose asked me earlier this week?"

"Yeh'll tell me, I'm sure."

"She asked which I'd hate less — learning to cook or learning to use a computer."

"And yeh had to think about it?" he said, smiling.

"Don't you start! Yes, I will agree that as a business owner I should know how to use computer programs — not that I would have been able to stop Rose's slip yesterday, and I don't blame her for it. And as a human being, I should be able to make food that other people might actually be willing to eat. But I don't think I'll ever be an expert at either. Still, I hate to have to depend on Rose so much. If she leaves, I don't know what I'll do."

"Has she said she wants to?" Mick asked.

"No, but you know I've been dangling the hope of fixing up the kitchen and letting her cook."

"Do yeh mean to do it? Because yeh keep saying it. Yer gonna have to decide, or Rose'll get tired of waitin'."

"Do you think it makes sense?"

"Could do. Yeh'd have to find your niche fer the place."

"Huh?" Maura spread more butter on her bread. She really liked the local butter, and she didn't have to do anything to make it.

"Look, you've got the Leap Inn across the street, then Ger's on the corner, and the bistro on the next corner, and that doesn't even take Skib into account. There's yer competition. What're you gonna do that's different?"

"Give the drinkers something that'll make them thirsty?" Maura grinned.

"Yeh're not far off. Yeh want yer people to stay in the pub and buy pints. They get hungry. If they leave fer food, will they be back? Mebbe, mebbe not. It's up to you to make it easy fer them to stay. They're not lookin' for gourmet stuff, or even a full meal. Just somethin' in their bellies to keep 'em from getting too drunk."

"Mick, have you been thinking about this too?"

"Now and then. Wouldn't take that much to fix up the kitchen, buy plates and the like. Mebbe a real dishwasher fer the back. Question is, what would yeh have to charge? And what would people pay?"

"Mick, I can't answer things like that!"

"So ask Harry."

"I will, I will — just as soon as I find the time." Maura stood up and took her lone plate and cup over to the sink and washed them. "You ready to go?" she called back over her shoulder. "Because Rose has a class this morning. Hmm — I forgot she slept over at the pub. I hope she doesn't have any trouble getting to Skibbereen on time. And there's another thing — we should make some sort of decision about those rooms upstairs."

"Why?" Mick asked, handing her his dirty dishes.

"I don't want to rent them out — that's a pain in the butt to manage — but they could be appealing to any staff we might find, at least in the short term, if we could offer them a place for cheap, or even free. I've already got the space, and it wouldn't take that much to make them livable."

"And where are we findin' the time to make that happen?" Mick asked, and Maura tried to read his expression.

"I don't know, Mick!" Maura finally told him emphatically. "It's just something I've been thinking about for a while. I'm trying to find ways to sweeten the deal for anyone I can find to hire, and I can't offer more money than other people around here. It's just an idea."

"Right now yeh've got a boatload of ideas. What's the most important?"

"Easy. Staff."

"And yeh've made a good start with that. It'll work out. We should go."

"You're not seeing Bridget this morning?"

"We've only the one car between us, remember? I'll be seein' her Sunday fer church."

"Okay, I'll stop in tomorrow morning."

Mick had done the driving the night before. When they reached the end of Maura's lane, she suddenly remembered that he probably hadn't seen the Sheridan caravan parked in the field straight ahead. Mick stopped abruptly when he saw it.

"So they're back," he said in a flat tone.

Maura debated about playing dumb, but she didn't want to lie. And there was something unsettling about his tone. "Peter Sheridan and his wife and kids. I met him day before yesterday."

"And yeh didn't mention it," Mick said in the same odd voice.

"Why should I? I figured you'd be stopping in anyway. What's the problem?"

"They're Travellers."

"I know that — Peter told me. So I'll say it again: what's the problem?"

"Most people don't trust 'em."

"Does that include you? Are they any kind of threat to Bridget? She told me they've been stopping here for years."

"The Sheridan's aren't so bad, but some of their friends aren't welcome around here."

Maura turned in her seat, despite the seat belt, and looked at Mick. As long as she'd known him, he'd been pretty openminded

241

about people. She'd never seen him act petty or suspicious about anyone. Why this particular group?

"Look, I don't know squat about Travellers, apart from what I learned this week. I've never seen them before. And I've never seen you act like this before either. Why?"

"They're most often thieves. Poachers. If they come upon a house that's vacant or they know the owner's away, they'll pass on the word and the owner will come back to find his telly missing and the place trashed. They'll offer to fix somethin' fer yeh, and they'll take it away and yeh'll never see it again."

"You sound like someone from another century. Is it really that bad, or is it because memories are so long around here? And Bridget didn't seem to have any problem with them."

"Bridget is a trusting person."

"But she's not stupid, and as far as I can tell she's a good judge of character. Now, tell me — are you going to jump out of the car this minute and march over there and tell the Sheridans to leave? They just wanted a place to park!"

"Just keep an eye on them, will yeh?" Mick mumbled.

"Sure, and if they're not around I'll break

in and search their home to make sure they haven't taken Bridget's spare teapot." Maura lapsed into silence, and neither spoke until they arrived in Leap. Before they got out of the car, Maura said, "Mick, I don't mean to be sarcastic, but I really don't understand why you feel the way you do about Travellers. You're usually pretty fair to everyone."

He didn't look at her but stared at the steering wheel. "I can't say I'm proud of feelin' that way — it has to be what I grew up with. But the Travellers haven't changed much since then — it's like they live in a different world. And they still use the same ways to get by."

Maura decided she'd said enough for now. Maybe she should wait until the Travellers moved on to their next stop, wherever that was. Maybe she could talk to Bridget some more. Right now she had other, more urgent things to deal with.

Inside she found a short note from Rose. "Cleaned up some. Going to class. Back by noon." She looked around the room and had to smile: Rose's idea of "some" cleanup beat hers by a mile. The place looked almost normal now. She checked the back room and it looked good too. Having Rose around — minus her lazy father — was a blessing, and Maura wished she could clone her.

As if to make up for his early departure the day before, Billy came in earlier than usual. "Mornin', Maura. Seems like the place survived. Good night?"

"It was, but kind of unexpectedly. Is it too early for a pint? Or would you rather have coffee?"

"Coffee, please — if yeh'll join me."

She smiled at him. "Since Rose did most of the cleanup I was going to do, I'd be happy to join you." She went behind the bar and started up the coffee machine and waited for it to produce two cups. Then she carried them over to Billy's seat and sat in the other chair. "Rose is at class at the moment. I envy her her energy — she went to bed well past midnight, and she was up early enough to clean the place this morning before going off to Skibbereen. I don't think I ever had that much energy."

"How'd yeh manage the night?"

Maura launched into the tale of the craziness of the crowds, and the band, and the appearing of an unexpected bartender named Niall. And how she wondered whether he was real. She finished up by saying, "Maybe he wasn't there at all — we just made him up. He appeared out of nowhere and started pulling pints and making change. And don't even think of asking if he emptied the cash box on his way out, because he didn't. I'd love to know where to find him, but he didn't leave much of a trail: twenty-something white man, dark hair, nice smile, name of Niall. He introduced himself and seemed pleasant enough, and we didn't have time to talk, but I trusted him."

"Accent?" Mick asked.

"You mean, was he Irish? I'm the wrong person to ask. He sounded Irish but not quite, you know what I mean? And that's all I know. Any ideas how to look for someone like that?"

"Pray to Saint Anthony that he'll come back?"

"Isn't he the patron saint of lost things?"

"That he is. And how'd yeh come to hear of that? Yer gran?"

"No, Bridget, I think." Maura leaned closer to him. "Can I ask you something?"

"Ask and I'll answer if I can," Billy told her quietly.

"What do you think of Travellers? I'm only asking because there's one Traveller family parked in Bridget's field. She says they've been coming there for years, but Mick seems kind of upset about it. What's the problem?"

Billy gathered his thoughts for a moment. "Most are decent people who happen to live a different kind of life than most of us. They believe in family, and they look after their kids. But they've always been outsiders, and there's people who don't trust them. Mebbe they do steal, for they've precious few ways of earnin' a livin'. But they're not beggars, and they're willin' to work for what you give 'em, only they don't stay around long after they're done. You've nothin' like them in the States?"

"Not that I knew of. I guess in the cities there are some people that are usually called gypsies, but I don't know where they came from, and I don't think they move around. Most of the homeless or the really poor — the ones who don't have jobs for one reason or another — don't go far. They kind of camp out in abandoned houses or under bridges — stuff like that. And yes, they steal, for food, or drugs these days. It's a real problem in a lot of places. Are the Travellers like that?"

"In some ways, mebbe. In other ways, not so much. I'd have to say they feel some pride in the way they live — they don't take anythin' from the government. And that's the way they like it, even though it means that they haven't much of their own. Let me ask you this, Maura. Are you troubled by them since they're new to yeh, or because of the death of that young man?"

"More than I would have been before? Maybe. But are they killers?"

"I'll have to answer that two ways. Among themselves, they might get into fights, and some don't end well. But their crimes are mostly petty theft. It's a rare thing that a Traveller will kill a man fer what's in his pocket. They know that would be a threat to their way of life, not just to the man holdin' the knife. Can yeh see that?"

"You know, I think I can. They kind of live outside the law, but they have their own rules."

"That's it. And the gardaí leave them alone unless they get too many complaints. But most people who've been here a while are used to them. Does that ease yer mind?"

"I think so. But what about Mick? He really seemed bent out of shape when he saw the caravan in Bridget's field. And then he didn't want to talk about it. That doesn't seem like him. Am I missing something?"

"That I can't say. Talk to Bridget — could be she knows somethin' about it."

"Thank, Billy." Maura stood up. It was past ten, and she should take another look through the place — she was still surprised that last night's crowd had passed through without leaving much of a trace. She should check the rooms upstairs, in the event she might need them shortly for her expanded staff. If ever she found anyone who wanted to work for her. Or she could look at the kitchen again. Mostly she avoided it. Rose had managed to make the sink and cooker work in the winter when they were snowed in, but Maura really didn't want to touch either of them.

To her surprise, she found Mick in the kitchen, leaning against the wall. "Taking measurements?" she asked.

"Wonderin' if it could ever work. Might be fine fer Rose, who's young and slender and can get around easily. But an older, stouter person, man or woman, might take one look and run. There's nowhere to expand — yeh've the rock wall behind. Might be that a more modern cooker would take up less space, but Rose or whoever worked in here would need at least one other person to help, and it would get crowded fast. And where's the storage, for food or for pots and pans and plates and the like?"

"I haven't a clue. You'd have to ask Rose those questions." Maura heard the outside door open and slam shut, and Rose called out, "Where is everybody?"

Maura and Mick joined her in the front room. "We were checking out the kitchen. What's got you so excited?"

"I saw the man! The bartender from last night!"

"And did you tie him up and drag him back here?" Maura asked, only half joking.

"I didn't have the chance. But he was meeting one of the other girls who's in my class at the café, and I can ask her who he is the next time I see her. I would have talked to them today, but the bus was just leavin' and I figured I should get back here. But at least now we've got a way to find him!"

CHAPTER TWENTY-ONE

Finally, a break, Maura thought. Maybe her luck was turning. "When's your next class?"

Rose's expression wilted. "Not until the day after tomorrow. I've no idea where else to look for 'em, and I only know the girl as Sophie."

"Rose, don't beat yourself up. It's a starting point. Heck, maybe we'll be lucky and the pair of them have a busload of friends who really want to work in an authentic Irish pub. Have you talked to her at the café at all?"

Rose shook her head. "All I can tell yeh is that she's got an Irish accent, or pretty near."

"Well, don't worry about it now. By the way, thanks for cleaning up this morning. You have any ideas about fixing up the rooms upstairs? The last time I took a real look at them was when we were snowed in, and since it was freezing I didn't spend a lot of time up there."

"As it happens, I do — I was lookin' about when I woke up. They need cleanin', of course, but mostly you could get by with a decent bed in each, maybe a rug fer the floor and a lamp or two. If yeh're not renting the rooms to guests, just your staff. I'd think of takin' one."

"Really?" Maura said, surprised. Although Rose had never mentioned where she lived, and Maura was embarrassed to admit she had never asked. She had no idea how much it cost, or how Rose got herself back and forth to the pub, or even how she paid for it. Had she really been so selfish? For that matter, she hadn't seen Mick's place, not that he had invited her there. But he brought a car to Leap each day, so it must be out a ways. Something to add to her mental to-do list: pay attention to the other people she worked with and their lives. Since she'd been more or less handed a place to live and the use of a car — one that Bridget had owned for years but no longer drove, and that Mick had maintained all along — she'd had no reason to look into things like rents. If she could only get her staffing issues straightened out, she'd have more time to check out all these things. And visit with Gillian more — she realized she hadn't seen her for days. Maura reminded herself to keep looking for child care for her — after she found wait staff and another bartender. Ireland might look simple on the surface, but there sure were a lot of details to take care of.

"Maura! Are yeh still with us?" Mick's voice pulled her out of her thoughts.

"Yes. I was just thinking about all the things I need to do, that I've been ignoring or putting off. What do we need to do right now?"

"I've got to check the kegs and figure out when we'll need to reorder. I'm guessin' if it's a busy night tonight, we could come up short by Monday."

"So you'll handle that?" When he nodded, she asked, "Any other supplies we're running out of?"

"Coffee," Rose said promptly. "Paper goods fer, you know. Some cleanin' stuff."

"In other words, everything. Want me to take care of it? I should stop at the bank with last night's take."

"Yeh're thinkin' like an American — the bank won't be open today. But yeh can go to the farmers market instead," Rose added enthusiastically. "It's a grand time of year fer it — lots of goods to sell, and lots of people who want 'em. Yeh can stock up on food."

"I guess. I could go now, before things get busy." Actually she was kind of dismayed, because she didn't know what to do with free time. Normally on any day she'd be at the pub, and when she wasn't at the pub, she'd be visiting Bridget or Gillian. She rarely took time for herself. Okay, today she could check out the famous farmers market people kept telling her about, and the next time she had a couple of hours free, she could visit the other restaurants in Skibbereen to see what they offered and what she liked. Maybe one a week. It was a plan. "You want me to bring anything back?" she asked.

"Jest enjoy yerself — if yeh can," Mick said, smiling. "Go."

Maura fled to her car before she or anyone else could change her mind.

Saturday. She knew it would be a busy day in Skib, so she decided to park outside the center of town behind Fields and walk — walking was another thing she didn't do enough of these days, although she was on her feet and moving most of the time. Once parked, she found herself walking fast and had to make an effort to slow down and actually look at things. For all that she'd lived near the town for over a year now, she still wasn't exactly familiar with the shops, much less the people who worked in them.

She strolled along, keeping her pace slow, and studying whatever was in windows. A store selling paper goods — she could use some pads to make notes. And pencils, And erasers. Then a shop with secondhand clothes, but nothing she saw interested her. She had to wonder where people wore dresses these days. Church? Weddings and funerals? A corner store selling appliances. Would she replace any of her ancient ones at her cottage, if she had the money? It seemed kind of a waste, since she hardly ever used them. But she should look at prices, if they decided to move ahead with the kitchen at Sullivan's. She crossed the street, passing the café where Rose had taken her. Half a block later she came to the farmers market.

On a beautiful day in June, it was mobbed, but in a good way. She perched on a low wall along the side and took it all in: ordinary people shopping, meeting friends, sitting down for a cup of coffee; families with small children, who seemed to be excited by everything they saw. Fish, meat, cheeses. Fresh vegetables, mostly the familiar carrots and potatoes and cabbage, but people were lined up to buy them direct from the farmer who'd harvested them that morning, and they chatted with each other while they waited. There were a few booths selling odds and ends, like discarded pots and pans, and even one with nice stuff like china that actually matched, and the odd piece of silver. There was something she had no use for!

She spied the Albertsons in the distance: Marv the strong anchor, Linda darting about pointing at things that caught her eye, Jannie dragging her feet behind them, pretending to ignore them as well as all the treats around her. Linda spied Maura and waved, so Maura stood and made her way through the crowd toward them.

"This is wonderful!" Linda gushed as Maura drew closer. "There's everything you could want here, and the people are so friendly. You're lucky to have a place like this nearby."

"Yes, it's great. You've been keeping busy? Seen anything interesting?"

"Well, we've been to Schull, and to Baltimore, and we've been the other direction too. But we've also spent some time just relaxing. It's really hard to get Marv to slow down back home."

Maura laughed. "I have the same problem.

I'm playing hooky right now, but I can tell myself I'm mixing it with shopping for food. How much longer will you be around?"

"Till next weekend. I hope we'll get to hear some music at your place." Linda leaned closer. "Jannie seems kind of interested, maybe. It's hard to impress a teenager these days."

"You can probably find which group will be playing next week if you look on your mobile phone, or so Rose tells me. We'd love to have you come."

"Thank you, Maura, and thanks for setting us up at the B and B — it's been really nice. I'll let you get back to your shopping now."

Maura resumed her wandering, eyeing the food stalls and wondering what she would actually eat. There were some cookies that looked really good, but then she got distracted by a booth selling a mishmash of secondhand kitchen items. At the cottage she had one lidless pot and one fry pan to her name, both inherited from Old Mick — plus the required teapot to boil water — which might explain why she wasn't interested in cooking. But she really could use a pot, couldn't she?

Fifteen minutes later she found herself the owner of three pots in varying sizes, complete with matching lids. Rose would be proud of her. As she was juggling her prizes, she backed into someone, and when she turned to apologize, she saw it was Sean Murphy. "Hey, Sean. You here to shop or are you on duty?"

"A bit of each. Can I buy yeh a coffee?"

"That'd be great. If we can sit down somewhere, before I drop one of these on someone's foot."

He pointed to a table with two empty seats in the middle of the lot. "That's a good place to watch the crowd," he said. "I'll bring yeh yer coffee."

Maura sat on one of the rickety chairs and parked her pots between her feet so she wouldn't forget them, while she jealously guarded the second seat. Sean was right: this was a great point from which she could see at least half the market, so she people-watched some more while she waited. She was surprised to find that she was smiling.

Sean was back in a few minutes and handed her a paper cup, then sat beside her.

"Are you looking for something? Or some-one?" Maura asked, careful to avoid being overheard.

"It's a busy season, and there are those who take advantage of tourists and the like."

"That reminds me — I wanted to ask you

about the Traveller family that Bridget has parked on her land. Says she's known him for years. Is there anything to worry about?"

Sean smiled briefly. "That'd be Peter Sheridan and his family, I'm guessin'. They pass through here each year." He suddenly perked up like a watchdog, and Maura followed his line of sight. A shabby-looking man was walking aimlessly, but as Maura watched, he tried to slide a hand into a woman's handbag from behind. Pickpocket, then. But even as she watched, another man she recognized as Peter Sheridan came up behind him and grabbed the man's arm before it reached the purse. Maura could feel Sean relax a bit beside her. "Didja see?" he asked her.

"I did. One man tried to grab something in the woman's purse, and Peter stopped him."

"Peter's an honest man, and he keeps an eye on his mates here, because he'd like to be welcome back again. Others aren't so particular."

"So, Peter's one of the good guys?"

"That he is."

"I hate to ask this, but could the group have anything to do with that man's death this past week? I mean, it happened just around the time they showed up here."

258

"It's not likely. The Travellers stick to the small stuff, because they know there'd be hell to pay if someone died at their hands."

"Any more suspects?"

Sean shook his head. "I wish I could tell yeh different, but we're no nearer to identifying the man who died, much less who killed him. Yeh do know they were face-to-face when it happened? The knife came from the front. So nobody sneaked up on him to rob him. It was more personal than that."

Face-to-face with his killer, then, Maura thought. Had they known each other? Because it still seemed like nobody had known either of them — strangers stood out around this area. Maybe the men had known each other from somewhere else?

"The killer must have had a lot of blood on him," she said. "Have any discarded bloody clothes showed up?"

Sean shook his head. "Too many places to get rid of such things. And the knife as well."

Maura picked up her bag, which clanked. "I hope you find him soon." She stood up. "I'd better be getting back to work, but Mick and Rose told me I had to go do something to get out of the pub, and everybody always says such great things about this market. And they were right. Maybe I'll take them some cookies as a thank you. Good to see you, Sean. Let me know if you find anything new."

She left him sitting and watching and wandered over to the booth with the cookies and bought a couple of small bags. By the time she found her path out of the crowded lot, she'd ended up with a few more odds and ends. It seemed that everybody had been right: this place was both fun and practical. She'd have to find a way to keep coming back, at least now and then.

When she got back to Sullivan's, she found Seamus sitting at the bar, nursing a coffee. "Where's your gang?" she greeted him.

"Busy. And discouraged. We've decided to give it another day — tonight's usually a big night fer most pubs, as you well know — but we've little to report. If we give it more time than that, our wives will have our hides."

"Hey, I've got something to report, although it probably doesn't have anything to do with the murder," Maura said. Seamus quirked an eyebrow. "What, you don't believe me? Last night we were crazy busy with the band and the place was packed. So at one point I looked up and realized there was a youngish guy behind the bar, handing

260

out pints, and he looked like he knew what he was doing."

"Didja not know him?"

"No, I didn't. I talked to him for a second, and he said his name was Niall, but that was all the time I had. Rose and Mick didn't recognize him either. At the end of the evening he just disappeared without a word."

"Takin' yer money with him?"

"No. Not even to pay for his time. But the point is, he was the same age as the . . . body. And Rose said she saw him in Skibbereen this morning with someone she kind of knows, and she'll look for him again."

"It's a long stretch between seein' an unfamiliar face behind the bar and accusing the man of murder, yeh know."

"Of course I know, Seamus," Maura protested. "Maybe I'm grasping at straws, or maybe I've been spending too much time with you guys, because you seem to know everybody who walks in. Now when I don't recognize someone, I figure he's got to be a stranger to the village or even the area and I'm not too sure I can trust him. Or her. Anyway, that's all I've got. One twenty-something guy who knows how to tend bar and stepped up without being asked and did a good job, then disappeared into the night. And Rose says he knows a girl who's taking classes at the café in Skib, who seems to know the guy pretty well. And that's all I've got. I'm sorry my pitiful crumbs don't impress you."

"Ah, don't get yer back up, Maura Donovan. It's a good effort." Seamus slid off the barstool. "I'd best be on my way home, before the missus sends out a search party herself. Me and my mates will be around and about tonight, and I'll let you know if we hear anything."

"Happy hunting, Seamus."

CHAPTER TWENTY-TWO

Saturday evening, the crowd at Sullivan's had returned to a more normal level. Maura hoped to see the mystery bartender again, but no such luck. Still, they could manage without him, at least for the night.

During a lull, she said to Mick, "Are you taking Bridget to church tomorrow?"

"I am. Do yeh want to come along?"

"No, thanks. I used to go with my gran, but it never really took, if you know what I mean. But it meant a lot to her that I went now and then."

"Didja have somethin' yeh wanted to do tomorrow? Yeh don't need to be in early."

"I hadn't really thought about it. The way I see it, we've got two possible big projects to look at: rebuilding the kitchen, and fixing up the rooms upstairs in case somebody like an employee needs them. I'm letting Rose worry about the kitchen, but the rooms would be easier anyway. I'm not asking anybody else to help, but I hate to sit still when there's something that needs doing and things are slow down here. If we could clear out the stuff up there that nobody's ever going to want, I could start on the cleaning part, when there's time, and maybe paint the rooms. And you can tell me the best places to buy furniture and stuff. Not too expensive, or maybe even secondhand. Isn't there a place that sells it down the street?"

"There is," Mick told her, "And another in Skib."

"Great. But I wouldn't want to put anybody up — even a temporary worker — in a place I wouldn't be willing to stay in myself."

"Shouldn't be hard, nor take too much time."

Maura hesitated for a moment, then said, "Can I ask you something?" When Mick nodded, she went on, "I realized that even after a year, I have no idea where you live. I mean, I guess I know the townland, but for all I know you could be living in a barn there. Or a tent."

"Yeh want me to invite you over?" he said with a half smile.

"Not necessarily, but I feel I should know. What if something happened to you, like

264

you fell down and broke your neck? And landed on your mobile at the same time, of course, so you couldn't call for help. Do you have neighbors who would notice? I mean, I'm not trying to invade your private space, but I'd like to have the information."

Mick still looked amused. "I'll draw yeh a map, when I have the time. Was that all?"

"No, I have the same question for Rose. I don't know where she lives, and I don't know how she gets here. I have to assume she walks, so I know it can't be far. But is it where she lived with Jimmy? And is it okay for her to stay there alone now? How's she paying for it? I know what I pay her, and it's not a lot. And I don't even know what rents are like around here, since I've never had to pay any."

Mick looked more serious now. "And yeh're thinkin' that if Rose wants this kitchen to happen, it'd be simpler if she lived over the shop?"

"Well, it is possible, isn't it? It would be good for everybody. But I'm not going to assume it will happen, and if she's happy where she is, that's fine. I just want to take the first step and clean up the rooms upstairs. Maybe I'll hate the results. Maybe Rose will hate them. Or maybe we'll find something else to do with them. But I have to see what they look like after they're cleaned up." Her only memories of the rooms upstairs were of darkness and a jumble of discarded items scattered on the floor — and the eerie view of blowing snow in the dim blue light out the window. *Curtains,* she reminded herself. And sheets and towels. Nothing fancy, just sturdy. *Maura, what is wrong with you? You don't put this much thought into the place you're living, which is as much yours as the pub. Why do you care about those old rooms above?* This was business, she reminded herself, but she wasn't convinced. Maybe she just wanted to keep busy until this murder business was cleared up.

"Up to you," Mick said. "I'll help yeh move the furniture, but you and Rose can see to the cleanin' between yeh."

"Fair enough. I'll take a look by daylight tomorrow, maybe take some measurements to find out what there's room for." Maura turned as a group of men came in, and she recognized Seamus and some of his friends. They headed for the largest empty table, then Seamus came over to the bar. "Maura, Mick," he greeted them.

"Hey, Seamus. You look depressed," Maura said.

"That I am, I'd have to say. Pints all

around if yeh will."

"Do I need to guess why?" Maura asked as she started filling pints.

"The poor dead man, of course. We'd been doin' so well, solvin' yer crimes fer yeh, up till now. Mebbe it started as a joke, but we had some luck, and we started to think it was easy. But this one's got us baffled. And the strangest part of it is, nobody at any of the other pubs is talkin' about any fights there that might have led to a death. Sure and the gardaí will have asked the same questions, but we're just guys talkin' to their mates after a few pints, and nobody's dropped a hint or a whisper. Fer all we know, the man was killed in Dublin and somebody delivered him here, dumped him, and went home again."

Maura topped off the pints and waited for them to settle again. "So you're giving up?"

Seamus shrugged. "Have I a choice? We've talked to everyone we can think of. Do the gardaí have anything fer yeh?"

Maura shook her head. "Not as of this morning. By tomorrow it'll have been a week since the man died. That's not good. But thanks for trying anyway, Seamus, and tell the rest of your crew that I appreciate it."

Maura set the pints on a tray, and Seamus

carried it back to his table.

Rose arrived shortly after that. "I've had me supper, Maura, if yeh want to go get a bite fer yerself."

"I might do that. Oh, wait — let me show you what I got at the farmers market today." She pulled out her bags from where she'd tucked them under the bar and unveiled her pots and pans with a flourish. "Ta-da!"

Rose broke into a smile. "Yeh've been listenin' to me! This is a grand lot of cookware. Are yeh going to try more than grillin' cheese now?"

"One step at a time," Maura grinned at her. "But I'm working on it. Oh, and I got us some cookies from one of the stalls. Don't flash them around or they'll be gone in a minute." She handed Rose the bags under the bar.

"True enough. Although I don't think biscuits and stout go together very well."

When Rose joined Mick behind the bar, Maura went out to the street. In June, she'd found, it stayed light what seemed like incredibly late, and there were plenty of people out enjoying the lingering sunlight and warm air. Where did she want to go? The Costcutter up the road, she decided — she wasn't in the mood for a real meal. She set off in that direction at an unhurried pace.

Had her resistance to cooking been a sign that she didn't feel she was here to stay? She hadn't done much with her cottage, taking things as Mick had left them — and he'd been an eighty-year-old man. She had, of course, gotten a new mattress and a lamp or two, but that was about all. Had she been so unsure when she arrived? And what did she think now?

The answer came through loud and clear: the place felt like home. Yes, she'd been raised in Boston, mainly in one neighborhood, and she'd had some happy times there. But she'd had few human connections, apart from her gran. No friends in the neighborhood. No friends at school, really — she'd hung out with a vague and shifting group, but after they'd all graduated, she hadn't seen any of them. Maybe once or twice, by accident. But here? In this tiny town at the far end of nowhere? She had friends. And Mick. People knew who she was and actually seemed to like her. They greeted her by name, which after being anonymous on the streets of Boston was kind of unsettling. And she knew them. She knew their families' names and where they lived. It wasn't just that the place was so small that it was hard *not* to know, but it was because she wanted to know.

Maura, get your bleeping sandwich before you start crying on the street! What had Ireland done to her? She'd gone soft. And, she realized, she kind of liked it.

When she got back to the pub, Billy was settled in his chair, and she waved to Mick and Rose and dropped into the one next to him. "Hey, we missed you earlier. Everything okay?"

"Don't worry yerself, Maura. There's days when I feel old, is all. Shame to waste this nice weather, though. Have I missed any news?"

"About the dead man? No. The gardaí are stumped. Seamus and his gang are stumped. You have any new ideas?"

"I don't get about as much as I used to, yeh know. My memory's grand fer the people I met half a century ago, but I don't often have the chance to meet the young ones comin' along now. And now they come from all over, not just the townlands here. Still, it's a sad thing, to die with nobody to mourn yeh."

"I know what you mean, Billy. But nobody's given up yet. Well, maybe Seamus and his pals — he told me the wives were getting mad that they were all spending so

270

much time hanging out in pubs 'investigating'." Maura made air quotes. "And they've come up with nothing."

"Might be we'll never know who he was, or who killed him," Billy said softly.

"I hope somebody figures it out!" Maura said. She looked up to see Sean Murphy come in. "You need another pint yet, Billy?"

"Nah, I'm grand fer now. Go talk to yer garda friend."

She stood up and approached Sean. "Are you on duty or can I get you a pint?"

"Coffee'll be fine. We're all workin' round the clock at the station on this murder, but we've little to show for it after a week. I've had an idea, though."

Maura slid his coffee across the bar and took the stool next to him. "And that would be?"

"Yer friend Gillian. The artist? Well, maybe I should start from the beginning. Yeh know the man's face was damaged."

Maura shuddered at the memory, and she hadn't even gotten very close to him. "Yes, of course. Where does Gillian come in?"

"She's an artist. I was wonderin' if mebbe she could take a shot at rebuildin' his face on paper."

"I thought there were computer programs that could do that now," Maura said.

"So I've heard, but that doesn't mean our little station has the money to get one."

"Okay. But what could you give her to work with? I don't think she'd be happy to look at pictures of what's left of the head and face."

"And I wouldn't ask her to," Sean hurried to tell Maura. "But we've got enough measurements and such to give her something to work with. Things like how close together the eyes were. How high his cheekbones were. Did his ears stick out. Most of the teeth were messed up, but we can say they didn't look like a rabbit's. I know the chances are slim she'll come up with something we can use, but we're that desperate."

"Are you going to ask her?"

"I was hopin' you'd do that, seein' as you know her better. And she's out near you. I don't want to disturb her if she's busy with the baby and all."

Hadn't Sean spent any time around babies? "Do you have a list of the details like you were telling me about?"

"That I do." Sean reached into his front pocket and pulled out a sheet of paper, folded in quarters. "It's not much, but it's the best we've got. Will yeh do it?"

"Sure, I'll ask her, and I'm sure she'd like to help. I can stop by in the morning, before

I come into Leap. But you've got to remember that she doesn't really do portraits of people. Mostly sort of abstract landscapes, or something like that. And pictures that tourists will like. I'm pretty sure there are no faces."

"If she's willing, it'd be grand. If nothin' comes of it, we're no worse off than we are now."

"Okay. Maybe she'd like the challenge. Or maybe anything that doesn't involve diapers and such would be a nice change for her. I'll take this to her tomorrow."

"Thanks, Maura." Sean drained his coffee mug. "I'll get back to checkin' the other pubs around. Might be somebody's remembered somethin'. Ta."

When he'd gone, Mick asked, "What was that about?"

"The gardaí's latest brainstorm is to try to get an artist's drawing of what the dead man looked like. Sean thought of Gillian, who's probably the only local artist he knows."

"I thought there was little left of the man's face."

"So did I, but they're getting desperate. They've taken measurements, although I don't want to know how, and he's hoping that Gillian can make something out of them. I guess there's nothing to lose. I'll drop off what they've got at Gillian's in the morning."

"What're the odds that she'll come up with something that looks human?" Mick mused.

"Hey, Gillian is a good artist, but I can't say how she handles faces. If I'm realistic, slim to none that she comes up with a guy that people could recognize. But you never know." Another group of people came in, and they were both swept up in pouring drinks.

The rest of the night was no more crowded. Billy took himself off after a couple of hours, and Maura watched with concern: was he really all right? He was moving slowly, but he smiled and raised a hand to her as he left. Other people came and went, but by midnight the place had cleared out, well ahead of closing time.

"Should we close?" Maura asked. "Anybody who comes in this late won't have time to finish his pint."

"True," Mick said, swabbing down the top of the bar. "Might as well. Yeh said yeh'd be stopping at Gillian's in the morning. I'll be picking up Bridget fer church around then — we can wave at each other as we cross on the road."

"Will do," Maura said. She left before

him, and didn't pass another car on the road to Knockskagh. As she chugged up the hill to her cottage, she saw the lights of the Sheridans' caravan, glowing golden in the night. That reminded her that she'd seen Peter prevent a small theft earlier that day. Had he known Sean was watching? Or had he done that simply because it was the right thing to do? She still had a lot of questions about the Travellers. What was their organization like — if there was one? Did they have a leader? A council? Some sort of justice system? She'd liked Peter, but maybe she had simply accepted Bridget's opinion of him.

She shook her head. Maybe she'd ask Gillian what she knew about Travellers when she stopped by in the morning.

CHAPTER TWENTY-THREE

Sunday was another sunny bright day. Where was all the Irish rain? Were the farmers worried? Or the dairymen whose cattle were proudly "grass-fed"? All the fields looked as green as ever. Maura couldn't complain — she preferred driving in sunny weather. Driving at night on the small winding roads still made her nervous. Driving at night in the rain was white-knuckle time.

It was still early, but she figured Gillian would be up and about — baby Henry would see to that. She didn't plan to stay long anyway. Right now she wanted to get out and walk — up over the hill, down the other side, and then a short distance to the old creamery. Would it always be called that, now that there were people living in it?

She had herself a quick breakfast and studied the page of details Sean had given her. It gave basic information like height and estimated weight. White male, probably in his twenties. Dark hair, brown eyes (Maura was surprised there were still two, after what she'd seen, but maybe the plural was what the form required). No obvious scars or marks. No tattoos — did that mean he wasn't a gang member anywhere? He had all his fingers and toes. His teeth were another issue — what with the deliberate bashing, some had gone missing, but there had been no obvious dental work done on the ones that remained.

Then there were the additions that Sean had mentioned — the dimensions and distances between parts of the ruined face. Maura had no idea what Gillian would make of this mess.

After washing her lone plate and cup, Maura set off on foot over the hill, enjoying the sun on her back. There were no cattle on this steep hill, but once she reached the crest she could see a small herd grazing down below. And plenty of flowers, most of which she couldn't identify, apart from the gorse, which she knew was prickly. She was surprised once again to see fuchsia blooming in tall tangled hedges. Back in the States, the stuff sold for ten bucks and up for a single basket. Here it was more or less a hedgerow weed. There was a small lake below to her right, on the near side of the road, and straight ahead she could see a few rowboats with fishermen out on larger Ballinlough.

It took her no more than ten minutes to reach the creamery, and she went around to the back to find Gillian sitting outside on a rickety chair, watching the fishermen and nursing the baby.

"Hey there," Maura called out. "Flashing for the crowd?"

Gillian turned her head without disturbing the baby. "I take my fun when I can. Mostly they're interested in the fish, though. What brings you here on such a bright and lovely morning?"

"Official police business, if you can believe it. Something they want you to do."

"Ooh, tell me! How do they think I could help? This is about that murder, right? They still haven't arrested anyone?"

"Yes, and no. Sean had this brilliant idea that since you're an artist, you could do a reconstruction of the face of the dead man."

Gillian sat up straighter, jostling Henry, who complained briefly before returning to his breakfast. "Seriously? I thought his face had been smashed. And aren't there computer programs for that?"

"That's what I said, but Sean told me they couldn't afford such a thing here. More likely they've never needed one before. And Sean told me they took detailed measurements of what they could of the face. So you don't have to look at any pictures."

"I'm glad of that!" Gillian shuddered, and the baby opened his eyes in protest. "There, there, *mo stór*. You just finish up while I talk to Maura here." Henry complied.

"That's Irish?" Maura asked.

"*Mo stór?* Yes. It means my darling or my treasure. I figured the kid should grow up hearing some Irish. He'll probably have to take it in school anyway, so he should get used to it. So, this idea of Sean's — they want it, like, yesterday?"

"Of course. The man's been dead a week tonight. Look, I didn't promise Sean anything. If you can't do it, I'll tell him. I've never seen anything of yours with people in it, much less a portrait."

"We all learn in art school, but that doesn't mean I can do it from some measurements. Now, if the man was sitting in front of me, I'd have a better chance."

"Trust me, you do not want to see him in his current condition," Maura said vehemently.

"That bad?"

"Yes," Maura told her. She did not elaborate.

"So. No indication that he came from somewhere outside of Ireland? Tags on his clothes? Tattoos, scars, fingerprints — all the usual stuff?"

"Nope. He's a clean as the day he was born, although Sean didn't say whether x-rays might have shown anything, like he's missing a rib or his leg was broken. But I'm pretty sure the gardaí have done the easy stuff like that. And here I was thinking everybody in Ireland knew everybody else."

"It does feel that way sometimes." Gillian looked down at her son. "Sleeping now. Why don't we go in, and I'll put him down and we can sit at the table in the kitchen, and I'll see what I can come up with?"

"That fast?"

"I'll know what I can manage quickly. I don't suppose you'll be looking for the mole under his left eyebrow?"

"I doubt it. By the way, he didn't have any facial hair either, unless the killer was a real pervert and gave him a shave before dumping him. Nobody's mentioned whether there was any DNA under the dead guy's fingernails, but it might take a while for whichever lab it is around here to process that."

"Huh." Gillian stood up carefully, to avoid disturbing the baby, and Maura followed

280

her into the house. Gillian and Harry had little money for improvements right now, but they'd cleared out the place, bought essential furnishings with clean simple lines, and hung some of Gillian's pictures around. Maura liked it. It was light and airy, and the lake cast flickering reflections on the walls.

Gillian settled baby Henry in a low cot, then led Maura to the kitchen table. "What've you got?"

Maura handed her the paper Sean had given her.

Gillian read it carefully, then sat back. "You weren't kidding when you said there wasn't much to work with. I can reconstruct a simple version of the face based on what's here, and then look at it. At the risk of sounding biased, it might give us an idea of where he came from, but only in a very general way. I can leave the mouth shut in the drawing, so we won't have to worry about teeth or the lack of them. I'll have to guess at a few things. The set of the eyes and nose and chin are pretty well fixed. Or maybe I can make a few different versions, like with different ears. Long or short hair, curly or buzzed."

"Do what you can, Gillian. They're not expecting miracles. How long will it take?"

"If my darling child will cooperate, I can have something for you by the end of the day. Harry should be back by then, and maybe we can stop by Sullivan's and drop it off. Unless you think I should take it straight to the gardaí?"

"The second might be the right thing to do, but I want to see the results first. Maybe I can ask Sean to come to Sullivan's to pick it up."

"Whatever. I'll call you when I've a better idea of how long I'll need."

"Thanks. So, how're things going with Harry?"

"Good. How're things going with Mick?"

"Pretty good. I think. I have nothing to compare it to. Other than that, we're still looking for staff for the pub — Friday night was a madhouse, with the music going on." Maura told Gillian the story of the vanishing bartender and Rose's sighting of him after. "I'm hoping we can track him down tomorrow. Have you found anyone to look after Henry?"

"No luck yet. If you run into anyone you think might fit — man or woman, old or young — lock him or her in your cellar until I can get there for an interview."

"You getting any painting done?"

"Nothing important. Pretty little watercolors that the tourists like, which helps pay the bills, but I know I can do better."

"I keep forgetting to push the one you gave us to hang in the pub. I'll try to talk it up." Maura checked the time. "Shoot, I've got to get to work. Mick's taking Bridget to church this morning. Have you seen her lately?"

"I try to get over there now and then. It makes her so happy to see Henry, and I enjoy talking to her."

"Did you notice the caravan in the field above?"

"Peter's? Yes. I've known him and his family for years. When I was young, it was his father who would come by in the summer. My sisters and I were fascinated by the caravan — which was horse-drawn back then — and we kept asking our parents why we couldn't live like that. That made them angry. They didn't like Travellers."

"Any particular reason?" Maura asked.

"Not really, or not that I recall. Just tradition. And they're still coming. Did you meet Peter?"

"I did, but just for a moment. He seemed like a good guy."

"He is, from all I've heard. It's an odd lifestyle, isn't it?"

"It is. I'd better go — I've got to get up

the hill and get my car and head to Leap. I hope I'll see you later today."

"I'll do my best."

Maura trudged up the long hill and stopped at the top, winded. She really did need to get more exercise — walking around the pub carrying pints was not enough. After she'd caught her breath, she started down the far side of the hill toward her cottage. When she reached her lane, she saw Peter Sheridan outside his caravan, trying to fix something mechanical she couldn't identify. "Car trouble?" she called out. "Or should I say, caravan trouble?"

Peter straightened up and smiled. "These old ones, it's hard to find the parts for 'em. This one's held together with string and chewing gum. Were yeh looking fer Bridget? Her grandson just came by to take her off to church."

"I know. I just stopped by to get my car, and then I'm going into Leap."

"Yeh own the pub now, I hear."

"I do. More than a year now. I never expected to be living like this. I mean, with a business and a house of my own, and in Ireland."

"Are yeh stayin'?"

"Looks like it. I'd better get going — not

that I expect business to be too heavy to-day."

"Because it's Sunday?" Peter asked.

"Partly. And because of the murder, and whoever dumped the body next to my place."

"Sad thing, that," Peter said, reaching down to the ground and picking up a tool. "But it's nothin' to do with you, is it? The gardaí still have no idea who the man was and who might have killed him?"

"Not that I've heard," Maura said. She wasn't about to explain her special relationship with the Skibbereen gardaí, but this time around it hadn't produced anything useful. "You wouldn't happen to know him, would you?"

Peter shook his head. "The dead man? He's not one of us. Word would have got round if he was."

An answer, Maura noted, that didn't quite cover her question. But now was not the time to get into it. "Will you be staying around long?"

"Tryin' to get rid of us already?" Peter responded with a humorless smile.

"No. I didn't mean it that way. Look, I'd never heard of Travellers until last week. I don't know much about your history, and I don't know why so many people distrust you. But I'm not one of them. I'm kind of an outsider too. Bridget knows you, and she doesn't have a problem with you. Should I?"

"Sorry," Peter said. "We're accustomed to being defensive. Don't take it personally. We'll probably be around another week or so, and then there's some fairs farther west, where there's horse tradin' goin' on."

"Maybe we can sit down sometime and talk. Although I'm almost always at the pub."

"Maybe we can work somethin' out."

"I hope so."

Maura raised a hand in farewell and walked back to where she'd parked, thinking about Peter. And his people. Who were, she'd been told, genetically Irish, but who had been living on the fringes for centuries. But there was this underlying hostility among the people toward Travellers that had also been going on a long time. Odd. They looked and sounded like most people in Ireland, but generations back they'd chosen — or been forced onto — a different path. Then it had become a way of life.

She parked near Sullivan's and unlocked the front door. Rose wasn't in, not that she had expected to see her so early. Mick was probably at church with Bridget. That meant she was the one who had to clean up, but that was only fair, since Rose had done it the day before. She wouldn't order her staff to do things that she wasn't willing to do.

Cleaning gave her time to think. Sometimes that was good, sometimes bad. Right now she had to admit she was frustrated. Somebody had dropped a body on her property a week ago, and still nobody knew who he was or who had dumped him. She couldn't accept that — it was wrong. She didn't think she'd ticked anybody off enough to leave a dead body on her doorstep. She didn't have any feuds going with anyone. Okay, then call it a coincidence. Somebody who needed to get rid of a body fast had thought the ravine would be a good place, and had known the bridge in the past. Or maybe there was some symbolic message that she just wasn't getting. Heck, maybe the dead guy was a Donovan. Had anybody asked Jerry or Tim in town whether they were missing a brother or nephew? But that long-ago O'Donovan who'd given his name to the village was sort of a local hero, and he'd been dead a long time. Almost nobody would understand the connection now.

Okay, maybe she'd left her gate open, and

plenty of people had to know it was never locked. Still, it wasn't exactly obvious to anyone on the street, especially in the dark. Which again led her back to the idea that somebody must have known the property well enough to know it was there.

She was going in circles. So were the gardaí. This was ridiculous. Worse, she was losing business. She hadn't done anything to deserve that.

She realized she was banging the mop harder than she needed to. She had no new ideas. At least Sean had come up with one, even if it seemed ridiculous. Yeah, maybe some high-tech computer scanner could take the dead guy's face and put all the pieces back where they belonged to see what he looked like before someone smashed his face. But that was not going to happen. So Sean had turned to Gillian. Couldn't hurt, right? Any small progress would be a good thing right now.

CHAPTER TWENTY-FOUR

The day crawled slowly by. The weather was beautiful and it was high tourist season — but where were the tourists? Weren't they here in Ireland to sample the authentic atmosphere of an old Irish pub with a lot of music history thrown in? No, more likely they were out frolicking in the meadows looking at cows or prehistoric stone circles. Or avoiding Sullivan's.

Rose came in shortly before official opening time. She scanned the mostly empty room and said, "Maybe when church lets out . . ." She did not sound convinced. Billy joined the crowd — if three customers could be called a crowd — just after Maura opened the doors, and he made his slow way to his usual chair. Maura poured him a pint and carried it over to where he sat. "How are you, Billy?"

"Much as I always am. And yerself?"

"Frustrated. Although I guess I shouldn't

be. Things will turn around, right? People will forget the dead man, mostly because nobody ever knew him anyway — he wasn't one of theirs. Oh, Peter told me the Travellers would be moving on soon — they've got horse trading to do, or something like that. Do they keep going in the winter?"

"Some do. Fer all that they're the same tribe, in a manner of speakin', they spread out and go their own way much of the time. But there's those that have settled campsites — there's one south of Cork city."

"Do the kids ever see the inside of a school?"

"Most don't, although that may be changin'. At least the government gives them the chance these days, but that doesn't mean they grab fer it."

Time to change the subject. "I saw Gillian earlier. She might stop by this afternoon, with Harry and the baby."

"That would be grand," Billy said, beaming, and Maura was reminded that he had no children and probably saw infants rarely. He would have been fun to have as a grandfather, she thought. "Is she settled now?" Billy asked.

"Yes and no. The place is livable — actually I kind of like it, because it's simple and sunny. But she doesn't have much chance

290

to work on her art because she can't find anyone to take care of the baby. At least Harry seems to be earning something now, and I think they got enough from the National Trust to buy the old creamery outright, so they're not paying any rent or mortgage."

"Word will get round in the townlands. It may be she won't find a person for the whole day, but if her time's her own, they could work out times when she could do her paintin'."

"I hope so! Hey, maybe we could get Rose to work on a website for her, if she can't travel far or spend time in Dublin these days. That might bring people to her instead."

"Can't say I know anythin' about these website things, but sure and yeh can ask Rose. And mebbe she could teach Gillian a thing or two?"

"Maybe while she's teaching me. We haven't even talked about a website for this place — she started with setting up a way to keep track of tickets for the music. Maybe we could combine the two? Give Gillian a page on the Sullivan's site?"

"Yeh've already lost me, Maura. Talk to Rose."

"I'll do that."

Pour drinks, make coffee, clean up used glasses and mugs, repeat. Mick came in around two, after returning Bridget to her cottage. Rose went out to buy some lunch and brought Maura back a sandwich. It was a very ordinary day, until Gillian, Harry, and Henry arrived in the late afternoon.

For the regulars, especially Billy, the sight of baby Henry was welcome. For the strangers, they glanced at the baby and returned to their pints. When the greetings died down, Maura pointed Gillian and Harry to the table by the window and followed them over. "I don't think we have any milk on tap. Are you still, uh . . ."

"Half and half. Don't worry about it. Harry, you want a pint?"

"I'll get it — you can talk to Maura." Harry went over to the bar and struck up a conversation with Mick. Maura took his chair. "So?"

Gillian grinned. "I thought you'd never ask. I rather enjoyed the whole process. I came up with several variations, but the only things I changed among the boys were the details nobody had mentioned. The pictures are different enough so that no one would say they're identical."

"Boys?" Maura asked.

Gillian sighed. "Well, men, I suppose, but

from my advanced age, they seem very young. Let's say I didn't add any wrinkles."

"Before I look, assuming you're going to share them with me, did you come to any conclusions about the man?"

"I'm thinking he's Irish, which doesn't help much. I don't think he's Italian or Spanish or even middle-European, but I can't claim I'm an expert. But he doesn't look foreign to me. Maybe I'm biased — after all, I'm the one who recreated him."

"You want him to be Irish, or everybody looks Irish to you?" Maura pressed.

Gillian didn't take offense. "Or the only faces I've every drawn were Irish and that's all I know."

"You didn't happen to recognize him, did you?"

Gillian shook her head. "You know I haven't been getting out a lot in the past few months. If he was new to the area, I wouldn't have seen him. If this guy had been around for long, somebody else will probably recognize him, if only from passing him on the street."

"Show me, then," Maura said. "Maybe he stopped in here a time or two." Anything to erase that awful idea of the smashed face from her mind.

Gillian pulled a manila envelope out of

the baby bag she carried, opened it, and fanned out three sketches on the table top. She didn't say anything but watched Maura's reaction.

Maura studied them carefully. Gillian was good: each picture looked like a believable person, but there were distinct differences among them. They could be brothers. But none of the images looked like anyone she could remember meeting. "Can I show Mick and Rose?"

Gillian shrugged. "If the gardaí won't be angry. But you don't have to tell them who's seen them."

Maura grabbed Rose as she passed with some empty glasses. "Does any one of these look familiar to you?" she asked in a low voice.

"Ah, Gillian's sketches." Rose looked at each, then shook her head. "I can't say I've seen anyone like this here. I don't think this is his kind of place. Good likenesses, though."

"Can you send Mick over?"

"I'll do that." Rose collected her glasses again and went to deposit them on the bar. She leaned closer to talk to Mick and nodded at the corner table, and he came over quickly.

"There are yer sketches fer the gardaí,

294

then?" he asked.

"They are," Gillian said. "See anyone you know?"

He, like Rose, looked at each, taking him time. "I can't say that I do."

"So it's unanimous," Maura said. "None of us knows him. Can I call Sean now and tell him to come collect them?"

"Might as well," Gillian told her. "My darling child will no doubt wake up sometime soon, and I'd like to explain to Sean how I approached his request before that."

"I'll do it now." She pulled out her phone and hit Sean's direct line, and he answered immediately.

"Maura, what've yeh got?"

"Gillian's here at Sullivan's, and she wants to show you what she's put together."

"I'll be there in ten." He hung up, and Maura could picture him running for his car.

She turned back to Gillian. "On his way."

Gillian smiled. "Now I know how you feel — I have only to snap my fingers and the gardaí come running. I hope the sketches live up to his expectations."

"Well, they're better than the nothing he has now." Maura went back to the bar to tell Mick and Rose what was going on. Rose looked excited, but Mick looked doubtful.

"Have yeh not noticed how much we Irish look like each other?"

Was he kidding? "Well, yes, but if these pictures don't look Irish to Sean, then we've learned something. Come on, Mick — you can't just complain. If you have a better idea, then tell us. Or shut up."

He threw up his hands in defeat and turned away. Maura felt bad for ticking him off, but she wasn't about to apologize for trying to do something — at the request of garda Sean — rather than just whining about how unfair the world was. She hadn't killed the guy in the ravine, but she was going to do her best to find out who had. She was taking this personally.

Sean arrived eleven minutes after he had hung up, but his delay was explained by the presence of Sergeant Ryan looming behind him. Sean was all business. He nodded at Maura, then greeted Gillian. Harry had joined her and was standing behind her chair. Henry was oblivious to the drama going on. "Gillian, you've met the sergeant here, am I right?"

Gillian nodded. "Of course. You helped us clear out the creamery. Sergeant Ryan, isn't it?"

The sergeant nodded. Sean went on, "We thought it might be a good thing to have a second set of eyes on the drawings, and Sergeant Ryan's from away, so he might see something we don't. What've yeh got fer us?"

"Sit down, the two of you — you're making me nervous, looming over me like that. Maura said she told you I don't do portraits, and that's true. But drawing faces is part of any art student's education. I've done my best." Like a fortune teller, Gillian laid out the drawings, one at a time. Since they were on standard-size paper, they took up a large part of the table, and she spaced them carefully.

Without speaking, the two gardaí studied each picture, one at a time. When they got to the third, the sergeant burst out, "Are yeh shitten' me? Oh, sorry."

Gillian smiled at him and said in a mock-stern tone, "Careful, sergeant, there's an infant present. Wouldn't want him to pick up bad habits. What do you see?"

Sergeant Ryan pointed to the middle picture. "Him. I'm thinkin' I know him from Limerick."

Sean was suddenly alert. "How do you come to know him?"

"You know I worked some with the Limerick gang unit — hard not to in one way or another. This one was new, just arrived

297

when I was leavin'." The sergeant nodded toward the picture on the table.

"No tattoos?" Sean demanded.

"No, he hadn't been around the gangs long enough. Mebbe that's what threw me off — I figgered 'no tats, no gang.' "

"So he's not local," Maura interrupted. "What would he be doing here?"

"Any number of things. Just passin' through — this is a main road, yeh know. Looking fer a friend. Transporting something that come by boat. Can't say without more information."

"Is this picture good enough to hand around, see who else might've seen him?" Sean asked.

Sergeant Ryan nodded once without hesitating. "It's close enough. I'd put money on it bein' him."

"What's his name?"

"Paddy Creegan. Could be he's still got family up toward Limerick — if they're not all dead. I'll make a call to one of my mates, see if there's any word about what young Paddy's been up to lately."

Sean picked up the picture and made a discreet mark on it. "This yer only copy?"

"I can't exactly afford copy machines, Sean," Gillian said. "Yes, it's my only copy of the sketch."

"I'll see to it yeh get a copy. More than one, if need be."

"Can we post one here?" Maura asked suddenly.

"Yeh may. But if yeh're thinkin' his killer might be hangin' about, yeh should watch out fer yerself."

"If he had half a brain, he's long gone. But somebody might have seen this Paddy with someone else. Can it hurt?"

Sean looked at her seriously for a long moment. "Just keep safe. All of yiz."

Sergeant Ryan interrupted. "Murphy, let's get back to Skib. I want to start this ball rollin', now that we've got something to work with. Oh, and Maura? Don't be spreadin' his name around, right? Show the face, ask if anybody saw him, but you don't know who he is, nor do the gardaí."

The Creegan family must be important in Limerick, Maura deduced, but she understood the sergeant's meaning. "Got it. We don't know him, but we welcome any information."

"Right so." He turned back to Gillian. "Gillian, yeh've done a grand job, and we appreciate it. You'll get proper credit for what yeh've done, at least within our station."

The two gardaí turned and walked out the

door as Maura and Gillian watched. "You'll notice he didn't say anything about paying me for my services," Gillian said wryly.

"True. But think of the publicity! 'Come visit the site of the crime, and you can buy an original artwork by the woman who broke the case.' "

"Good point. We might polish it up just a bit, though. And he did say to keep it quiet, did he not?" Henry began to make mewling noises, so Gillian picked him up and said to him, "You missed all the fun, little man. Are you ready for your supper?" He answered with a cranky wail. "I'll take that as a yes. I guess we'd best go home. Let me know if anything exciting happens." She waved across the room to Harry, who made his good-byes to Mick and came over.

"Ready to go?" he asked.

"I may not be, love, but the little one is."

"Go, the two of you," Maura told them. "And thanks for going along with the crazy idea, Gillian. It's great that it paid off. Harry, you'll keep an eye open?"

"What?" he asked, bewildered.

"I'll explain on the way," Gillian said. "Besides, who'd come after me? The gardaí have the picture, and I'm sure they'll spread it around. My part's done."

She stood up and gathered Henry and his

baby things. "Mick!" she called out. "Take care of her" — she nodded toward Maura — "and Rose. And say hello to Bridget for me."

"I'll do that. Safe home."

Maura sat down on a barstool. "Wow, that was unexpected. I need a pint, since we don't have any champagne."

"The case is far from solved," Mick reminded her.

"I know that, but this is the first break we've had. I'm glad I don't know who the guy is personally, but if he's a Limerick thug known to the gardaí, it's no surprise somebody wanted him dead. And now at least our gardaí have something to work with."

"What was he doin' here?" Mick asked.

"Hey, you want me to figure out everything all at once?" Maura protested. "This is a start."

"It is that," Mick agreed, and raised his glass.

CHAPTER TWENTY-FIVE

As the evening wore on, Maura's original excitement about their discovery of the dead man's identity wore off, and she started gnawing at the next set of questions: what was this Paddy doing in Leap, or more likely Skibbereen; who had killed him; and why had he been dumped here? Maybe someone in Limerick had wanted him dead and killed him there, but why drag the body down this far? There were plenty of other places to get rid of a body (funny how often she found herself thinking or even saying that). Or had he come on his own and gotten killed in Leap? But why? Something personal? Drugs? Smuggling? Was his gang involved in those, or something else? What else was there?

People?

She felt a tickle of excitement. As the world had become more troubled, especially in countries she was now closer to geographically than she had ever been before, she had heard that there were more and more immigrants around. But they weren't exactly visible, which she assumed was their choice — they wanted or needed to stay out of sight, or maybe they were just passing through. The problem there was, if they wanted to stay below the radar, they couldn't get real jobs, except off the record, like farm jobs. But Maura knew personally that there weren't enough workers to go around at the moment, not in what she would have called service jobs, like waitressing or washing dishes. Or child care, which probably required more detailed documentation.

Had the Limerick gangs moved beyond drugs into smuggling illegals into the country? Who could she ask? Sean, maybe, but Sergeant Ryan would probably know more, after his time working in Limerick. But it was kind of late to run a vague idea past them — it could wait until morning. Billy? No, he didn't get out much anymore, as he had said, so he wouldn't notice a rise in the number of unfamiliar faces on the streets. Which left Mick.

When the pub had cleared out (early closing night, with nobody interested in drawing it out or begging for a last pint) and

Rose had left, promising she'd talk to Sophie in the morning about the guy she'd been with, Maura went to him. "Mick, can I ask you a weird question?"

"Wouldn't be the first time," he said, focusing on wiping the top of the bar. "What?

"Well, Sergeant Ryan said he recognized the man in Gillian's drawing, right? And he knew him from Limerick, as part of a gang. But probably a kind of new member, because he didn't have the ink yet."

"So?" Mick asked.

"So he's new to the gang, or new to the area, okay? Now, when he joined up, what would the leaders do with him?"

"Yeh're right, yeh're askin' odd questions. Whaddaya mean, 'do' with him? A ceremony? A swearing in, like?"

"No, not that. Where would they put him to work?"

"Ah. Depends on his experience, right?"

"What if he didn't have much? Look, we've seen a little of the basic stuff — smuggling, drugs, that kind of thing. But is that all they do?"

Mick gave up any pretense of cleaning, leaned his elbows on the bar, and looked at Maura. "Yeh're thinkin' I know the answer to this?"

"No, but you must hear stuff from other people. Look, I could have given you a quick rundown of which bad guys managed what back in Boston, and this place is a lot smaller. So what were they into here?"

"Like yeh said, drugs and smuggling, mostly — pretty standard stuff. In the bad old days it might've been guns. What're yeh lookin' for?"

"Well, you know what trouble we've been having finding any staff for this place, and Gillian's had the same problem finding child care, even part-time. So I was thinking, maybe somebody saw an opportunity there. And the world's been so messed up these days, and all these countries fighting each other, that somebody might have found a way to bring in people without papers and find them jobs that nobody would look too closely at. Like working on a farm. And around here, I'd guess the gardaí are pretty cool about checking papers, until somebody commits a crime."

"Let me get this straight. Yeh're thinkin' the gangs of Limerick have set up some sort of people-smuggling operation, bringing the undocumented folk over here — for a fee, of course — and finding them jobs, and then letting them sink or swim?"

"Yeah, that's about it. Only it's kind of

new. Paddy Creegan just showed up recently, but he might have brought the idea with him. We know there's a need for workers. The guys in Limerick saw the opportunity and jumped on it."

"Could be. Yeh should talk to the gardaí about it. But there's a hole in the idea: why is it Paddy who's dead? He was the guy who was makin' it happen, according to yer idea."

"You think I know any more than you do about how this kind of operation works? Say Paddy was bugging one of his passengers for his fee and things got out of hand."

Mick countered quickly. "Seems like he would have demanded payment up front. I don't think the gangs wait fer their money."

"Good point. Maybe Paddy was doing *too* well, and another gang member wanted to teach him a lesson? Or wanted a cut of Paddy's business?"

"And stabbed him with a knife, more'n once? More likely he'd have given him a beatin' and left it at that. Paddy was no good to him or the gang if he was dead."

"One of his passengers was angry at him? He felt cheated? Or he couldn't find a job?" Maura was rapidly running out of logical ideas.

"Mebbe. But what was Paddy doin' down

here? If someone had come over and paid the fee, he wouldn't think to find the man here. Maybe in Skib, but even that's a small place compared to Limerick. What would make it worth Paddy's while to make the trip?"

Maura felt tired. And frustrated. "Mick, I don't know. I'm just trying to come up with any kind of idea that fits. Maybe I'm trying too hard. Here's what we think we've got: Limerick gang member smuggles illegal aliens into the country, then sets them to working at low-level jobs. He probably doesn't share his home address with them, and if they're illegals, how're they supposed to know how these things work here? I can't even guess how they find him. Maybe there's some message board somewhere. But say they contacted him somehow — what on earth would make Paddy come down here? Those aliens wouldn't blow the whistle on him, no matter how he'd treated them, because then they'd probably get sent back to wherever they came from. So, who would be angry enough to kill Paddy, and how would he get him to come down here to do it?"

Mick smiled, if sadly. "Maura, I've no more idea than you do. Maybe the man has a favorite pub in Skibbereen. Sleep on it. In the mornin', mebbe things'll look clearer to yeh, or maybe yer ideas'll look foolish. But there's nothin' to be done now, and it's late."

All too true, Maura thought. "So, uh, are we going home together?" She still didn't know how to do this stupid dance with a man. *Hey, Mick, you wanna do it tonight?*

His mouth twitched. "Is that what yeh want?"

"What, you're going to make me ask you? Okay, yes, that's what I want."

"Then I'll drive yeh home. No use wasting the gas."

"What a romantic thing to say!"

Monday morning, Maura woke up far too early and lay in bed starting at the ceiling and finding all the holes in her half-formed theories of the night before. Okay, gangs and illegal workers made some sense, and that was something she could confirm with one talk with Sergeant Ryan. That still left a lot of questions: How many people were involved? Where did the new arrivals go? Did they stay in West Cork or keep moving? What were the legal issues? And were those so complicated that the gardaí found it easier to look the other way?

All of which was nice and interesting, but

didn't explain what had gone wrong and resulted in a dead man in the ravine next to her pub. Had he been a "good" smuggler or a jerk? Had he played fair with the people he brought in, or just dumped them when they got off the boat and let them fend for themselves? If that last bit was true, it was unlikely he had shared his real name with any of them, and in that case, how could anyone have found him? He was Joe Average, based on his description, and the illegals weren't likely to walk into the nearest garda station and demand that something be done.

Which left her right back where she had started. Why was Paddy Creegan dead? Did anybody stand to gain from his death? His gang buddies? Someone who knew him? Or a total stranger he'd met when he was drinking at a pub?

Mick's voice startled her — she hadn't realized he was awake. "Yeh're like a terrier after a rat, Maura O'Donovan. Yeh just don't give up."

"Not when it affects me directly. You don't notice me chasing after any old criminal, do you?"

"Can't say that I have."

"Good, because I haven't been. Look, all I want right now is a couple more employees that I can count on, at least for a while. The fact that Sullivan's is smack in the middle of a murder investigation doesn't make that easy. If the gardaí would wrap that up, I could go on with business as usual. I'm just trying to help."

"I know. No one would call yeh a busy-body. Yeh're not after the excitement of it, either."

"I'm glad you see that. So we'd better get our act together now. Remember that Rose has a class in Skib this morning. If we're really lucky, she might get a line on finding that new bartender we need, if this girl Sophie is there."

"So I'll go make the coffee," Mick said, bounding out of bed quickly. He pulled on a shirt and his jeans and headed down the stairs.

One more thing on the to-do list, Maura reflected as she listened to him bang her few pots around downstairs: sort out what this relationship was and what they wanted from it. But she wasn't going to push it. Figure out the death of Paddy Creegan first.

They managed to arrive at Sullivan's just before ten. There wasn't much cleanup to take care of, since there hadn't been much business the day before. Maura found herself staring at the picture that Gillian

310

had asked her to hang in the pub quite a while earlier. Maura had hung it in what she thought was the busiest corner, but she realized it was kind of dark there, and it would be hard to see the image. No place for it behind the bar. What about the short wall over the bar, in front? Then people would see it as soon as they walked in — a bright splash of color. They might even ask about the artist. "Mick?" she called out. "Can you help me move Gillian's picture? Nobody even looks at it where it is."

He came out from the back, and Maura pointed to where she wanted it now. He looked at it and said, "There's already a hook there. Might be somebody's had that idea before."

"Well, I'm not going to ask who. I just want people to see Gillian's artwork, and maybe even think about buying it."

"Consider it done."

Billy came in before eleven, and he and Maura chatted for a few minutes. Maura was startled when her mobile phone rang — few people had her number. It seemed to be Rose, so Maura answered quickly. "What's up?"

"I'm here talking with Sophie, the girl from the café? But she doesn't have the time to come talk to you there. You think you

311

could stop by, just fer a bit?"

"That's fine. Where are you?"

"The café at Fields Supervalu in Skibbereen. It's not too busy yet. Will yeh come?"

"Sure. It's quiet here. I can be there quickly."

"Grand!"

She smiled at Billy as she turned away. "Mick, Rose wants me to meet the girl with the bartender friend in Skibbereen like right now. Mind if I run over there?"

"Go," he said. "I'll handle the crowds."

"I'll let you know if I get caught up in something." Maura grabbed up her keys and went out to her car. Ten minutes later she was parked in the lot behind Fields, and she came in the back way. She headed for the café in the front, overlooking the main street, and quickly saw Rose and a girl her own age sitting at a corner table. Rose saw her and waved her over.

"Maura, this is the girl I told you about, from the café. Her name's Sophie O'Riordan. I've told her yeh're lookin' for help at the pub."

"Hi, Sophie." Maura held out her hand, and Sophie looked confused, then took it. "Good to meet you." Maura took a seat.

"Yeh're American?" Sophie asked. "Rose

didn't mention that."

The girl's accent was definitely Irish, although with some odd inflections. "I am. I inherited the pub in Leap last year, and I'm still learning to run the place. Are you taking classes here in town?"

"That and workin' some hours to pay fer the classes. It's a good place to be."

"Do you want to be a chef?"

Sophie shrugged. "I've no idea. But I like the cookin' part. Why was it yeh wanted to talk wit' me?"

"Rose didn't explain? Then I'll let her tell you."

Rose launched into a short version of the story. "Well, I messed up bookin' the band last week and we had a flood of people, and . . ."

While Rose explained, Maura watched Sophie's expression, and she saw the color leach out of Sophie's face. *Odd.*

"I barely know him," Sophie said, then stood up abruptly. "Sorry, but I have to be somewhere now. Thanks fer the coffee, Rose." Before either Rose or Maura could answer, Sophie dashed out the front door.

"What was that all about?" Maura asked Rose.

Rose looked bewildered. "I couldn't say, but I'd guess somethin' scared her."

"About the guy you saw her with?"

"Mebbe. I can't think what else it might be."

I might have an idea, Maura thought. No, that seemed impossibly unlikely. But still . . . "Rose, were you going to take the bus back to Leap? I'd offer you a ride, but I want to stop by the garda station and talk to Sean for a minute. You can wait for me if you want."

"Shouldn't I be at Sullivan's?"

"When I left, Billy was the only customer. I think Mick can handle things for a bit longer."

"Does this have to do with Sophie and the guy?"

"Maybe," Maura said cautiously.

"Then I'll be comin' with yeh."

CHAPTER TWENTY-SIX

Since Maura was already parked behind the Fields market, she and Rose walked the block to the garda station. In the tiny vestibule there, Maura asked, "Is Sean Murphy here?"

"Hi, Maura," the officer behind the desk greeted her. "Yeh're lucky to catch him. I'll let him know yeh're here."

Maura and Rose studied the assorted posters and announcements tacked on the walls while they waited for Sean, who appeared only a couple of minutes later. "Is this official business, or did the two of yiz just want to pay a call?" he asked, smiling.

"A bit of each, maybe," Maura told him. "It might become official sometime, but right now it's just a couple of questions about . . . things."

That seemed to make sense to Sean. "It's a fine day — let's sit outside somewhere." He led the way out of the building and pointed them to the stone wall bordering the property. "Will that do?"

"Sure. This shouldn't take long, and we both need to get back to Leap. Let me just throw this out there: what do you know about smuggling illegal or undocumented aliens into West Cork?"

Sean stared at her a moment, then burst out laughing. "If it was anybody else, I'd think yeh were pullin' me leg, but since it's the two of yiz, I'll listen to yer questions. What do yeh want to know, and why?"

"Let me lay this out, and then you can comment, okay?" Maura proceeded to outline her early-morning thinking, about the man Sergeant Ryan had identified as a low-level Limerick gang member, and how he had ended up dead in Leap. "I mean, I thought about all the other crimes you've had around here, and that was one we've never talked about."

Sean nodded. "The sergeant would be the man to ask. We've never had anyone come to the garda station here to complain about illegals. But why do yeh think this girl at the café is involved, and the guy you saw her with? Rose, was this your idea?"

Rose swallowed before answering. "Look, all I wanted to do was find the guy who took over the bar at Sullivan's to ask him whether

316

he'd like a bartending job. And Sophie was the only person I know who seemed to know him, not that I know her well — I only saw them talkin' together. So I got Sophie and Maura together this mornin', but when we mentioned the man I saw with her — whose name may be Niall — Sophie seemed to get scared and left in a hurry. Which made us wonder if she was hidin' something?"

"Is that the way it seemed to you as well, Maura?" Sean asked.

Maura nodded firmly. "Yes. The three of us were having a nice chat, but when I asked about him, Sophie turned white and left fast. I know this is a real long shot, but if she's so anxious to hide him, maybe she has a good reason. Either he's doing something criminal, or he shouldn't be here. And maybe she shouldn't either. What happens if one or both of them is actually illegal?"

"Yeh mean, if yeh ever find them again?" Sean said. "Depends. I don't know the details, but there are different choices, accordin' on the circumstances. Let's take this one step at a time. Why are yeh so interested in the pair?"

"Because I need another bartender!" Maura said. "And he seems to be a good one. But that's the only reason I was look-

317

ing for him. When I saw him at the pub, he seemed like a great guy, and he was good at the job, but then he disappeared and it turned out that he never gave his name to anyone. Heck, I'd be happy to pay him for his time that night, if I could find him. But the whole thing started me thinking: I know there are jobs available because I've got a couple open, and I've already figured out that there are not enough people to go around. So it seemed logical to me that it would be a good business for someone to bring people in from somewhere else, if there were jobs waiting. But it's illegal, right? Assuming the people coming in don't have the right papers or are criminals or terrorists or something?"

"And from there you made the jump to yer dead man? That he was killed by someone here illegally?"

"Maybe by someone he brought in, and things didn't work out well. Why was a man from Limerick here in this area? Why Leap? Now that we know this Paddy Creegan was in a gang, it makes it even more suspicious. Someone killed him, and it wasn't an accident. Someone dumped him in a place he didn't belong and made sure it wouldn't be easy to identify him. So maybe our mystery bartender could tell you something about that death, if Paddy had something to do with bringing him here. I mean, why wouldn't he wait around to see if he could pick up some cash that night, just for helping out, unless he didn't want to be seen?" Maura tried to read Sean's expression. "Look, I've told you my idea. I admit it sounds ridiculous. You can tell me I'm crazy, and I'll go back to work. But there seems to be something odd going on here, and it might all be connected. And I really need to prove that this death had nothing to do with me or with Sullivan's, and to find some more staff. What do you think?"

Sean sighed. "I think it might, maybe, possibly mean somethin'. I think I need to take this to the sergeant. If he laughs in me face, that's the end of it. Do yeh know where to find the girl, Rose?"

Rose shook her head. "I've only seen her at the café in town here. And now we might have scared her away and she won't even go back there. Maybe Sinéad there has some information on her. Or you could ask the other girls, if they know her better than I do."

"I'll see what the sergeant says, and we might give that a try." Sean stood up. "Thank you for bringin' this to my attention, ladies," he said formally. "I'll let yeh know if anything comes of it."

"That's all we wanted, Sean," Maura said, standing up herself. "And if you find our bartender guy, lock him up until I can talk to him, will you? I want to hire him before he disappears again."

"Yeh're jokin', I take it?" Sean asked.

"Of course I am, Sean. I just want to know where to find him," Maura told him.

Sean smiled. "Then I'll do my best."

Sean went back to work, and Maura and Rose walked toward the parking lot. "Well, that was kind of a bust," Maura said. Had she expected more? Hoped, maybe.

"I know it seems odd, that all these pieces should fit together somehow," Rose said slowly. "Are we that hard up for ideas?"

"About the murder? Or about finding staff?" Maura thought for a moment. "Look, here's what I think. I've gotten used to everybody knowing everybody else around here. Now suddenly we've got a dead man that nobody around here knew, and an experienced bartender that nobody had seen before, who appeared out of nowhere and then disappeared without leaving his name. If he was just visiting, wouldn't he have stayed to talk, or come back the next day? Why did he disappear so fast? So since we have two things that happened that involved two strangers, I kind of want to lump them together, you know? Because almost everyone else is accounted for."

Rose nodded. "I see what yeh're sayin', but I don't know what yeh can do about it. Yeh've given what yeh know to Sean and he can handle it. If he talks with Sinéad, maybe she can point him in the right direction."

Maura sighed. "You're right, I know. So we'd better get back to Sullivan's and hope another bartender walks through the door."

"In yer dreams!" Rose responded, smiling.

Nothing appeared to have changed when they walked into Sullivan's: Mick was behind the counter, Billy was dozing in his chair, and otherwise the place was empty. Maura tried to convince herself that that was normal for a midday Monday. but she wasn't sure she believed herself. Maybe she was kidding herself about this whole murder/illegals/gang stuff, hoping there would be some easy answer that would make everybody feel better and then business would pick up. Maybe she was bored silly and was making up stories to keep her mind busy.

"Did yeh talk with Sean?" Mick asked.

"We did. He might have taken us seriously. Maybe. He said he'd talk to the sergeant. I'm not going to hold my breath. Did I miss anything?"

Mick shook his head. "It's been dead quiet."

It stayed that way until midafternoon, when Maura looked up to see Sinéad storming through the front door. She looked angry. Why?

"We need to talk," she told Maura. "Someplace private?"

"The back room," Maura said, and led the way.

Once they were there, Maura shut the door. "What's the problem?"

"You sent the gardaí to my place."

Maura wondered why this bothered the woman so much. Was she hiding something too? She simply didn't like police? "Not exactly. I'm looking for one of the young women who works at your place, because I want to ask her how to find somebody she knows. Rose and I met her at Fields earlier today. When I asked her about him, she got panicky and left in a hurry, which I thought was odd. I happened to talk with Sean Murphy right after that, mostly about the body that was found outside here, and we were talking about people who are here and working illegally. I wasn't pointing a finger at you. I only told him that Rose had met

Sophie at your place." Maura watched as a variety of expressions crossed Sinéad's face.

"You're not working for the gardaí, then?"

"No. I know some of them, Sean in particular, because I've gotten mixed up with a couple of crimes, but I'm not a spy or a mole or whatever you want to call it. Like I told you, all I want is to hire a couple of part-timers to work here, before we all wear ourselves into the ground. You should understand that."

Sinéad's shoulders seemed to loosen up just a bit. "I overreacted. Look, can you keep what I tell you to yourself?"

"As long as it doesn't involve the dead man, sure."

Sinéad hesitated, then went on. "I've had the same problems with staff as you're having now. For me, summers aren't bad because the kids are out of school, but during term I'm always scrabbling to cover the shifts. So, yes, maybe I've hired some people without demanding to see their papers, as do others around here. I pay them in cash. As long as they can do the job, I don't ask too many questions. You must know how hard waitressing can be, and if someone is willing to work hard, that's all I need."

"I can understand that. How do you find these people?"

"Mostly word of mouth. Somebody knows somebody and says, 'Go talk to the chef at the café.' "

"What's Sophie's story?" Maura asked.

"She's Irish born, but there's something messed up about her documents — she hasn't told me much. She's been in the country maybe six months and worked for me for the last couple. She's got some talent as a cook, so I let her sit in on a class — that's where she met your Rose."

"Where does she live?"

"That I can't tell you. Like I said, I pay her in cash. There's no paperwork. She comes in on time and she does her job. She's dropped a few hints that she's had a couple of other jobs since she got here and they didn't all work out well."

"And the man?"

Sinéad shook her head. "He doesn't work for me, and I don't know him. I've seen him outside waiting for Sophie now and then, but that's all."

Sinéad seemed to have calmed down, and Maura thought her story made sense. Should she go the next step? Maura wondered. Well, why not? "Look, I told you I'm not working with the gardaí, but you must have heard about the body that was found right out there just a week ago." Maura waved vaguely toward the ravine outside. "I think it's made people nervous to come here, so my business is down. Now, please don't spread this around, but the gardaí have more or less identified the dead guy as a gang member from Limerick, but there's no reason why he should be here in Leap, much less be found dead here. The new sergeant in Skib is looking into his connections with Limerick. But if it turns out he's not involved with drugs, maybe he was here for another reason, like smuggling people."

Sinéad cocked her head at Maura. "Interesting way of thinking you've got. Which is either good or bad as far as figuring out why he's dead. Could be something to do with his Limerick mates. Could be something with the people he's brought in, if that's what he's been doing — someone thought they'd gotten cheated. Or it could be personal — an old enemy who showed up out of nowhere and things got out of hand after that."

Maura had to smile. "I think you've got the hang of this. Look, I don't want to make trouble for anyone, and I'm not into sticking to the letter of the law. I only wanted to find this one guy, because he knows his stuff, and he stepped right in and helped out without being asked. If — still an if —

he's not quite legal, where do these people stay? Are there people who rent to them? Or to one of them, and then the rest pile in? Do they get together somewhere to talk about what jobs are open or who's looking?"

Sinéad was shaking her head again. "I don't usually bother myself with things like that. I've got more than enough work cooking to keep me busy. They do the work, they get paid, and that's it. But I'll tell you, it's summer and the weather's as good as it's going to get. They may be sleeping rough."

"You mean outside?"

"Yes. But that's only my guess. There's often some kind soul that gives them shelter — maybe an old barn or cottage that nobody's using. These illegals, they're good people mostly — not criminals or beggars. They want to work and pay their way, and they had to get away from something bad back where they came from."

"If the gardaí or someone else finds out you're hiring illegals, do you get in trouble?"

"It depends. On a lot of things. It's not simple." She stood up quickly. "I've got to get back for dinner prep. And I've told you just about all I know. I don't want to know too much."

"I can understand what you mean, and

thank you for being honest with me. This is all new to me, and I must sound stupid. I'm happy to give a job to someone who needs it. Although I have to say that a pub on the main street is pretty public, and the gardaí are in and out a lot because we're friends, and it's hard to hide behind the bar when you see them coming. Someone here illegally might feel kind of overexposed."

"I can see that," Sinéad said. "Look, I'll have a word with Sophie and tell her you're no threat to her or her friend. Assuming I ever see her again."

"Thank you. And if you hear of anybody else with some basic experience, who's looking for a job, keep me in mind."

"I'll do that. By the way, that Rose of yours has real talent in the kitchen."

Maura smiled. "I know. I'm worried I'll lose her too before much longer. Let me walk you out."

When she turned from saying good-bye to Sinéad, she found both Rose and Mick staring at her. "What was that in aid of?" Rose asked.

"Seems that Sean went to talk to her about hiring illegals and she took it the wrong way."

"Is she?" Mick asked abruptly. "Hirin' them, I mean."

"She said that if someone comes in and can do the job, she doesn't ask questions about their papers. But we talked about the hiring scene in general, and she knows there are illegals looking for work. Mostly they hear about a job from someone else and just show up — looks like most don't have anything like a fixed address. She said she'd ask Sophie about her mystery friend, now that she knows I don't want to turn anybody in or make trouble. Assuming Sophie goes back to work at all. But there's probably some network and they can find each other. So, I guess it's back to business as usual. Unless you happen to know where illegal immigrants are hiding out in this part of Cork?"

"That I don't," Mick admitted, "but I'll keep my eyes open. There's plenty of places to stay out of sight."

CHAPTER TWENTY-SEVEN

The day passed somehow. Maura went home alone at the end of it, and Mick went his own way. That didn't trouble her; she didn't feel like she was very good company at the moment. Had Mick had any idea about the presence of illegals in the area? She wasn't sure. He'd been kind of operating on autopilot for a few years, and maybe he hadn't been paying attention. Besides, during Old Mick's time, she had the feeling that business had amounted to Old Mick's friends, with few outsiders coming into the dark and none-too-clean pub. No need for extra staff, then. Or maybe the arrival of the illegals had been more recent than any of that.

She ate a quick breakfast, cleaned up, and was heading for her car when she remembered Sinéad's comments about sleeping rough. She couldn't say she'd noticed anybody bedding down in a hedgerow in the time she'd been in Ireland, but if they'd wanted to remain hidden, they would have been careful not to be seen. But where would they go? Plenty of open land in West Cork, but much of it was filled with cattle, who might not like one or more strangers sleeping in the middle of their food supply. Not too much in the way of stands of trees for cover in a lot of places. A few abandoned buildings, certainly, but most were so tumbledown that they wouldn't provide much protection from rain and wind. Maybe they crashed in vacant houses? There must be a fair number of holiday homes around. Maybe there was some unseen network to get the word out that the house on whichever lane was empty and looked like it might be for a while. And so the squatters moved in. Again, she hadn't heard much about that, but she hadn't been paying attention. Maybe she should, since there were a couple of long-vacant houses just up the hill from hers.

She debated about asking Bridget what she knew, but she had a feeling that this was something that had begun to happen about the time Bridget had stopped getting out much. But what about Peter and his family? She hadn't noticed the night before whether the caravan was still there, but she could look. She didn't feel comfortable with the idea of stopping a random Traveller — assuming she could identify one, which was doubtful — and asking what they knew about where the illegals were staying at the moment. But Peter should know, and she thought it would be safe to ask Peter, and he might give her the truth. Or not — he didn't really know her, and he had no reason to trust her, apart from Bridget's friendship. Still, it was worth a try. Her mind made up, Maura walked quickly down the lane. Yes, the caravan was still where it had been. Nan and her children were outside stringing up wet laundry, and Nan looked up warily when she saw Maura approaching, which made her sad. Did she look like a threat to the family? The children ignored her.

"Hi, Nan, is it? I'm Maura, remember? Is Peter around?"

"Inside," Nan said tersely, nodding toward the caravan. "I'll fetch him. Kids, come on — we'll finish this later." The three of them disappeared inside, and a moment later Peter came out, looking cautious.

"Maura? Is everything all right? Bridget?"

"Sure, everything's fine. I just had a question and I thought maybe you could help."

"If I can," Peter said, still sounding hesitant. "Will yeh walk with me?"

"Sure." *He doesn't want his wife to hear? Or is he just naturally secretive?*

He led the way halfway up the hill and gestured toward a stone wall. "Why don't we sit?"

Maura complied. When they were both settled, she dove straight in. "I'm trying to find the guy who filled in behind the bar at Sullivan's last week, the night we had the music and more than two hundred people showed up. He gave his name as Niall and that's all, and he disappeared before closing. I'd like to find him and ask if he wants a job."

Peter turned his head to look at her. "And why do yeh need me to find him?"

"I'm not asking you to find him, just to tell me where to look. See, Rose saw the guy before he disappeared, and then she saw him again in Skibbereen with a girl she takes a class with, but she couldn't catch up with them. So today she fixed it so she and the girl — Sophie's her name — and I could have coffee in town and see if she could tell us where to find him. But when we got around to talking about that, she got spooked and left in a hurry."

Peter's expression gave nothing away.

He was certainly careful, but Maura

pressed on. "Well, you must know about the dead man outside Sullivan's, right?" When Peter nodded, she said, "So Gillian over the hill here helped the gardaí by making some sketches of the guy, based on measurements of what was left of his face, and the sergeant at the station thought he recognized the man from Limerick, which is where the sergeant was before he came to Skibbereen. I'm sorry, am I confusing you?"

"No, yeh're not. Go on."

"Look, I probably shouldn't be telling you this, and maybe I'm making a lot of guesses, but I got to thinking. I know there's been a problem with drugs coming through this part of Cork, and smuggling of who knows what else, but when I started asking around about finding a couple more people to work at Sullivan's, I realized that there are some people who come here off the record, kind of — refugees and people looking for asylum, or maybe just trying to find a way to make a living that they can't back wherever they came from."

"Illegals, yeh're sayin'," Peter said flatly.

"Yes, I guess. I'm not talking about Travellers like you and your family. But maybe a lot of these are newcomers who paid to come over and don't know what to do now. Maybe there are plenty of farmers who need help in the summer and won't ask questions."

"Maura, have yeh buried a question somewhere in here?" Peter asked, his expression still neutral.

"Yes. I guess in part I'm still trying out the story to see if it makes sense, by telling it to you, but I know it sounds like I'm rambling. So here it is: when Sophie left so fast, I got to wondering if maybe she was in this country illegally. And maybe her friend or boyfriend or whatever he is was too, so they both have reason to hide, especially from the gardaí. But I'm not here to help the gardaí. All I want is to talk to him, or both of them, and see if they really do want jobs. Sophie's working some shifts at the café in town, and I've asked the chef — Sinéad — if she knows where to find either of them, but she told me she was careful *not* to find out, in case anybody official came asking. But then she said maybe since it's warm enough now, they'd be sleeping outside? Only she called it sleeping rough."

Peter seemed to relax just a bit. "Ah, now yeh're makin' sense. You think they're camping out or squatting or call it what you will, and you're wonderin' if I or any of the Travellers might have seen them around here, or know the good safe places?"

334

Maura felt a surge of relief. "Yes! Exactly. And I hope I haven't offended you by thinking you'd know something about them. I know there are people who think badly of Travellers, but I'm not saying that you or your friends are involved in any sort of crime, or even know about it. I'm sorry — this is all new to me."

Peter finally smiled. "If yeh're trying to offend me, yeh've a long ways to go. Yeh're guessin' that the two of them are a couple, or going around together, mebbe fer their own protection?"

"Yes, I think so. Is there a settlement or a camp or something nearby, where they might be?"

"And all yeh want is to give them a job? One or the both of 'em?"

"Yes. I need people to work at the pub. Sinéad tells me there aren't a lot of people looking for jobs around right now. These two might be available — and the guy is very good at serving drinks, from what I saw. That's all. I don't want to get anybody in trouble, and if they're not interested in working for me, that'd be the end of it."

"How wouldja square it with the gardaí, if they find out?"

"Peter, I've helped them out before, and they've helped me. I trust them, or at least

335

the ones I know best. But I'm not ready to tell them about this — I need to know more before I say anything to anybody."

"I doubt it's so simple as that." Peter leaned back and looked up at the sky for a few long moments. "I can't say as I know of a camp right now, but I know others who might. Let me ask around a bit and get back to yeh, all right?"

"Thank you — that'd be great."

"I can't say as I'll find 'em, either, but if I do I'll tell them yeh're no threat to them."

"That's all I'm asking for. Thanks, Peter. I appreciate your help."

"Not a problem. Yeh're off to Leap now?"

"Yes. You want a ride? Or does Nan?"

"I might. I need some nails and other supplies. If it's no trouble."

"Of course it isn't."

"Then I'll let Nan know where I'm headed. Half a minute." He stood up, then disappeared into the caravan, while Maura admired the view. There was a trickle of smoke coming out of Bridget's kitchen. Bridget had no interest in a modern hot pot and still boiled her water on an old stove each day. But why not? It worked for her, and it saved clutter in her small kitchen. She didn't have time to see Bridget today — and then she realized she hadn't told Gil-

336

lian that her sketches had done the trick with the gardaí. She hoped Sean had called her to tell her, because she didn't have time right now.

Peter came out again, still alone. "Shall we go?"

"Sure, I'm ready." They walked back to Maura's cottage.

"Nice place, this," Peter said. "Did Bridget tell me you'd inherited it?"

"Yes. Long story, and nothing I ever expected. I never met Old Mick — he's the one who left it to me — and I haven't changed much of anything since I moved in. It still doesn't feel quite real. What's it like for you, moving all the time?" Maura climbed into the driver's seat and started the car.

Peter settled himself in the passenger seat. "I've never known any other way of life. And we — by that I mean Nan and the kids — are not alone, nor lonely. We Travellers tend to travel together, and we know others like us wherever the old paths take us. Our extended families are strong, and we stick together. We raise our children to be strong, and fair and honest as well."

As Maura navigated the lanes toward Leap, she said, "Why do some people think you're dishonest and shifty?"

"They don't understand our way of life, mostly. To tell the truth, there are those among us who've been known to help themselves to things that weren't theirs. Maybe more than in the general population, like. But we don't steal — and we don't kill, if yeh're wonderin' that."

"I can't think of any reason why you'd have anything against a guy from Limerick. Are there Travellers near there?"

"There are, and they're no more popular there than anywhere else."

Maura kept her eyes on the road. "I feel like I should apologize, although I'm not sure for what. There's nothing like you back in the States, or at least, not in Boston, although maybe I just never noticed. But I have heard that in the cities, there are groups that people call gypsies, and mostly they pick pockets and mug tourists. And there are a lot of homeless on the streets, so the lines are kind of blurry."

Peter didn't say anything, so Maura asked, "Where do you want me to drop you?"

"Skib'll be fine — say, at the corner at the Drinagh Road? I'll find me own way back."

"No problem. And thanks for talking with me. I spend so much time working that I don't know half of what I should about the rest of this part of the world, and that makes me feel stupid."

"If yeh don't mind my sayin' so, yeh've got a good heart. Wantin' to help those two."

"Hey, we'd be helping each other. I need people to work for me, and I'm guessing they need work. And the guy certainly knows how to handle a crowd in a bar."

Maura dropped him off at the intersection of the two main roads, then turned toward Leap. Would Peter get the word out? Would it make a difference? She was fast running out of ideas. She'd give Peter some time to ask around, and try to figure out what her next step might be.

CHAPTER TWENTY-EIGHT

The day proved to be the most boring one yet, Maura thought, checking the clock for the seventeenth time since lunch. No one had stopped by bearing important or even trivial news — no sign of Sean or Seamus or anyone else. She wondered if the slow business was due to something other than finding what Sergeant Ryan believed to be Paddy Creegan's body next to the pub. From all she'd read or been told, West Cork was a hot area for both celebrities and tourists — so where were they? Maybe she should do a tour of local pubs, to see how well-filled they were and how they were attracting business these days. Or maybe it was her engaging personality — that thought made her snort — that was driving them away.

Then she was struck by a new thought. Maybe she and the rest of the local population hadn't known who the dead man was

— but maybe his pals in Limerick (if Conor Ryan had it right) did, and they were sniffing around the area themselves. She'd have to find out just how important Paddy was to them, or if he was no more than a junior member of the gang who had somehow messed up and gotten himself killed. The rest of the gang wasn't about to ride in and avenge his death, were they? She hadn't seen many unfamiliar faces on the streets of Leap recently, and certainly no one who looked like a city gang member.

"Somethin' yeh ate?" Mick said. He had come up behind her without her hearing, and his questions startled her.

"Huh?"

"Yeh've a sour expression on yer face."

"Oh, no, nothing like that. I'm just trying to figure out where all the customers are."

"Business'll pick up soon enough," he said.

"And how do you know that?" Maura demanded, turning to face him.

"It always has."

"But we haven't always had a body in the back yard," Maura countered.

"That's true enough," Mick said, then turned and started polishing already-shining glasses. Maura debated about swatting him but decided it wouldn't help anything. It wouldn't even make her feel better.

Rose came in about noon. "Sorry, sorry," she said breathlessly. "After class, Sinéad asked if I could help out with lunch prep, since Sophie didn't come in today."

One more complication. "Do you think she's gone for good?"

Rose shrugged. "I don't know her well, so I can't say. But Sinéad said she's always been on time before. Maybe Sophie thinks we've turned her in to the gardaí. Yeh didn't say anythin' more to Sean, didja?"

"No, I haven't seen or talked to him since we met with him. Look, Rose, you've lived around here all your life. Do you have any idea where people go to hide out? Seen any strangers in unexpected places?"

"That I have not. Yeh're thinkin' about Sophie and Niall? No one's ever really talked about the illegals, but I'd say it's because there've never been many, not that people are lookin' the other way. The odd man who passed out on his way home, or the young tourist who didn't bother to book a room anywhere — you'd see them slee-pin' in a field now and then. But now there's so much goin' on with politics and such in so many places, and you know well how easy it is to land in a quiet cove, if yeh can find yerself a boat to bring yeh across.

So it might be there's more than there was."

"But do people land here and keep going, or do they settle in and look for work here? Try to fit in?"

Rose shrugged. "Maura, if I don't know if they're here, I can't tell yeh what they're doin', now, can I? I'm not hiding anythin' — I simply don't know."

"I'm sorry — I'm not accusing you of anything. Or Sinéad. And we aren't even sure if the dead man was involved in anything like smuggling people in — we could be completely wrong about him too. And Mick hasn't been any help either."

"Why could he? He spends most of his time here or at his grannie's. Or at yer place." Rose flashed a brief smile.

Maura still wasn't comfortable with everybody knowing what felt like her private business, like how often Mick stayed overnight. But as he'd reminded her, Rose was family in a way, and a smart girl as well. "There's a family of Travellers camped out in Bridget's field — they've been there a few days."

"They come round every year," Rose said.

"That's what they told me. I asked if maybe they knew where people could camp out."

"They might not be willin' to share that

343

information — they keep to themselves."

"I know. It's a long shot, but I keep feeling I have to do something to get business back on track. I'm hoping that I can prove that the dead man has nothing to do with us."

"People will forget — give 'em time," Mick said. Apparently he'd been listening all along.

"Maybe," Maura muttered. She decided to talk with Old Billy, who never seemed to mind if business was busy or slow. She walked over to the fireplace and dropped into the old chair next to his. "Anything new with you, Billy?"

"Ah, Maura, me days don't change very much, from one to the next. So yeh're stuck on findin' out about yer dead man?"

"He's not mine!" Maura snapped, and then added quickly, "Sorry — I didn't mean to bite your head off. We — and the gardaí — think they might know who he is, but that doesn't explain why he was here and why somebody killed him. What can you tell me about Limerick? I've never been near there."

"It'd be the third-largest city in the country, and one of the worst fer crime. Mostly the lads from up there don't come down here and bother us — there's not enough profit in it fer them. Which is not to say they aren't after looking fer new opportunities."

Maura laughed briefly. "Well, I don't see many here. And Sean didn't seem to think there was much to worry about in Skibbereen." She glanced quickly around the nearly empty room, then leaned closer to Billy. "We were wondering if he might be smuggling immigrants into the country. Have you ever heard anything like that?"

Billy smiled to himself. "Ah, Maura, there was many years when people were more eager to leave than to sneak in. Mebbe that's changed, but I haven't been going around as much as I used to, so I could've missed it. The world's a different place now. Smaller in some ways, but bigger too. But you'd know yerself — a foreigner would stand out around here, and I'm not talkin' about tourists. He'd be more like to travel to one of the cities, not stay in the country. He'd fit in better."

"Makes sense. So if somebody sneaked in, or was helped to, he'd just pass through and keep going?"

"If he looked — or sounded — out of place. I don't mean to say that we don't trust strangers, only that we'd remember them."

"And it'd be hard for them to hide or find

work. Do a lot of farms need extra hands this time of year?"

"They might do. In the past, there were always enough sons in a family to take care of the farm, but now families are smaller, and the lads may be lookin' fer somethin' more than life tendin' to the cows. So it could be that a farmer would welcome some help, if only fer the summer, and wouldn't ask too many questions."

"That makes sense," Maura said. A lot of things seemed to be changing fast in Ireland these days, even in the short time she'd been here. Wars and conflicts often drove innocent people out of their homes, and no doubt Ireland looked like a safe, peaceful place to head for. But that offered an opportunity for illegal business, getting them into the country — for a fee. She herself had come in legally, with all her papers in order. But what about the others? What documents did they need to have to come in legally, or how could they get them if they arrived under the radar? What were the penalties if they were caught? That was a question for Sean.

Maura stood up. "Thanks, Billy. I don't always understand how things work around here, but I'm learning, and you're a big help. You need another pint yet?"

"I'm fine fer now, but yeh can ask me again in a bit."

It was a couple of hours shy of closing time when Mick told Maura, "Go on home — there's little happenin' here."

"But I feel guilty doing that. It's my pub, right? If anyone should be here, it's me."

"I think Rose and I can manage. If yeh want, yeh can take the early shift tomorrow."

"Fine. See you then."

Outside it was still barely light. Near the summer solstice, she'd been told — something that nobody in Boston had seemed to care about. Maybe a few Druids, but she couldn't swear to it. There didn't seem to be any weird ceremonies around Leap, so the only clue was the length of the days. Past nine o'clock and it was still light.

She drove back to her cottage, enjoying the weirdness of the late light, but when she approached the building, she saw someone leaning against her front door. It was only when she got fairly close that she recognized him as Peter. What did he want with her? Did he have news?

She parked, got out, and walked toward the door. "Hey, Peter. What's up?"

"I've found the people you were lookin' fer."

"You mean Sophie? And the guy? That's great. Where are they?"

"Right now they're inside yer cottage."

It took Maura a moment to process that. "What? Wait — didn't I lock that door?"

"You did. But a child could open it. I thought it might be best to keep the two of 'em out of sight until you could hear their story, and then you can decide amongst yerselves what to do."

"Oh. Well, okay, I guess that makes sense." She was miffed that Peter had gotten in so easily, but no doubt he was right, and her lock was more for psychological purposes than any kind of security. But instead Peter had brought in people and parked them in her house. "So let's go talk to them. You coming?"

"If yeh want. I'll let them tell yeh their story — I've nothin' to do with it."

Well, it was her home, so she should take charge. She pushed past Peter and opened the door. Inside, Sophie and the guy she recognized as Bartender Niall were sitting stiffly at her table, but they jumped up as soon as the door opened.

"Hi, Sophie. Hello again, Niall." Maura nodded toward the man. "Good to see you."

Sophie spoke quickly. "Yeh might have got the wrong idea, Maura — Niall's my

348

brother."

"Ah." A new and interesting fact. "Niall, I recognize you from the pub the other night — thanks for stepping in."

"Happy to help," Niall mumbled.

They both looked wary. Maura went on, "Look, you know I own the pub in Leap. I talked with Sophie yesterday and told her why I was looking for you, Niall. I don't work for the gardaí but I know some of them, and I trust them to listen and be fair. So I'm not going to turn you in or report you or anything like that if you're not quite legal here. But I've got to figure you're in some kind of trouble, or you wouldn't be hiding. And I'm guessing it's got to do with the dead man that somebody dumped next to my pub. Am I right?"

Niall and Sophie exchanged a glance, then both nodded, looking miserable.

"Okay, who's going to tell the story? But first, you want something to eat? Drink? I don't have a lot, but you're welcome to it. Tea, maybe?" She thought maybe doing something so ordinary might help them to settle down and make them more willing to talk.

"That'd be grand," Sophie said.

"Okay, let me put the kettle on." Maura turned her back on all of them and went

349

over to the stove, where she went through the familiar ritual of tea-making. None of the others spoke, and she began to feel like she was in some sort of weird avant-garde play — one without words. She tried to sort out what questions she needed to ask, fast, before they disappeared again.

When she'd assembled everything, she put the pot, cups, milk, sugar, and spoons on the table, then took a seat at the head of the table. "Okay, who wants to start?"

She was surprised when Peter spoke first. "Maura, Bridget said you could be trusted, and I have faith in yeh. Bridget's always done right by me and my family. She doesn't know about these two yet, though. Nor does anyone else. I respect the secrets of others. If they want me to leave, I'll go."

Sophie reached out a hand. "Peter, no. Please stay. It's time we got all this out into the open. We can't keep on hiding forever."

Niall spoke up then, and he sounded angry. "And who's to say we can't? Nothin's holding us here."

"Apart from the fact that we have no money?" Sophie shot back. "And no plan, and nowhere to go? We came back to Ireland to sort things out, not to make things worse."

"And look how well that's worked out,"

Niall shot back.

"That was not our doing!" Sophie protested. "Or at least, nothing we asked for."

Maura slapped her hand on the table to get their attention. "Hey, you two, why don't you stop arguing and start at the beginning? I haven't been in Ireland very long, but I can tell your accent is Irish, but maybe with something added? Are you Irish?"

Niall looked at Sophie, and nodded to her to go on.

"We are. Or at least, we were born here." Sophie stopped.

At this rate, this discussion was going to take all night. "Are you here legally?" Maura prompted.

"Not exactly," Sophie said, then stopped again.

Niall jumped in. "We are by birth Irish citizens. But our parents took us abroad when we were very young, and we never came home. For the past several years, we all lived together in Syria. Our father taught English at a small school in a rural area, and nobody bothered him. Our mother simply followed him, dragging us along."

"Why there?" Maura asked. "Isn't there a war going on?"

"There is, but we were there well before

that started. When it all began, our father believed that the conflict would be resolved quickly. He was wrong. But he was there legally, with all the appropriate papers."

"Couldn't you have gotten out earlier?"

"We might have done, but it was difficult. And our father held on to the belief that things would get better. And paid the price."

"What happened?" Maura asked.

"One of the many local groups attacked the village where we were living — it's hard to say which group. The small house we lived in was torched, and our parents were killed in the fire. Everything we owned was burnt, including our documents. We had no way to prove who we were, and we didn't know who to trust, and that included the so-called authorities. So we started looking for ways to get out of the country. We thought coming to Ireland would make it easier to replace our documents, and we could sort things out when we were here, but we've had little luck so far. And that was before . . . the death."

"How long have you been here?"

"A few months. We took what little money we had, and we begged from the friends who were still talking to us, and then we headed toward the coast. And that's where we met Paddy Creegan."

CHAPTER TWENTY-NINE

"How did you find him?" Maura asked.

"We got to the nearest port and started asking around. Carefully, you know? We're not stupid. When we found Paddy, he wanted Sophie."

"For the obvious reason?" Maura asked.

Niall looked disgusted. "Yeah. He wanted to sell her, uh, favors. We led him on a bit, and said if she went with him, I did too. He wouldn't charge for her passage, since he figgered he could make money off her, but I paid my way. And after that I wouldn't let her out of my sight. Pissed him off, all right."

"He had a boat?"

Niall shook his head. "He knew a man who had a boat. They were mates, and it looked like they'd worked together before. And there were other girls on that boat."

"Where did he take you?"

"Limerick."

That matched Sergeant Ryan's suspicions. "There's a port in Limerick?"

"Yeh haven't been here long, have yeh? There is — a small one on the river. Good place if yeh want to keep yer business quiet."

"So you arrived in Limerick with this Paddy. What happened?"

"We gave him the slip when we got off the boat," Niall told Maura, not without pride.

"After you knocked him down and bloodied his nose," Sophie protested. She turned to Maura. "He didn't know that we knew our way around here. So we just fled, and made our way here."

"Why here? You have family here?"

Sophie shook her head. "No, we've no family anywhere. But it was near, and we were guessin' that Paddy Creegan wouldn't be lookin' fer us in the country — he figered that we'd head for Cork or Dublin."

"How'd you get by?"

"A bit of farm work and the like," Niall said. "Day jobs. We tried to stay out of sight as much as we could."

"Until you got to Skibbereen. Why'd you stop?"

"We were tired and dirty and we needed a bit of a rest," Sophie said. "If I was goin' to find a job, I had to look clean, at least. I was lucky to find a place at Sinéad's café —

someone had left only the day before. I told her I was visitin' fer the summer but my cash was low."

"So she didn't know about Niall?"

"Not by name, nor that he was connected with me. She paid the goin' rate, and she let me sit in on her classes. That was all a coupla months ago."

"Where were you staying?"

Niall took up the story. "We found a group of people . . . like us," he said carefully. "They'd found an old house that still had runnin' water from a well, but we didn't dare cook for fear that someone would notice the smoke. But it was summer, right? Didn't matter much, and Sophie brought us some of the food that was left over at the cafe."

"How many more of you were there?" Maura asked. When she saw the distrust on their faces, she added quickly. "I told you, I'm not working for anyone else. I just wanted to know how big a group there was. Three? Ten?"

"More like ten, I'd say, but people came and went. We stayed the longest of any of 'em."

Maura had never noticed a group of ten people skulking around in this general area, but she did know there were plenty of abandoned houses down dead-end lanes. Maura looked at the time and saw it was getting late — and her guests, if she could call them that, looked exhausted. "Look, I know there's a lot more to tell, but you two look wiped out. I've got a spare room and a couch — why don't you stay here tonight and we can pick this up in the morning?"

Niall and Sophie exchanged glances, and Sophie won the silent battle. "That's kind of yeh, Maura. If it's no trouble. And I'd kill fer a bath." She realized what she had said and put her hand over her mouth. "Sorry, I didn't mean that."

"Yeh won't turn us in?" Niall demanded.

"I've said I won't, haven't I? And so far I don't know that you've done anything wrong except enter the country illegally, but you tell me you have the legal right to be here, and I believe you. So let's leave it at that. I won't tell anyone you're here, and I'll feed you breakfast, and you can tell me the rest tomorrow. But early, since I have to be at the pub by ten. You think you'll be going back to your job at Sinéad's, Sophie?"

"I hadn't thought that far ahead. I didn't go in this mornin', which wasn't fair to her, after she'd been so kind."

"We can sort it out in the morning. I think she'd understand."

After doling out sheets and towels from her pitiful supply, Maura followed Peter outside. "You were quiet in there," she said.

"Do yeh know what yeh're lettin' yerself in for?" he asked in a low voice.

"No, of course I don't. But what I said was true: I don't know of any crime they've committed, except for sneaking into Ireland. I'm sure there's a lot more to the story, and we haven't even gotten to what happened to Paddy Creegan, but I was worried that they'd clam up or just leave if I pushed it. You think I should be handling this differently? I won't tell anyone that you found them and brought them to me, in case anybody asks. I'd ask you where they were, but I probably wouldn't know what land or house you were talking about. So I guess sometimes being ignorant helps."

"This is dangerous business, Maura. I know yeh think it's safe here, but if the Creegan man was involved here, there's others that may follow him. You don't take the Limerick gangs lightly."

"Why would they come chasing after Niall or Sophie? Maura asked. "So what if one girl gets away from him? There are plenty of others, aren't there?"

"Maybe this one was special to this Paddy. Maybe it was his first run, and he looked like a fool to his mates for letting her get away from him. Or maybe he was related to someone important — they take family seriously. I can't tell yeh what the answer is — most Travellers I know steer clear of drugs and trafficking and all that. We may not be completely honest, but we're not involved in the really bad stuff. And Limerick's not a good place."

She seemed to be getting in deeper and deeper without even knowing it. "Thank you for the warning, Peter. Will you and the rest be moving on soon?"

"It's time. Yeh're worried the gardaí will come lookin' fer us?"

"No, I hadn't thought of that. And you're not involved in this other thing, and I can tell them that with a straight face."

"And they'll believe yeh?"

"I've earned that much from them. Will you be back next year?"

Peter smiled. "Will yeh be here next year?"

"I think so."

"Then I hope I'll be seein' yeh then. Good-night." He turned and vanished into the dark.

Maura went back inside. She could hear splashing from her bathroom, so she retreated up the stairs to her bedroom, wondering what she'd find in the morning.

She heard the sound of movement in the kitchen below her bedroom before she opened her eyes. After a brief spurt of panic, she remembered the night before. It had to be Sophie, although for all she knew Niall was as good a cook. At least one of them hadn't disappeared during the night, leaving things as unsettled as they had been before she found them. Her clock read seven o'clock — plenty of time yet to hash out the rest of the Paddy Creegan story. She hauled herself out of bed, pulled on some clothes, and went down the stairs.

Sophie heard her first, and turned to smile at her. "Good mornin'. Yeh weren't kidding when you said you had little food here. How do yeh keep yerself alive?"

"Most people who visit me here ask the same question, but I seem to have survived for a year. Of course, mostly I eat lunch and supper at the pub. Your brother awake?"

"Not that I've heard. He thinks he needs to look out fer me, so it's harder for him to get to sleep, and I'd like to let him sleep in this mornin'. Coffee?"

"Please." Maura sat down, and Sophie presented her with a full mug. "Listen,

Sophie, are there some things you don't want to talk about in front of your brother?"

"Yeh mean the sex stuff? He knows what goes on, but the two of us haven't talked about it. Creegan wanted me to use me for, well, you know. Niall stayed close and kept me safe. But Creegan wasn't going to wait forever. I was worth money to him, and he figgered I owed him."

"And it was worth it to you to risk . . . all that, just to get back here?" Maura asked.

Sophie nodded, watching the bacon in Maura's lone fry-pan. "It was. We've no family, apart from each other. Syria was never home to us, and we didn't want to stay, even before all the fightin'. This was where we wanted to be — as much a home as we ever knew. We knew it might be difficult, but we thought we could fix it once we were here. We never counted on anyone dyin'."

"Do you know what happened?" Maura asked carefully.

"We do. Mostly. Can we wait fer Niall before we start in on it?"

"Sure. I've got plenty of time. And I'm starving!"

Sophie presented Maura with a full plate and she dug in happily. "Sinéad said you were a good cook," Maura told her after swallowing her first bite.

"She's a kind woman, but I do like the cookin'. I used to do it fer the family, before. It's funny — fer most people the food there would be exotic and strange, but fer me it's the other way around. I don't recognize half the things I see in the shops here, much less know what to do with them."

"But you enjoy it. Have you talked with Rose much?"

"When I see her. She has only her da now, right?"

"Yes, and he's just gotten married and moved in with his wife — she has a farm. She was doing all the cooking for him, and I think she's not sure whether she's enjoying her freedom. She keeps making noises about serving food at the pub. Hey, where did Niall learn to tend bar?"

"There's bars in Syria, particularly in the cities. It was hard fer him to find work sometimes, and he picked up a lot of things. And he likes bein' around people."

"Well, I can tell you that we all noticed him when he filled in at Sullivan's. What was he doing there?"

"He shouldn'a been there, but he wanted to know if there was any word about Paddy and he figgered a local pub would be a good

361

place to listen."

"It was a crazy night. We had a band playing but we were way overbooked, and nobody could see or hear much of anything," Then the coffee kicked in and Maura realized the timeline was wrong. She'd found dead Paddy on the Monday, although it had taken a few days to identify the body. Niall had showed up at the pub and filled in *before* that ID had been made. Had he known or suspected the dead man was Paddy? Maura decided to wait until Niall was part of the conversation to ask awkward questions like that. "How would Paddy expect to find you, camped out in the country?"

Sophie shrugged. "Mebbe he knew people around here. Or mebbe one of the people he'd brought over had let something slip. The guys at the farm, they'd paid their way, so maybe Paddy already knew where it was and pointed people in that direction. You found us, did you not?"

"Yes, because I asked Peter. I don't know this area well, so I wouldn't have found you on my own. And Peter said he trusted me. Well, I trust him too, from what I've seen of him. I figured if he didn't want to tell me he'd found the two of you, he wouldn't. In fact, he never did — he just brought you here. I'm not very good at all this sneaking around and trying to remember who knows what about who." Maura took another sip of coffee. "Were any of the people you were . . . camping out with come over from Syria with you?"

Sophie shook her head firmly. "No. We never met them till we got to this part of Cork."

Maura smiled ruefully. "There is so much going on around here that I don't know anything about."

"Where is it yeh're from?" Sophie asked.

"Boston. In America. My father was born right about here, but I don't remember him. My gran raised me, and fixed it so I'd inherit the pub, and this house. All that was over a year ago. So in a way I'm homeless too. I never thought of Ireland as a place to come home to."

"Are yeh goin' back to Boston?"

"I don't think so. I like it here. I've got friends, and work, and it's all new and interesting. Sophie, if you could go anywhere you wanted to — forgetting about how much it cost — where would that be?"

"Here. In Ireland. We've lived in a foreign country, and that was fine. But our mother was always talking about the farm and the cows and her friends."

"Sounds like she was homesick," Maura said.

Sophie nodded. "She was that. She loved our da, and she agreed to go with him when he went to Syria, but it never felt right to her. And then the place changed, of course. She would have left if she could, but I guess you'd say our da was a dreamer and always hoped for the best."

The door to the parlor opened, and a rather scruffy Niall was standing in the doorway. "Givin' away all the family secrets, are yeh?" he asked Sophie, but he softened it with a smile. "Shower available?" he directed at Maura.

"It is. All yours."

"Yeh wouldn't happen to have any clean clothes, would yeh?" he asked.

"For a guy? Not hardly. Although you could look in the loft up above the bedroom. The guy who lived there before might have left something. Of course, he was in his eighties when he died, so I can't claim the stuff will be fashionable."

"I'll take a look. Right now clean sounds a lot better than fancy."

CHAPTER THIRTY

Sophie ate her own breakfast in silence while Niall poked around the rafters upstairs, then came down and took a surprisingly fast shower. Maura didn't say anything, trying to work out in her head what questions she needed to ask now. She figured Paddy had found the pair of them wherever they'd been hiding — that was clear enough. But what had happened next?

Niall emerged from the shower looking significantly less scruffy than he had going in. He seemed to have found a moth-eaten sweater of Old Mick's and a pair of shapeless cloth pants that barely clung to his slender hips. He looked younger now, with his curly hair wet and tousled. He nodded toward the empty plates on the table. "There more of that?"

"On the stove," Sophie said.

Maura corralled her patience and waited until he had filled a plate for himself and

365

sat down. Finally she said, "Are you ready to tell me the rest of the story?"

Niall glanced at Sophie, who nodded, then answered. "We are. Then yeh can decide what yeh need to do."

"Fair enough. But I promise I won't do anything without talking it over with you two first."

Niall nodded once, swabbed up the last of the egg on his plate with a piece of bread, and sat back in his chair. "Yeh can guess that Paddy managed to find where we was camped out. It was night, and dark. Most of us were there, and some were sleepin'."

"Hold on — *how* did Paddy find you?"

"We figgered he knew someone in the town, someone he'd brought over, who ratted us out. Mebbe even led him to the place. Or mebbe he'd sent people there before. We didn't stop to ask him."

That was more or less what Sophie had guessed. "Okay. Go on," Maura said.

"So Paddy shows up and wants to know where Sophie is, because she owed him. She stands up and faces him, and he tried to grab her. So of course I stand up and get between them, but Paddy, he was bigger than me, and tougher, and it didn't take much to push me down. But I wasn't about to let that stop me. Sophie's me sister, and what he wanted from her was wrong. So I came at him again, and he shoves Sophie away and pulls out a knife. 'She goes with me' was all he said.

"By now everybody in the place is awake and comes out to see what's happenin.' Turns out more than one of 'em had come over thanks to Paddy, and had paid dearly for it. But Sophie was the only woman in the lot of 'em. So Paddy's wavin' his knife around, and trying to grab Sophie again and back away, and somebody in the crowd says, 'Leave her be.' And Paddy's gettin' more and more angry, but he's not backin' down — thinks he can scare the whole lot of us, at least long enough to get away from 'em." Niall fell silent.

"And then?" Maura prompted, although she was already pretty sure things weren't going to end well for Paddy.

To her surprise, Sophie spoke up. "I picked up a log and hit him over the head with it."

"Sophie! Keep out of it," Niall said urgently.

"I will not! He came fer me! I wasn't going to sit back and let him hurt any one of you because of me. And I sure as hell wasn't going to go with him. I didn't stop to think — I just wanted to stop him."

367

"Was he dead?" Maura asked softly.

Niall shook his head. "Nah. He got up right fast, and now he was mad, 'cept he couldn't seem to make up his mind who to take it out on first. He tried to grab Sophie again, but she was standing well away, still wavin' the log at him. And then . . . it's hard to say what happened. Like I said, it was dark. And it was like the guys, or most of 'em, saw Sophie, a young girl, defending herself, and they figgered they should help her out, and everybody grabbed somethin' or mebbe nothin' and went for Paddy. They got the knife away first, and then they all kind of piled on him with whatever they had, and minutes later he was layin' on the ground and not movin'."

"Were you part of that? Either of you?" Not that it would have mattered much, Maura thought.

"Sophie was well out of it, but I might have gotten in a blow or two. We were all angry and lashin' out. It's a wonder more of us weren't hurt."

"Then what happened?"

"Took us a bit to calm down and back off. Then someone took a hard look at Paddy and said, 'I think he's dead.' He was right."

"And?"

Niall shook his head. "We didn't know

368

what to do. Go to the gardaí? We'd all be taken in fer it then, even if we explained, and then we'd end up in a cell or sent back to wherever we came from. Hide the body? Mebbe. There's plenty of places where a body'd never be found, you'd think. Leave him where he was and go our separate ways? We could've done that. Sophie here was the only one of us who had anything like a real job, and the others could find more short-term work elsewhere."

Had Sophie convinced Niall to stay? Maura was getting impatient. "Okay, I get it: Paddy is lying there dead, and nobody's quite sure who killed him, or maybe you all killed him. I understand why you didn't want to go to the gardaí. Maybe dumping him in a ditch somewhere would have been a good idea, and that's sort of what you did. But how the hell did you decide to dump him in my backyard?"

"It wasn't personal!" Niall protested.

"Well, it sure felt personal to me, when I found the body. So what happened?"

"Well, we blathered on fer a while, and finally one guy — mebbe the oldest among us — stepped up and said, 'The man's dead. It's best if nobody knows about all of yiz. If yeh leave him here, and mebbe some of his mates from Limerick know about this place

369

and come lookin' fer him, you'd best be gone by then. I'll take care of gettin' rid of him.' And nobody had a better idea, so we gathered up what little we had and went our separate ways. It was a different place where yer pal Peter found us — I guess he knows the places round here to lay low."

Maura still wasn't satisfied. "So unless this mystery guy of yours was a bodybuilder, how'd he get the body away? Did he tell you?"

Niall shook his head. "He was the only one of us who had a car, an old junk heap but at least it ran. He had us help him roll Paddy up in an old blanket and stuffed him in the boot of the car before we left. He didn't say where he was takin' him. Seems like he saw your bridge and thought it'd be a good place to dump him, without knowin' the lay of the land, like. Then Sophie heard there was a body found in Leap, but we couldn't be sure it was Paddy. That's why I came to yer pub, after a bit, to see what the talk was about the man. And it turned out nobody had figured out who it was yet, and I thought we were safe, or mebbe it was some other body."

"Hey, Leap's a quiet place — we don't get a lot of bodies," Maura protested. "So you thought it was safe enough that Sophie

370

could keep her job, except then Rose and I came along and spooked her by asking questions. Right, Sophie?"

Sophie nodded. "That's so."

Maura thought for a moment. "You probably don't want to hear this, but if you could find this guy with a car, or even some of the others in your group, it would help if they could support your story. You don't know where they went?"

Niall shook his head. "We didn't really trust anyone, yeh know. At least Sophie and I knew we had a chance here, but the others had no ties and no money. They were desperate, and they couldn't get tangled up with the gardaí and a murder. We didn't know more than their first names, and we don't know where they scattered to."

"So all we have is you two and one bloody body. Who did in fact get identified, purely by chance, by a local garda who happened to have been stationed in Limerick. At least he can back up your story about smuggling people."

Maura tried to think through the details of their story. The worst part was that everybody and nobody had killed Paddy Creegan, who from what she'd heard had not been a particularly nice man and probably already had a criminal record. No loss to anyone, except maybe his mother, but his death was still a crime. Could the gardaí find the anonymous guy with a beat-up car who had dumped the body? Would anyone even try? But should she — and the gardaí — worry that if Paddy's Limerick pals found out what had happened, they would want some kind of revenge? What form would that take? She shuddered to think.

This was beyond her abilities to fix. The logical thing would be to tell the gardaí — or at least Sean or Detective Hurley — and figure out what the legal channels were. The problem was, she kept asking them for . . . well, not quite favors, but to bend the law, or look the other way in some cases, and she really didn't have the right to do that, certainly not if it involved a lot of other people plus violent gang members. She was pretty sure that the right and just thing had gotten done in the end, but she was an ordinary citizen messing around with the laws in this country, and that didn't seem right either. So what now?

She realized that Niall and Sophie were both staring at her, waiting for some kind of answer. She didn't have one. She wasn't a wise old woman — heck, she probably wasn't more than five years older than these two. And she couldn't ask the wisest people she knew — Bridget and Old Billy — because these were modern problems. Their experience in smuggling people probably ran to IRA members and such, not thugs looking to make money from people to get away from wherever they were. But she had to say something.

Maura took a deep breath. "Sophie, Niall, I wish I could tell you what to do. Or hand you a wad of money and send you on your way, and keep my mouth shut. That last part I can do, if it makes sense, but I don't have a lot of money. I should tell you to talk to the gardaí, but I can understand why you don't want to. They're good people, and I think they can help you, but you don't know them and you can't trust them. I can look into getting your papers replaced, which might help a little, but it wouldn't solve the bigger problem."

"Paddy," Niall said bluntly.

"Exactly. Look, even if you admit he brought you here illegally, and then you tell them, gee, it was some guy whose name you never knew who killed Paddy and dumped his body in Leap and disappeared into the night, I don't think they'll be convinced. Unless they have proof, or a very good reason to believe the story. I believe you, but I'm not in charge here. You have any ideas?"

Sophie and Niall looked at each other, and finally Sophie spoke. "I think yeh're right — I should go to work and act like nothing's happened. I can make up some excuse fer Sinéad, and this is the first time I've messed up with showin' up fer work. As fer Niall . . ."

And then Maura had a brainstorm. "Niall can hide in plain sight. I'll hire him part-time to work at Sullivan's. He, or both of you, can have the rooms over the pub until we sort things out." She was surprised when she realized that both Sophie and Niall were looking at her as if she'd gone mad. "Let's think this through. Did anyone else around here ever see either of you and Paddy together? I know there might be people in Limerick who did, but here?"

Both shook their heads mutely.

"Okay, that's a start. Rose saw you and Niall together on the street in Skibbereen, but she didn't know who Niall was, except that he helped us out here that one night. I'm not saying this fixes anything permanently, but it gives us two things: one, we can see what direction the murder investigation goes, and two, we can find out if anybody from Limerick is going to come looking for their man and cause trouble here." Maura paused to study their expressions. "You don't expect any of your buddies out at whatever farm it was will come back — ask you for money, blackmail you, whatever?"

"No," Niall said. "They were decent people who'd somehow gotten themselves into a mess. They wouldn't come back lookin' fer a handout. I'd bet they're as far away from here as they could get."

"So that leaves us with a couple of different outcomes. One, the gardaí don't push hard on solving the murder and it goes away quietly. You two get your papers sorted out and go on with your lives, here or somewhere else. That's the easy ending. Two, the gangs of Limerick ride into town and threaten to tear the place apart until they find out what happened to Paddy, and then we're going to have to come clean, at least with the local gardaí, because that's too big for us to handle on our own. Three, maybe — we all spend the rest of our lives, or at least a few years, looking over our shoulder waiting until it all blows up in our faces. I don't have a four."

"We can't ask yeh to do that fer us," Sophie protested. "Yeh're puttin' yerself at risk — and yer pub, and yer friends."

Sophie was right, Maura knew. "Then let me talk to the gardaí — off the record, no names. I can get a sense of what the Limerick guys might do, and maybe what the charges would be against you and anyone else they could track down." Damn, but that would be a tricky conversation, Maura knew. Telling Sean didn't worry her so much, but he was kind of inexperienced and probably hadn't had much to do with gangs. Conor Ryan would be the best person to ask, but he didn't know her well, and from what she'd seen, he was a harder man and kind of went by the book, and he was still trying to make his mark in the Skibbereen station. But he knew Limerick and the gangs there. Did she have a choice?

"You're right, Sophie. So I'll say it again: this is too big for me or us to handle. Let me find out what the gardaí think is the best way to go, and I'll tell you what they think. That's the best I can offer. Will you stay around long enough for me to get some answers?"

"We owe yeh that much, fer bringin' this trouble down on your head," Niall said.

"Thank you. Let me make a phone call." Maura stood up and retrieved her phone from where it was charging, then walked out the front door. Such a beautiful sunny summer day, and now she was supposed to be consulting with the gardaí about how to avoid being attacked by angry gang members. How had that happened?

She hit Sean's speed dial number, and he answered quickly. "Maura? It's early yet — I'm not at the station. Somethin' wrong?"

"Kind of. Look, I don't want to talk about it on the phone. Can you meet me at the pub, say by nine? And can you bring Sergeant Ryan with you?"

"Why . . ." Sean began, then said. "I'll do my best. See yeh in Leap."

CHAPTER THIRTY-ONE

Maura dropped Sophie and Niall in Skibbereen — Sophie to go to the café, Niall to go somewhere, anywhere — and then she headed for Sullivan's. Along the way, she wondered how she had come to be in the middle of this mess. A bloody murder, angry gang members, human trafficking? She'd been minding her own business, and *blam,* there was a body. One that had nothing to do with her. And yet that, coupled with Niall's unexpected appearance behind the bar, had started the whole thing. And now she was supposed to explain it to the gardaí in order to keep Limerick thugs from attacking her and maybe burning down her business and killing most of her friends. Okay, that was the worst case, but the other cases weren't much better, and somebody could get hurt or even killed.

She parked and walked toward Sullivan's, where she found the door unlocked. She was getting ready to panic when she saw Mick inside, cleaning up. Damn, she hadn't counted on having to explain — or not explain — everything to someone else, much less him. But if they were together, whatever that meant, she owed it to him to tell him what was going on, particularly if he might be at risk in some way.

"You're in early," she said as she closed the door behind her.

"I could say the same to yeh," he said. "What's wrong?"

Was she so obvious? Now she had to tell him. "Sean and Conor Ryan will be here soon. I have news about the dead man, but I don't know that I want to go public with it right now, so I thought I'd run it by them first, off the record. I don't have time to explain it all to you now, but I think — no, I *want* you to hear it too, so you might as well sit in. And I want your opinion, because I don't know where to go from here."

He studied her face for a moment before speaking. "Thank you. Yeh think yeh know what happened, with the death and all?"

"I do, but it's complicated. I can't *not* say anything, because too many people are involved, but I don't want to make trouble for people either, not if they don't deserve it. It's a mess."

"So of course yeh're right in the thick of it," Mick said with a half smile.

"Funny thing about that — it seems to keep happening."

Maura looked up to see Sean and Sergeant Ryan — Conor. She still had trouble thinking of him on a first-name basis. She went to open the door, let them in, and locked the door behind them. They both saw Mick leaning against the bar, and all the men nodded silently at each other.

Maura was surprised when Sean spoke first. "Yeh sounded worried on the phone, Maura, so I figgered whatever it was, it was important. This is a private conversation, am I right? Not official?"

"Yes, and I'd rather talk in the back room, without an audience. But I want Mick to hear this too, and I'd rather say it all just once. Anybody want coffee?"

Conor Ryan shook his head. "We've got to get to Skib — let's just get this over with."

That suited Maura, so they trooped into the back room and settled around a table. Maura began, "Let me tell you what I know — which I've only just learned — and you can ask questions at the end." And with that she launched into the whole story, beginning with finding the body — had that been only last week? — and helping the sergeant

380

put a name to the body, and trying to track down the mystery bartender, only to find that he and Rose's friend were connected, and then searching for him and finally finding them together, with Peter's help, and through what Sophie and Niall had shared with her at breakfast only an hour earlier. It took half an hour to cover it all, and Maura was exhausted by the end of it from trying to keep the timeline and the details straight in her head. She was both surprised and relieved that Conor Ryan had listened intently throughout, without interrupting. Maybe the story made more sense than she had thought.

"And that's all I know," she finished, "and I've barely had time to digest it. Your turn, guys. What now?"

Sergeant Ryan took the lead. "We've had the name of the dead man only since the weekend, as yeh know, Maura. And I told yeh I recognized him. From all I've heard since I arrived, your lot in Skibbereen and the villages live in a bubble, where there's little crime or even danger. I spent years at the big station in Limerick, and it's like another world. Maybe not as rough as it was a few years ago, but there's still plenty of trouble. Paddy Creegan was kind of attached to one of the gang families, trying to break his way in, but he didn't have the smarts to rise very far or fast, though he was impatient. He's been nabbed fer a few smaller crimes, but he's done no serious time yet. From what I'd been hearing before I was transferred here, he saw this trafficking thing as his territory, but he was still feeling his way into it.

"If yeh don't know it, there's two lots of people comin' in — women and workers. But the transport's the same. Paddy knew guys with boats, and he could get people to Limerick, which is a small port. Then they split off from there. Seems he made a mistake takin' on this Niall and Sophie — maybe he took a personal interest in Sophie and was planning to dump Niall along the way. But Niall and Sophie were smart to keep things back from him — they weren't your typical scared refugees. Could be they could have come into the country legally, but I can see that it would be complicated fer 'em, so they took the shortcut to get here, with Paddy."

Maura nodded. "And they told me they got away from him as quickly as they could, in Limerick, but they got only as far as Skibbereen, and then they kind of hid out in a place that was probably too well known to others in their situation — including

Paddy. And he found them."

"And yeh're tellin' us that because he was makin' a grab for Sophie — a young and pretty girl — the men hidin' out there all took up against him to defend Sophie, and Paddy died at their hands. Is that the story they gave yeh?"

"Yes. And nobody really knew the guy who disposed of the body — they were kind of careful about revealing any details about themselves, I gather. I know, it sounds like a fairy-tale story, with the Nameless Hero stepping up and cleaning up the mess and then disappearing into the night with the body — although if I'd been writing this, I would have dumped the body somewhere else. I might as well ask, Sergeant: do you believe Niall's story?"

"I can't say without meeting the boy, but it rings true."

"And what would he be guilty of? Apart from arriving illegally, but that can be cleared up."

"You mean, should he be charged with murder? That's harder to say. If his story's to be believed, he wasn't the only one to take part in the killin,' and who knows whose blow did in Paddy, but Niall's only witness is his sister, and she has every reason to lie to protect him."

"That's what I was afraid of," Maura said. "No other witnesses, no proof of his story. You guys can probably find proof that he and his sister were born in Ireland, but that's only part of the story. And that's not the part that worries me."

Ryan came to the obvious conclusion. "The gangs, yeh mean. When word that Paddy's dead in Leap gets out, are they gonna come pokin' around here to find out what happened?"

"I was hoping you could answer that, Sergeant."

Ryan stared up at the ceiling for a couple of moments. "The man was family, so the guys in Limerick will want to know what happened to him. How they'll take the news of the way he came to die, I cannot say. Could be he was a beloved relative, or could be he was a thorn in their side. Could go either way, and I can't say right now which might be true."

"Can you find out?" *Is that completely unrealistic?* Maura had to wonder.

Ryan looked at Sean now, who had remained silent. "I'd have to talk to our boss. It's got to be handled carefully, so we don't bring trouble down on our heads."

"And can you do that?" Maura pressed. "Get the word to the right people? Would they come after Niall and Sophie because they need some kind of payback?"

"Depends. That's not the answer yeh want, but it's all I've got. Let me talk to Hurley and put out a few feelers, and we'll get back to yeh."

Not a perfect solution, but at least it was a start. "That's all I can ask, Sergeant."

"Can yeh persuade the two of 'em to come in and talk to me directly?"

"I don't know. They're scared. Sophie was going to work at the café this morning, so you could find her there, but I'd hate to mess up her job if she has a chance of keeping it. She might know where Niall is hiding out, or maybe he didn't tell her or didn't know himself where he was going. Maybe they're both safer if they're apart?"

"Again, depends on how the men from Limerick feel about Paddy. I'll have to see what I can find out." Ryan stood up, and Sean followed suit. "But tell the two of 'em not to leave the area, not that they'll listen to yeh."

"If I see them again, I'll do that." Maura escorted them out, then closed the door, locking it, and leaned against it. It was still half an hour shy of opening time. From the other side of the room, Mick was staring at her. "Are yeh all right?" he asked.

Maura considered for a moment. "I'm more all right than I was when I walked in, I guess. Look, I would have told you before, but this only came together late last night, and this morning they seemed ready to talk. I figured it was important to get the story to the gardaí, if there's any way they can help."

"I understand," Mick said. "So yeh're tellin' me that a gang family might show up here at Sullivan's at any time and demand the whole story?"

"That's what scares me. I ended up in this mess for no reason, but now I'm trying to do the right thing for the largest number of people, and I'm not sure what that is. I don't want anyone to get hurt, or anyone else, at least. And I hate it that there are so many parts of this I can't control. I hate feeling helpless."

"Yeh're far from helpless, Maura. Yeh found the kids and yeh got the story out of 'em, and you gave it to the gardaí. Like yeh said, yeh can't do everything, and this is dangerous business, so yeh shouldn't try."

"I'll have to tell Rose. I'll tell Billy too, but I think this is outside of his experience. Although I've been wrong before. When did the gangs start up in Limerick?"

"Before yeh were born, Maura," Mick said.

"So what do we do now? Close up and hide until the sergeant sniffs around Limerick?"

"Do yeh honestly think it would make a difference? They'd find yeh wherever. Half of Skibbereen knows where yeh live."

"So it's business as usual?" Maura wasn't sure how she felt about that.

"I'd say so. Look, I've got yer back. Yeh can give Rose the choice of stayin' away if yeh want."

"Damn. She's a smart girl and independent for her age, but she's only seventeen. Do I have the right to let her make that decision? Or do I send her home?"

"Maura, I wish I knew what the right thing would be." Mick sighed. "I've no more experience with this kind of thing than you. I fact, you've probably more, since yeh were raised in a city. I think Rose needs to know what's goin' on. Sophie is by way of bein' her friend, and she's goin' to ask."

"I guess. Look, this may be a stupid question, but do gang members carry guns here?"

"They could do. Guns are rare hereabouts, as yeh know, and they must be registered, but if yeh're ignorin' one law, why not others? I'd be surprised if they thought they'd need them here. Could be they think we're all livin' in a fairy-tale world here and they think they can scare us into givin' up whatever they're after."

"The Big Bad Limerick Wolves, eh? Well, for now, I'd like to think that Conor Ryan can keep things from getting any worse. We're lucky to have someone with Limerick experience in this." Maura thought for a moment, "Here's another dumb question. How long does it take to drive from Limerick to here?"

"That's right, yeh've never seen the place. Less than three hours, say."

"That far? Anyway, once the identity of the body is released, we've got just over three hours before somebody could show up here. Or maybe all the relatives would have to get together to talk about it. Or maybe they'd put together a convoy and arrive all at once."

"Yeh're soundin' a bit hysterical."

"I know. Should we close, at least for a day or two? Or put up a sign that says POSSIBLE GANG ACTIVITY — ENTER AT YOUR OWN RISK?"

Mick looked as confused as she felt. He spread his hands but said nothing.

Then Maura heard a key in the lock and

Rose walked in, and the clock ticked forward to opening time, and it was kind of too late to do anything. Maura sent up a small prayer that she wouldn't regret opening this day.

prayer that she would not regret opening that

CHAPTER THIRTY-TWO

"Something wrong?" Rose asked as soon as she saw their faces.

"I really have to work on my poker face," Maura said, exasperated. "Okay, Rose, the short answer is yes. I found Sophie, and the guy turns out to be her brother Niall. They came over to Ireland illegally a few months ago, with the help of a guy from Limerick who wanted to, well, sell Sophie's services. She and Niall got away from Limerick fast and ended up here, and they stayed in Skibbereen because Sophie found the job at the café. I told her to go back there today — if there's any trouble I'll explain it to Sinéad."

When Maura paused for a breath, Rose said, "That's not all, is it?"

"Smart girl. No, it's not. The guy who brought them to Ireland is the same guy who was found dead under the bridge, Paddy Creegan, and apparently he was a gang member in Limerick. He tracked down Sophie and Niall where they were squatting near here and wanted to take Sophie with him because he figured she owed him or he had the hots for her or something. But the rest of the guys at the place didn't like the way Paddy tried to drag her off and kind of ganged up on Paddy and he ended up dead, and nobody could be sure who killed him, or maybe they all did. So they decided to let one of the guys, who had a car, take care of dumping the body, and the rest of them scattered, except for Sophie and Niall. When they didn't hear anything about the body, they thought maybe they were safe. Niall got behind the bar here that night because he wanted to know if people were talking about the body. Only we didn't know who he was then."

"Slow down, Maura," Rose protested. "So, let me see if I've got this right: the dead guy was from a Limerick gang, and came looking for Sophie and Niall, and ended up dead under the bridge. And I'm goin' to guess that the two of yiz are looking so worried because yeh're wonderin' if his gang mates will come lookin' fer revenge?"

"Yeah, I am worried about that," Maura told her. "So after I heard what Sophie and Niall had to say, I asked Sean Murphy and

Conor Ryan to come around before we opened, and I told them everything I just told you, only with all the details."

"And what did they say?" Rose demanded.

"They took it seriously, and the sergeant said he'd touch base with his old pals in Limerick and see if he could learn who might be looking for Paddy or even come after him for some reason. And that's all I know. To tell the truth, Rose, Mick and I aren't sure it's safe for you to be here, if there's going to be trouble."

"And how are these guys going to know where to come lookin' fer yeh?"

"This is where the body was found, and that was in the news."

"Oh. That's right. But why are they to think you had anythin' to do with the poor man's death?"

"Shoot, I don't know!" Maura said, more loudly than she intended. "Until this morning I didn't know much of anything. Now I know too much. All I want is to protect everybody — Sophie, Niall, us here."

"And yeh're not sure the gardaí can handle it?"

Maura smiled ruefully. "I'd put my money on Sergeant Ryan — he's tough. Sean's a good man, but he's out of his league with gangs from the city."

Rose faced her, hands on hips. "And yeh really think I'm going to go home and sit stewing about what might be goin' on here?"

"I was kind of hoping you would," Maura told her. "I don't want to be responsible for anything happening to you."

"That's a kind thought, Maura, but I can take care of meself — I've been doin' it for a couple of years now. I'd rather be here."

"Let her stay, Maura," Mick said quietly. "She's safer here with us. The gardaí know what's goin' on."

Maura's shoulders slumped. "Fine, stay. If something bad happens, it's not my fault."

Maura looked up to see Billy making his slow way into the pub for his first pint. She went over to see him settled in his chair. "Ready for a pint?"

"I'm thinkin' a coffee would suit me."

"Fine. I'll get it."

"Come back with it and sit with me, will yeh?"

Maura dredged up her first smile of the morning. "Of course I will, Billy."

A couple more people came in, and while Rose served them, Maura made Billy's coffee. A nice normal day, right? Ha! She hadn't seen Gillian since she'd made the pictures. Heck, she hadn't seen Bridget for nearly a week, and that was not normal. Not

393

that Mick neglected his gran, but Maura enjoyed Bridget's company and knew that she didn't get as many visitors as she once had. But Maura had been so twisted up about this body and what it meant that she hadn't felt like paying a call. She wouldn't lie to Bridget, and if Bridget brought up something she'd heard from someone else, she'd have to answer honestly. But, as she'd thought earlier, this business of gangs and killing had come after the time that Bridget and Old Billy were out and about, and apart from sharing nuggets of human wisdom, they couldn't do much to help her now.

"Yeh're looking upset," Billy said when she returned with his coffee.

Maura had to fight not to explode. "Why does everyone keep saying that? What is it that gives me away, anyway? Should I shave off my eyebrows? Start wearing glasses?"

"So there *is* somethin' wrong," Billy said in a low voice that only she could hear.

"Yes! There, you got it out of me. I know you'd like to help, but I really don't think there's anything you can do."

"I'm sorry. Will the trouble be endin' soon?"

"I hope so. Tomorrow, maybe even today."

"It's to do with the dead man, I'm guessin'."

"Yes, you're right. And please don't tell me he's a fourth cousin of yours and you grew up with his mother."

"Sorry, m'dear, but I'm not related to the whole of Cork. You've identified the man?"

"We have."

"And he's nothin' to do with you?"

"Not a thing, unless you count bad luck."

"Then I'll say no more."

As the went on, Maura flinched each time someone walked through the front door, even though they all proved to be innocent citizens looking for a quick pint. When she went out to pick up something to eat, she found herself looking closely at everyone on the street, not that there were many. What about that car parked up the block that had been there for a while: was there anyone watching Sullivan's? Friend or enemy? If the coast was clear, would someone come in and confront her about Paddy? Or would a random gang member just toss a firebomb through the front door and take off?

She tried to shake off her fears, but it wasn't working. Thank goodness there wasn't music this week, because that would have complicated everyone's safety — although it would have been a welcome distraction.

It was close to four when she saw Sergeant

Ryan walk in. But instead of approaching her, he found himself a corner table and sat. Nobody else in the room seemed to recognize him, except Billy, Rose, and Mick, or react to his presence. Maura went over to the table and asked, "What can I get you?"

"A pint would suit me nicely," he said.

"Coming up," Maura told him, and went back to the bar to pull his pint. Mick raised one eyebrow, but Maura gave a small shake of her head as she filled a glass. When it was ready, she took it to Ryan's table. "There you go," she said with false cheerfulness.

"What do I owe yeh?" Ryan asked, paying a lot of attention to sorting coins he'd pulled out of his pocket. But while he was looking at his hand, he said quietly. "Might be yeh'll be havin' a visitor shortly."

"From Limerick?" Maura said in the same tone, then raised her voice. "That's five euros."

"Here yeh go," Ryan said in his normal voice, then lowered it again. "Just tell him what yeh know. All of it. He's expecting yer news."

"Thanks for the tip," Maura replied, and returned to the bar. Mick gave her a long look, then went out to get himself some food, so she didn't have to explain to him, though he'd probably already guessed that something was up. Rose gave her a quick glance, but when Maura didn't volunteer any information, she went back to clearing the tables. And if one more person asked Maura if something was wrong, she might hit him over the head with a bottle.

She didn't have long to wait. The next time she looked up, a guy came in alone — not short, not tall, but solidly built, with graying hair cut short. He was dressed like everyone else in the pub, but somehow he looked out of place. Maybe she was jumpy and was overreacting, but he looked . . . dangerous. No, that was silly. He looked like he knew what he was doing and what he wanted, and it wasn't just a pint.

She watched as he scanned the room — Billy dozing by the fire, a couple of guys at a table in the corner. She noticed that he didn't looked directly at Sergeant Ryan in the opposite corner, but she was pretty sure the man knew who Ryan was and exactly where he was sitting. Finally he walked over to the bar and leaned his forearms on it. "You'd be Maura Donovan," he said. It wasn't a question.

"Yes. What can I get for you?"

"A bit of yer time, if yeh don't mind."

She looked briefly at Ryan, who gave her

a very small nod. Then she said, "Rose, can you cover? I need to talk to this guy."

Rose didn't comment but nodded and slid behind the bar. Maura turned back to the man at the bar. "The back room's private."

"I was thinkin' we might have our chat outside. I hear there's a nice view of that famous ravine from there."

"Fine." If she'd had any doubts of the man's identity, that statement erased them. He knew about Paddy and where he'd been found. How much more did he know? She led him out to the back, to the small paved area that had a slice of a view of the river. "Have a seat," she said.

"I'd rather stand. But sit down if yeh want."

She did. Maybe it was cowardly to play the weak woman whose legs wouldn't hold her, but getting in this guy's face wouldn't do her any good.

"Yeh know who I am?" he asked.

"I think I can guess, but I don't know your name."

"Danny Creegan of Limerick. Paddy was my brother's son."

"You know I found his body. Right over there, under the bridge." Maura pointed and was pleased that her hand wasn't shaking. "I didn't know who he was then.

Nobody did. His face was . . . damaged."

"But yeh know now. I take it his mother won't be happy with his looks now."

"I doubt it. What do you want from me?"

"Right now I'm gatherin' facts. If yeh know who I am, you know my line of business. Young Paddy was after joining the family business."

Maura nodded without speaking.

"I'm told yeh're American, but yeh had family from around here." Clearly the man was in no hurry. And he'd done his homework, or he and the sergeant had talked about her.

"Yes. I only knew my grandmother, but she still had friends and relatives here. That's why I ended up with this pub."

"So yeh have some idea of the importance of family hereabouts."

"Yes. I do." Maura held his gaze, but she still had no idea what he wanted.

The man settled himself against the stone wall he'd been leaning on. "Paddy was my own blood. I don't know what yeh know of Limerick, but it's safe to say that we look after our own."

This conversation was going nowhere. "Look, Mr. Creegan, I've never been to Limerick, and I never knew your nephew Paddy. As far as I know, he never came into

Sullivan's, but I could be wrong. It seems to be purely a coincidence that his body was left here and I was the one who found him. So what is it you want from me? Why are you here?"

It almost looked to Maura as though he smiled. "I have been informed by a reliable source that you possess information about the manner of Paddy's death."

She guessed that Sergeant Ryan was the reliable source, or one of his prior Limerick colleagues. "If that's so, why do you want that information?"

"Wouldn't you, if it was yer family?"

"I suppose." Maura squared her shoulders. "Look, I don't want trouble, for me or anybody else. If I share what I know, can you promise me that you won't just kill everybody involved and dump them in a bog somewhere? Or take the bodies back to Limerick and toss them in the river?"

Danny Creegan raised one eyebrow. "Would it upset yeh if I said it would depend on the circumstances?"

"I was raised in Boston. Let's say it wouldn't surprise me."

The man smiled. "Miss Donovan, let me tell you something in confidence, and I'll trust you not to spread the story around. For all that he was my nephew, Paddy was a danger to himself and to anyone who crossed him. I won't claim that I and my business associates are all angels, but Paddy wanted results and fast, and he had no patience. Worse, he liked causing people pain. He thought he was owed something, and he didn't care who he hurt when he went after what he wanted."

Maura took a moment to digest what he'd just told her. "Are you saying you and your people saw him as a problem? Or to put it simply, he was messing up your business?"

"You could say that. But as you might guess, blood still outweighs business, and my brother loved his boy."

"Then what the heck are we talking about here?"

"Let me boil it down for yeh. I want to be sure that the boy was not killed by any of my family's business rivals, or anyone who thinks they're righting a wrong that's been done to them by the Creegans. Because that would require a certain course of action on our part. But if we were to learn that he had died accidentally, or that those who were a party to it had no connection to our family or anyone else in Limerick, then we can lay the matter to rest. Do you under-stand what I'm sayin'?"

Maura felt a strange mix of hope and

relief. Maybe there was a light at the end of this tunnel after all. "I think I do. I can tell you that this is a crime that happened only because Paddy was involved, and you could say he brought it on himself. Can I trust you that this will go no further, and there won't be any bad consequences, if I tell you what happened?"

"If you tell me the truth, I'll take the tale back to Limerick. I will give you my word, which I hope is still worth something in Cork."

"Then here's the story . . ."

CHAPTER THIRTY-THREE

When she was finished telling the story yet again, Maura felt drained. It was simple and it was complicated at the same time. But she was pretty sure that no one had set out to kill Paddy Creegan, and it would be hard to tell whose blow had been the final one, much less find that person, who could be anywhere in Ireland by now. At least she'd had the brains to involve Sergeant Ryan in the mess: she could let him explain it all to the higher-ups of the gardaí. They'd already heard too many strange stories from her.

Danny Creegan had listened without interrupting, his eyes on her face, his expression neutral. When she had finished, he didn't speak immediately, and then he said slowly, "I'd always feared he would end like this. He had little control of himself, and he didn't think things through. I won't say I'm glad he's dead, but it's one less worry fer me."

"What happens now?" Maura asked.

"I go home and tell the family that Paddy's death was the result of a fight among strangers and had nothin' to do with us. I might not be so forthcoming with our enemies — let them stew a bit, thinkin' we suspect them."

"Am I in the clear? And the pub?"

"The news said the boy had been killed elsewhere and the body dumped along the road here. There's nothing that points to your lot."

"And Sophie and Niall? Are you going after them?"

"And why should we be doin' that? Niall paid fer his crossing. Mebbe Sophie might owe somethin' in theory, but Niall was only protecting his sister. In a way it's a part of the business — Paddy just didn't look closely at the two of them, and they outfoxed him. What happened after wasn't their fault."

"So they can stay here, if they want? In the clear?"

"Yes. You'll tell 'em?"

"I will."

Danny Creegan leaned back and looked at her with some curiosity. "Can I ask why that matters so much to yeh? You've no connection to the pair of 'em."

Why did she? Maura had to ask herself, and took her time putting it into words. "Because they're good kids who got caught up in something at a difficult time in their lives. All they wanted was to come home, and to stay together. They might have taken an illegal shortcut, with Paddy, but they had good reasons. I think they like it here in Cork, and I'd like to see them stay, but not if they have to keep looking over their shoulders all the time. Did Paddy have brothers?"

"Who might try to finish what he started? No, he was the only boy, to his mother's great regret. Maybe that's why he felt so . . . entitled, I'd say." Danny pushed himself off from the wall and stood up. "See me out?"

"You want to go through the pub, or slip out the back way?"

Danny Creegan looked at Maura and almost smiled. "I might want to give a nod to my mate in the corner, let him know our business is done."

"Did he have to call in any favors, or shouldn't I be asking that?"

"Let's say he stopped what might have been trouble in its tracks, which is a good thing for all of us. It's been a pleasure meetin' yeh, Maura Donovan."

She finally smiled. "I can't say quite the

same thing, but it's been interesting. Thank you for sorting things out, and for doing it in person."

"It's best yeh don't mention yeh've seen me, much less here."

"I'll try, but I have to tell my staff — Mick and Rose — because they've been involved from the beginning, and they know you're here. But they do know when to keep their mouth shut."

"A good quality fer someone working in a pub, I'd say." He followed Maura out through the main room, gave a nod to Conor Ryan in the corner, and left, in no particular hurry. Maura turned around and found Mick and Rose staring at her, although Sergeant Ryan didn't look troubled. She decided to deal with the garda first and headed for his table.

She leaned over and said quietly, "Thank you."

"So it's all fixed?"

"It is. If he keeps his word, and none of his gang decides to do something on their own. Can he control them?"

"I'd say he can. And in truth, Paddy died because of his own stupidity and pigheadedness, which I'd guess was well known in certain circles. Yeh can rest easy, Maura." He stood up. "I'll see myself out."

Which left Mick and Rose waiting to be filled in. Better get it over with before more people arrived. She walked over to the bar and said, "If I was a drinker, I'd ask for a straight whiskey about now. But that's not a good idea, so I'll settle for a coffee."

"Will yeh see to it, Rose?" Mick asked, then turned back to Maura. "Was that who I think it was?"

"Probably, if you're thinking of a Limerick gang boss. But he was never here and you didn't see him. Conor fixed things, and I'd say we're in his debt, but we shouldn't expect any trouble from the other side. The man, who will stay nameless, said that no one would come after Sophie and Niall, and he'll spread the word among his friends — and his enemies — that Paddy died in a pointless fight, which probably won't surprise anybody up that way."

Rose slid the coffee across the bar, and it was obvious she'd been listening. "So yeh'll tell Sophie it's safe, and she can tell Niall?"

"That's what the guy said. I think he was honest about it, and Conor says he'll keep his word. And we're pretty small fish down here — not worth bothering with." Maura took a fortifying gulp of her coffee. "So it looks like we're back where we started. I hope Sophie managed to explain to Sinéad

407

why she missed a day, but if there's a problem, I'll explain things to Sinéad. And can I offer Niall a job here? If he wants it, that is. Even if he doesn't stay long, maybe he can fill in long enough to get things sorted out for the summer."

"I've no problem with that," Mick said. Rose nodded in agreement. "Yeh can tell him as soon as Sophie finds him." He hesitated for a moment. "A word with yeh? In the back?"

"Okay," Maura said, and followed him to the back room. What did he want? She couldn't take any more complications in her life, not right now. She was startled when Mick grabbed her and pulled her close, and then she felt something untangle inside her — which made her realize how intense her conversation with a mob boss had been, and how lucky she was to have come out of it on the winning end. But for the moment she was content just to lean against Mick and try to relax her muscles.

"I could've gone with yeh," he said, without releasing his hold.

"And he probably wouldn't have been as straight if there were two of us." Now Maura pushed back, just a bit. "Look, Mick, this was my problem to take care of. I found the body, and I had to protect the pub, and the rest of you. That's nothing against you, but sometimes I need to handle things alone. Now if a bunch of drunken partyers barge in some night, I'll be happy to let you deal with them."

"I was worried, is all," he replied. "I know yeh're yer own woman and can take care of yerself, but I care fer yeh — so I worry. Sorry — it's something of a new feelin', thinking about somebody else."

"I know, believe me. But maybe things will calm down now, if Niall can help out at least part of the time. And Rose and Sophie have hit it off, and Sophie's a good cook, so maybe they can figure out something to do with our kitchen. Oh, and can I offer Niall and Sophie the rooms upstairs? They don't have any way of getting around, but we're right on the bus line . . ."

"Maura, will yeh stop tryin' to solve every problem at once?" He finally stopped her from talking with a kiss, and Maura was more than happy to simply let go of everything else.

The sound of new voices in the front room finally interrupted them some time later. Gillian's was one of them. When had she last updated Gillian on what was going on? Probably not since Gillian had handed her the sketches, which had been important.

And now there were things she had to edit out of the story, that would make sense to Gillian, who wasn't dumb. But since she'd played a part, she deserved to know at least part of the story. Reluctantly Maura backed away from Mick. "I'd better get out there — I've got to figure out what to tell Gillian."

"Less than the whole truth?" Mick asked.

"That's what I promised . . . that man. Not that I don't trust Gillian, but the fewer people who know the full story, the less loose talk there'll be."

Maura left the back room and found Gillian, a sleeping young Henry strapped to her chest, chatting with Billy. Gillian waved her over. "Big doings, I hear. You've identified that poor man?"

"The gardaí did, thanks to your sketches. Turns out he was from Limerick, not around here. The gardaí think he got into a fight with someone — or maybe more than one someone — and when they found he was dead, they panicked and dumped him here. They're satisfied it's nothing to do with Sullivan's."

"Will they arrest someone for the killing?" Gillian asked.

"Right now they don't have any suspects. But you know that an unsolved death is never closed in Ireland."

"That I do."

Maura looked at Billy, and he winked at her. She didn't doubt she knew the full story, one way or another, but he wasn't going to be spreading it around. Maura smiled back at him, then turned back to Gillian. "Can I get you something?"

"I've been told that a Guinness helps with, uh, Henry's dinner, so could I have a small one?"

"Coming up. Billy, you ready for a pint?"

"I won't say no," he told her.

Maura went over to the bar and started filling the glasses. Rose said quickly, "I'll take care of 'em, if yeh want to talk to Gillian."

"Thanks, Rose." Maura turned to find that Gillian had stood up and was standing across the room looking at the space above the bar, where Maura had hung several of Gillian's smaller paintings.

"They do look cheerful there, although maybe that's not the feeling you're looking for in a pub. Has anyone shown any interest?"

"No offers yet, I'm sorry to report. But please don't start painting dark, gritty art just to put in here — that's not your style. Any word from the Crann Mor people

411

about buying some for the place?"

"I think we've worked out the terms, but I haven't seen a contract yet."

Maura grinned. "Well, if they drag their feet, I have connections."

"That you do. Any word on that front?"

"Nothing new. Helen will probably be back in the next few months, and we'll take it from there. But Harry's already looking at the books, right?"

"That he is. And all's well here at Sullivan's?"

"I think so. I've got a line on one or two new staffers, which should help. As long as people forget about the body — and I can keep Seamus and his pals from poking around too much — business should get back to normal."

"I certainly hope so!" Gillian said, raising the glass that Rose had just delivered to her.

When the door opened again, Maura saw the Albertsons surging into the pub. "Oh, good, you're still here," Linda said. "We wanted to thank you for helping us with a place to stay and pointing out some good places to go. We've had a wonderful time! I wish now that we'd planned to stay longer. Isn't that right, Marv?"

"Sure is," he said heartily. He leaned in closer, "Don't let her hear it, but I think even Jannie enjoyed herself, not that she'd admit it."

"I'm glad. Ireland does have a way of getting under your skin. Can I get you something? Are you leaving tonight or tomorrow?"

"Maybe sodas all around," Marv told her. "I've managed to stay out of trouble with all this driving on the left this long, and I'd hate to blow it now. Linda, that okay with you?"

But Linda was distracted, looking up at the paintings hung over the bar. "Look, Marv, aren't these pretty? And didn't we see some of these very places?" she asked, pointing.

"Could be," Marv agreed carefully.

Maura suppressed a smile. "Well, you can find out easily, because the artist is sitting right over there."

"Really? She's a local artist? I'd love to talk with her."

"I'll send her right over." Maura crossed the room and leaned over so only Gillian could here. "If you talk nicely to them, they might even buy something. They're the Albertsons, Linda and Marv, and they've had a wonderful time and no doubt want something to remember it by. Want me to hold Henry?"

"Please," Gillian said, and handed over the baby.

Maura took her seat when she stood up and placed the baby on her lap. "Hi, Henry. How're things?"

Henry stared at her, then reached out to try to grab her nose. Maura fended him off and watched as Gillian introduced herself to the Albertsons and began identifying the sites of the various pictures. After several minutes, Linda seemed to have decided on one in particular, a small watercolor that Maura recognized as Bridget's cottage. "And I'm sure we can fit it in our carry-on, Marv."

"Of course we can," he told her, then turned back to Gillian to finish the transaction.

Finally Gillian cadged some Bubble Wrap from Mick and handed the Albertsons a carefully wrapped package. The family waved their farewells, and Gillian returned to her earlier seat. "I think our luck has changed, Maura Donovan. They didn't even quibble about the price. Join me in a drink? And maybe Mick as well? I think we should celebrate."

"Sounds good to me."

ACKNOWLEDGMENTS

I love to do research of all kinds, and for the County Cork Mysteries, much of that research means talking to people in West Cork. I've been visiting long enough that I've made friends there, and others who see me only rarely remember who I am, which delights me. It means that they're happy to talk with me, and quite often there's a story idea lurking in our casual conversations.

Travellers in Ireland, who play a significant role in this book, occupy an odd niche in Irish society, for a number of reasons which go far back in local history. Even today there are many people who don't trust them, and much of the information I've gathered about the group has come from such people. I've tried to use that information sparingly and without judgment while staying true to the reality of where the Travellers fit in contemporary Ireland.

Many of the details about the region have

come from people I've been talking to for years now: garda sergeant Tony McCarthy, who is a valuable resource; Eileen Connolly McNicholl and her son Sam, who have brought the pub Connolly's of Leap back to its former glory as a music venue (and I was lucky to watch it happen); Carmel Somers, founder of the Good Things Café, who let me play fly on the wall and see how a small restaurant kitchen really works; my cottage neighbors, who like me have spent much of their lives in other countries but who have chosen to live in rural Ireland; and a wonderful range of strangers in shops or at the weekly farmers market or on the street, who are more than happy to talk to me about almost anything.

I owe many thanks to the wonderful people at Crooked Lane Books: Matt Martz and the great team of editors and marketers he has put together, who have given the County Cork Mysteries new life. Thanks also to my longtime agent Jessica Faust of BookEnds, who brought the series to Crooked Lane, and who has made so many things possible.

ABOUT THE AUTHOR

Sheila Connolly is the Anthony and Agatha Award-nominated author of over thirty titles, including the Museum Mysteries, the Orchard Mysteries, and the County Cork Mysteries, in addition to the Relatively Dead paranormal romance e-series, the standalone books *Once She Knew,* a romantic suspense, and *Reunion with Death,* a traditional mystery set in Tuscany, as well as a number of short stories in various anthologies. She lives in Massachusetts with her husband and three cats and visits Ireland as often as she can. This is her seventh County Cork mystery.

√L 7/19